A Hobby of Murder

A Hobby of Murder

E. X. Ferrars

FELONY & MAYHEM PRESS • NEW YORK

All the characters and events portrayed in this work are fictitious.

A HOBBY OF MURDER

A Felony & Mayhem mystery

PRINTING HISTORY
First UK edition (Collins): 1994
First US edition (Doubleday): 1995

Felony & Mayhem edition: 2023

ISBN: 978-1-63194-294-5

Manufactured in the United States of America

Cataloging-in-Publication information for this book
is available from the Library of Congress.

The icon above says you're holding a book in the Felony & Mayhem "British" category. These books are set in or around the UK, and feature the highly literate, often witty prose that fans of British mystery demand. If you enjoy this book, you may well like other "British" titles from Felony & Mayhem Press.

————•◦•●•◦•————

For information about British titles or to learn more about Felony & Mayhem Press, please visit us online at:

www.FelonyAndMayhem.com

Other "British" titles from

FELONY&MAYHEM

MICHAEL DAVID ANTHONY
The Becket Factor
Midnight Come
Dark Provenance

ROBERT BARNARD
Corpse in a Gilded Cage
Death and the Chaste Apprentice
The Skeleton in the Grass
Out of the Blackout

SIMON BRETT
Blotto, Twinks and the
  Ex-King's Daughter
Blotto, Twinks and the
  Dead Dowager Duchess
Blotto, Twinks and the
  Rodents of the Riviera
Blotto, Twinks and the
  Bootlegger's Moll

CAROLINE GRAHAM
The Killings at Badger's Drift
Death of a Hollow Man
Death in Disguise
Written in Blood
Murder at Madingley Grange

ELIZABETH IRONSIDE
The Accomplice
The Art of Deception
Death in the Garden
A Very Private Enterprise

MAGGIE JOEL
The Second-Last
  Woman in England
The Past and Other Lies

SHEILA RADLEY
Death in the Morning
The Chief Inspector's Daughter
A Talent for Destruction
Fate Worse than Death

LESLIE THOMAS
Dangerous Davies:
  The Last Detective

L.C. TYLER
The Herring Seller's Apprentice
Ten Little Herrings
The Herring in the Library
Herring on the Nile
Crooked Herring

E.X. FERRARS
Something Wicked
Root of All Evil
The Crime and the Crystal
The Other Devil's Name
Last Will and Testament
Frog in the Throat

A Hobby of Murder

Chapter One

'What you need, Andrew, is a hobby,' Peter Dilly said.

He was the nephew of Andrew Basnett, retired professor of Botany from one of London University's many colleges. They were having lunch together in a small restaurant in Charlotte Street. Peter was thirty-five, a small man who in a neat, small way was good-looking. He had fair, straight hair which he had a habit of thrusting back from his forehead with one of his small, fine hands, but which instantly tumbled forward again, almost into his grey eyes. His pale face was deceptively expressionless, but lit up very charmingly when he smiled.

'I've never had a hobby in my life,' his uncle replied, 'unless you count collecting stamps when I was ten years old. It's true I wanted to collect birds' eggs too. I liked climbing trees. But my parents wouldn't allow it. They said it was cruel.'

Andrew was in his mid-seventies. He was a tall man, and if he had taken the trouble to stand erect would have been even taller than he looked, but in the last few years he had allowed himself to stoop increasingly. He was of spare build, with bony features in a narrow, thin face, short grey hair and grey eyes under eyebrows that were still black. Under his sharp chin the skin was sagging. However, his long sight was still good and he needed glasses only for reading. He had just put them on to read the menu and had ordered an avocado vinaigrette and goulash. Peter had ordered the same and the wine, a bottle of Côtes du Rhône.

'But you had a hobby for years,' Peter said. 'That life of Robert Hooke that you were writing and which nobody thought you'd ever finish. You really shouldn't have finished it. It gave you a nice undemanding occupation in which you were really interested. Now you've nothing to do and I understand that you're finding life rather boring.'

'But I got a contract for the book,' Andrew said, 'and half the advance paid on signing it. I had to finish it to earn that.'

'I doubt if authors are always so scrupulous,' Peter said. He was an author himself who had written ten highly successful science fiction novels. Before he had discovered that he had the ability to do this he had been a teacher on a very small salary. Now he was a fairly rich man who spent most of his time in a small villa that he had recently bought in Monte Carlo. His visits to London were rare and brief, but he was fond of Andrew and always managed to see him two or three times while he was there.

'Well, my editor gave me lunch a couple of times, to keep me moving,' Andrew said. 'And I never had any doubt myself that I'd finish the book in the end, though it's true I was a little afraid of doing it. But not to have had that in view would have seemed too futile.'

They were talking about the book that Andrew had started writing soon after his retirement, a life of Robert Hooke, the noted seventeenth-century natural philosopher and architect, celebrated for pioneering microscopical work in a variety of fields. Andrew had actually begun work on this before retiring, soon after his wife Nell had died of cancer and he had felt a desperate need to fill his lonely evenings. But it was not until after the trip that he had made round the world after retiring that he had let the book become very nearly a full-time occupation. And now it was out of his hands. He had been told that he would be receiving proofs in the next few weeks, though publication was still a long way off, but there was something intimidatingly final about the thought that soon he would be seeing his work in print.

He sipped some sherry.

'I'm thinking of writing a life of Malpighi,' he said.

'Who's he—another seventeenth-century botanist?' Peter asked.

'Well, yes, as a matter of fact.'

'No, don't do that. Do something quite different. If you don't, you'll simply feel you're repeating yourself.'

'But I really don't know what to do,' Andrew said. 'I'm not interested in collecting things. I'm not clever with my hands. I can't paint or draw. Photography has never much attracted me. I might try writing a murder story perhaps, but I've had one or two brushes with the real thing, and that's rather put me off. I shouldn't even care for golf.'

'Well, come and stay with me in Monte Carlo and see if that doesn't give you some ideas,' Peter suggested. 'You might find that you enjoy a little quiet gambling.'

Andrew shook his head.

'Whenever I've gambled I've invariably lost. It doesn't whet the appetite. But thank you for the invitation, I'd like to come sometime. Meantime, as it happens, I'm going to stay with some old friends for a week or two in the country. The Davidges. Did you ever meet them? Ian Davidge was my accountant for years. He handled the mysteries of my income tax for me and kept me out of trouble, then slowly we somehow got to know one another apart from all that and became very good friends. He's retired too now and lives in a village near Rockford in Berkshire.'

'And has he got a hobby?'

'Well, there's his garden, of course, and I've an idea he's taken to bird-watching. Very interesting, I expect, but not much use if you live in St John's Wood.'

For over twenty years now Andrew had lived in a flat in St John's Wood. He and Nell had moved into it and for the two or three years before the dread disease had struck her, they had lived very happily there, and since then Andrew had never thought of moving from it. Besides being comfortable and easily managed, it held a few memories of her, things that she had chosen for it, arrangements that she had made, and it happened to be in a very convenient part of London.

Peter knew how Andrew felt about the place, but all the same he said, 'Have you never thought of moving into the country yourself, Andrew? If you don't any longer need to spend half your time in libraries doing research, mightn't you find it easier to develop a few hobbies in some nice cheerful village, even perhaps the despised golf? I think you ought to consider it.'

Andrew shook his head.

'In my view London's the best place for the old, and I'll probably stick to Malpighi.'

Peter nodded with a little grin.

'Of course, I knew you'd say that.'

All the same, Andrew was looking forward to his visit to the Davidges, in their house in the village of Lower Milfrey near the town of Rockford. Early September was a pleasant time for it, he thought, not likely to be too hot or too cold. At his age, extremes of temperature were always disagreeable, but he was safe from both in September.

When the time came he set off by an early afternoon train from Paddington to Rockford, where Ian Davidge met him. Ian was sixty, a man of medium height and robust build, with a round head set on a thick neck and a round, cheerful face. He had a short nose, large dark eyes that were observant and shrewd and a wide mouth that smiled easily to show teeth that were still his own. The little hair that he had left was dark. He was wearing a dark blue knitted pullover, light grey slacks and sandals. Seeing Andrew getting out of the train, he came loping along to help him with his suitcase.

'Your train's dead on time,' he observed. 'Very remarkable these days. Did you have a good journey?'

'Since it was only fifty minutes, I don't see that it would have mattered if it had been very bad,' Andrew said. 'How are you? You look very well.'

Ian had the sort of tan that comes from spending a lot of time out of doors rather than from sunbathing, and which gave him a look of sturdy health.

'Oh, I'm fine,' he said. 'And you?'

'Getting old,' Andrew said. 'Increasingly incompetent. And that makes life rather boring.'

They were walking towards the exit.

'Well, we'll try to keep you entertained while you're here without involving you in anything too strenuous,' Ian said. 'Apart from that, be sure to do just what you like, as Mollie and I will get on with our normal lives. It's very good to see you again. You don't actually look any older than when I saw you last.'

This could hardly be true, for it was nearly two years since they had last met. It had been just before the Davidges had moved to Lower Milfrey. But Andrew allowed himself to feel flattered, accepting the intention behind the kindly lie. They settled into Ian's car, a BMW, and started the seven-mile drive to the village.

It was along a twisting road through fields and woodland. The fields which had been harvested were mostly a pale brown, but no tinge of autumn had yet touched the leaves of the trees. A light breeze stirred them and the sky was a pale blue with a few small clouds drifting across it. Ian, it was obvious, would have liked to drive fast. He kept speeding up, then having to slow down because he had caught up with a van too wide to pass on the narrow road or some placidly slow driver. He talked a good deal as he drove, asking Andrew all the usual questions about his book on Robert Hooke and expressing the surprise felt by nearly all Andrew's friends that it was actually finished and asking him what he intended to do next.

'Perhaps you'll give me some ideas,' Andrew said. 'I believe you've taken up bird-watching, yourself.'

'That's right, but of course, I'm only a beginner,' Ian answered. 'The amount some of these chaps know is phenomenal. But I've joined the Rockford branch of the RSPB—that's the Royal Society for the Protection of Birds—and I've made a few friends in it and sometimes go out with them. It's been getting me into the habit of getting up early, which pleases Mollie. The times to go out are early in the morning, when the birds start singing, and late afternoon, when they feed. But I won't drag you out with me. You can be as lazy as you like.'

'I don't usually need much tempting to be that,' Andrew said. 'But perhaps I might go with you sometimes if it wouldn't be a nuisance. It's always interesting to learn a little about what makes other people tick. How's the garden? When I saw you last you were looking forward to having a garden.'

'Still rather a mess, but I'm beginning to learn my way about in it. We've a neighbour who keeps an eye on me and gives me good advice. Did I tell you about our having a cottage as well as the house, and which we've let to an excellent tenant? At least, Mollie says she's excellent. I find her a bit overpowering myself and when she gives me advice about the garden I get a perverse desire to do something quite different. But I try to control it, because it seems she really does know what she's talking about.'

'How is it you've this cottage besides the house?' Andrew asked.

'Well, the house was once a farmhouse, and the cottage was for a labourer. The land, of course, was sold off some time ago, leaving just a fair-sized garden round the house, with the cottage at the end of it. We tarted it up a bit when we first moved in and now for about two months we've had this Miss Clancy living in it.'

'Is it furnished or unfurnished?'

'Oh, she's got all her own things in it. But I don't think she's too well off. She's told us she started life as a teacher. A games teacher, I believe.'

'Retired?'

'Yes, but not because of old age. She's only about fifty. You'll certainly be meeting her during the next few days. Look—there's the cottage.'

They had just passed the notice at the side of the road that said that this was the village of Lower Milfrey and the first building that they came to was a low thatched cottage with white walls plentifully criss-crossed with dark beams. It had no front garden and only a step leading straight from the road to the front door. But a high wooden fence, on which a number of creepers were growing, among them a splendid purple late-flowering clematis, jutted out behind the little house and presumably enclosed a garden. A car, an old Renault, stood in front of the cottage. There was no sign of a garage, or any special parking space, so it looked as if the car must spend most of its life in the road.

As Ian drove past the cottage, the house came into view, and beyond it there were more houses, cottages and bungalows. But they were all on one side of the road and opposite them, on the other side of it, was an open green space, a common, Andrew supposed. A turnstile led on to it and a part of it had been turned into a children's playground, with swings and slides. The Davidges' house stood a little back from the road, with a square of gravel in front of it, across which a paved path led up to a white front door with an elegant fanlight above it. The house itself, which had a modest but Georgian look, was painted a pale grey. Its garden was enclosed by a high wall of mellowed red brick that had the door of a garage let into it. Some beech trees showed from behind the house. Ian stopped the car at its door and tooted gently on his horn.

The door opened immediately and Mollie Davidge came running out. As Andrew got out of the car she flung her arms round his neck and kissed him warmly.

'It's such ages since we've seen you!' she exclaimed. 'Why has it been so long?'

She was a small woman, a good deal younger than her husband. She was his second wife and his marriage to her when he was in his late fifties had taken all his friends by surprise. His first wife had died of a stroke, which had kept her paralysed for the last two sad years of her life, and after her death Ian had waited for three years, then had married his secretary. Mollie was slender, delicately built, but full of energy and stronger than she looked. Her face was small and pointed, with big long-lashed eyes of an unusually brilliant blue and a small, pouting mouth. Her hair was fair and straight and cut very short. No one would have called her beautiful, but she gave an impression of great charm. She was wearing black jeans and a scarlet shirt.

'Why *has* it been so long?' she repeated, linking an arm through Andrew's and drawing him into the house while Ian followed with Andrew's suitcase.

The answer, Andrew thought, was simply that the Davidges had been so fully occupied with settling into their new home that they had not thought of inviting him, though when they had done so, they had implied that he ought to have invited himself.

However, he answered, 'Time flies, doesn't it? And it seems to go faster and faster with advancing age. You're happy here? You've settled in all right?'

'Oh yes, I feel as I've lived here all my life,' she said. 'We did just the right thing to come, though d'you remember how doubtful of it I was when Ian first suggested we should move to the country? I thought he'd be terribly bored. And in fact he's so busy he has hardly a minute to spare. Now, you'd like some tea, wouldn't you?'

Mollie had led Andrew into a long room, with a great open fireplace along one side of it, though there were radiators too for when real warmth was needed, for most of the heat from the fire, when it was alight, would certainly go straight up the wide chimney. There were two tall windows, one of which overlooked the road and the other a moderate-sized garden that consisted mostly of lawn and the beech trees that Andrew had seen from the road, though a rose-bed was making a fine show of September blossoming. There were several comfortable-looking chairs in the room, in gaily flowered covers, one or two small tables, a corner cabinet filled with china that Andrew thought was Spode, a bookshelf filled with obviously well-read paperbacks, a floor of dark polished oak with one or two rather homemade looking rugs on it, and no pictures but two or three framed embroideries on the walls. Indeed, a muddle of a room but with a friendly air about it, one in which it would come naturally to relax.

Andrew said that some tea was just what he was wanting and Mollie went off to the kitchen to make it.

'Perhaps you'd sooner go up to your room first,' Ian said. 'It's small, but it's got a bathroom of its own and we're rather proud of it. In fact, as you may have gathered, we're rather proud of the whole place. It's a great improvement on the flat in Holland Park. And it's funny that Mollie should have been afraid of my being bored, because, as she told you, I've never been so occupied, while my fear was that Mollie might be bored and not make many friends. After all, she'd lived in London most of her life. But she's joined in a number of village activities, including an embroidery circle run by a woman who's really a professional, and it's turned out Mollie has an aptitude for it.'

'Are those her works up there?' Andrew asked, nodding at the framed embroideries that he had noticed on the walls.

'That's right,' Ian began, but broke off, looking out of the window that faced the road to call out, 'Mollie, we've got a visitor.'

❀ ❀ ❀

Mollie came into the room carrying the tray, put it down on a table and went to the front door, just as the bell rang. The woman she brought into the room was about fifty, tall, slim, in a somewhat bony way, with strong, bony features in a long, tanned face. She had small, dark, deep-set eyes and dark brown hair which was cut in a heavy fringe across her forehead and bobbed round the rest of her head, so that it looked rather like a cap. She was wearing black jeans, like Mollie, and a black and green tartan shirt. Long green plastic earrings dangled from under her thick cap of hair and she was carrying a jam jar filled with something dark, which she held out before her.

'Chutney,' she announced. 'Peach chutney. I hope you like it.'

'For us? Oh, how sweet of you!' Mollie exclaimed. 'Eleanor, this is an old friend, Professor Basnett. Andrew, this is Eleanor Clancy, our tenant.'

Giving the jam jar to Mollie, Eleanor Clancy held out a hand to Andrew.

'Of course I've heard about you, Professor, from Mollie and Ian,' she said. 'They told me you were coming.' She had a gruff voice and a singularly penetrating gaze, which she fastened on Andrew as if she were trying to fix an image of him lastingly in her memory. 'I must say they told me the truth, you've a splendid head. Splendid. Don't look so surprised. It's the first thing I notice about people. But perhaps they haven't warned you about me.'

Andrew, who had just sat down before the visitor's arrival, had risen to his feet to shake hands with her and said rather nervously, 'No, I don't think they have.'

'You see, I've gone crazy about photography, specially portraits, ever since I retired down here,' she explained. 'And the moment I saw you I thought: I've got to get him to come and sit for me. You will, won't you? Tomorrow or the day after or any time, but you will come?'

'Well, I…I don't think… I don't really feel…'

'This chutney,' Mollie said, doing her best to rescue Andrew from his embarrassment, 'you made it yourself, of course.'

'Oh yes, and it's to a very reliable recipe,' Eleanor Clancy said. 'And I've made some raspberry jam. Pounds of it from my garden. Great fun. I'll bring you some of it too.'

Mollie, from what Andrew remembered of her, probably already had pounds of jam in her store cupboard, but she only said that that would be lovely and that Eleanor would like a cup of tea, wouldn't she? Eleanor said that indeed she would, and Mollie disappeared to the kitchen to fetch another cup. Eleanor dropped into an easy chair, crossing her long legs. Andrew and Ian also sat down and she at once returned to the attack.

'I can see you're one of the people who're afraid of being photographed, Professor,' she said. 'Some people enjoy it, but some feel sure they'll only show the worst side of themselves to the camera. It's just self-consciousness, of course, but you really needn't feel like that with me. I won't sit you down in some carefully planned position and tell you to smile or say "cheese". We'll just have a comfortable chat and from time to time I'll point my little camera at you and click, it's done, almost before you know it's going to happen. It'll probably be when we're talking about something that really interests you. What are your interests? Music? The theatre?'

'As it happens,' Ian said with a chuckle, 'one of Andrew's interests is cheese. He believes that it's important to start the day with some protein, and that it's much easier to get himself a lump of cheese to eat than to boil himself an egg.'

'How wise,' Eleanor said. 'I'm sure that's very sensible.'

'My own opinion about it is that it's almost certainly a superstition,' Andrew said, 'and the truly sensible thing would be to break myself of the habit. That's all it is now—a habit. I don't actually believe in it at all. I hope Mollie hasn't gone to any trouble about it.'

'I happen to know she's got in half a pound of the best Cheshire,' Ian said, 'so you'd better eat it when she brings you your breakfast. Breakfast in bed is one of our rules for visitors, incidentally, because I may be out early after my birds and have my coffee and my toast when it happens to fit in with that, and Mollie likes to have some quiet time to herself, doing *The Times* crossword.'

Mollie came in as he spoke with the fourth cup and poured out tea for them all. There was a sponge cake that looked home-made on the tray, and some chocolate biscuits. Andrew was not accustomed to eating in the middle of the afternoon, a cup of tea being as much as he really wanted, but the cake looked tempting.

'Of course you're coming to our party tomorrow evening, aren't you, Eleanor?' Mollie said. 'Andrew, that's something else we haven't warned you about, besides Eleanor's photography. We've a few people coming in for drinks tomorrow evening. I do hope you don't mind.'

'I'm sure I shall enjoy it,' Andrew said, hoping that he did not sound too dubious. Once he could have said those words with sincerity, but as age had crept up on him, he had found himself more and more reluctant to face numbers of people whom he had never met before, particularly if he knew that he was never likely to see them again.

'Sam and Anna Waldron are coming,' Mollie went on. 'They're just back from Scotland. You haven't met them yet, have you, Eleanor?'

'No, but I used to know a girl called Waldron when I was teaching,' Eleanor replied, 'though I don't think her name was Anna. Perhaps a relation, though come to think of it, she'd have been a relation of Mr Waldron's, wouldn't she, not his wife's? My mind's wandering. Well, I'm glad they're back home. That great house of theirs has seemed so empty-looking while they've been away, though I suppose the servants were there. Imagine having servants living in these days! They must be awfully rich.'

'We're going to a dinner party there on Saturday evening,' Mollie said. 'And Andrew, of course you're invited. And when they meet you here, Eleanor, they'll probably invite you too, because when they give that kind of party they like to get as many people to it as possible. It'll be a rather peculiar kind of party.'

'Peculiar?' Eleanor asked, while Andrew began to wonder if coming to Lower Milfrey had been a grave mistake.

'You'll probably find it very interesting,' Ian said. 'You see, Sam has made a kind of hobby of a certain eighteenth-century parson, Parson Woodforde, who wrote a voluminous diary, and one of his characteristics was that almost every day he wrote down what he had to eat, and Sam wants to lay on a dinner as close as possible to one the old boy described in his diary. He'll cook it himself, he and Anna together. He's a splendid cook.'

'A hobby, you said?' Andrew asked. 'You say your friend's made a hobby of this parson?'

'Well, more or less,' Ian said. 'It's something quite difficult to get him to talk of anything else.'

'I'm beginning to feel I shall have to find a hobby for myself,' Andrew said. 'I'm beginning to feel it's eccentric not to have one.'

But that brought them back to Eleanor Clancy's hobby, photography. She was still gazing at Andrew as if she were taking him in inch by inch, so that she could draw a diagram of him.

'Of course you are going to let me photograph you, aren't you?' she said.

'If you really want to...' he began.

'Oh, grand,' she broke in, 'and I've got some photographs to show you that I'm sure will interest you. You see, my great-grandfather was one of the early photographers and I've not only got some volumes of his work, but some of his negatives too. All glass, of course, quarter-plates, but they're as good as new. He spent most of his life in Burma, where he was a forest officer, and most of his pictures are of local scenes. They're history now, of course, and I've been thinking of making up a volume of them, with some commentary taken from some of his letters that I've got. Do you think that's a good idea?'

'Yes, indeed,' Andrew said, thinking that the old photographs might really be interesting, and that if he could keep her occupied with showing them to him he might escape the ordeal of being photographed himself.

'I'm so glad you think so,' she said, then turned to Ian. 'And about Mr and Mrs Waldron, Ian, do you think they'd make good subjects? And would they let me arrange to photograph them, especially Mr Waldron, because on the whole I'm more successful with men than with women, I don't know why. I can manage a woman if she's got a very intelligent face and doesn't want to smile too much, but the kind whom I'm told are perfectly beautiful and would make splendid subjects never seem to come out successfully.'

'I expect Sam will leap at the chance of being photographed,' Ian replied. 'And he's a handsome chap in his way, the aquiline type, very distinguished-looking. But I tell you whom you ought to try to get hold of while he's staying here—Luke Singleton. His brother, Brian, told me yesterday he's coming to him on a visit in a day or two.'

'Luke Singleton!' Eleanor exclaimed in a tone of excitement. 'And he's Brian Singleton's brother! I never knew that. Oh, I must get hold of him somehow. I'll telephone Brian this evening. I must fix something up.'

'Luke Singleton?' Andrew said on a questioning note. 'Is that the writer? There is a writer called Luke Singleton, isn't there?'

'Of course there is!' Eleanor cried. 'Don't tell me you haven't read anything of his. Why, he's simply marvellous. He's managed to turn the thriller into literature. Real literature, I do assure you. And he's enormously successful. Oh, he's absolutely my favourite novelist. Haven't you seen any of his films? Not that they do justice to the books, but that's because they aren't really written by him. They just state beforehand that they're based on a book by him with a main character he's created. I do think that's a shame and I wonder he allows it.'

'As long as it keeps the money rolling in, I don't suppose it worries him,' Ian said.

'But he must be an enormously rich man already,' Eleanor said. 'You wouldn't think he'd have to stoop to agreeing to it. The funny thing is, I used to know him a little before he became so successful. We both belonged to the same tennis club and I never dreamt he had a literary talent. But he was very good-looking in a rather fierce, intimidating sort of way. I wonder if he'll remember me. We used to go out together occasionally, but of course it's years ago. And to think he's Brian Singleton's brother. I wonder why Brian's never mentioned him. Could it be jealousy, d'you think?'

'I suppose it isn't impossible,' Ian said, 'though it might be a kind of modesty. I think that's more likely. Brian isn't the kind who goes in for name-dropping.'

'This Brian Singleton,' Andrew said, 'he's a friend of yours, is he?'

'Yes, and quite a near neighbour,' Ian replied. 'He lives in a bungalow a little way down the road. But he works in Rockford. He's a biochemist with a post of some sort in the Rockford Agricultural Institute. You'll meet him at our party tomorrow. You'll probably find him interesting.'

'Will Luke Singleton be coming too?' Eleanor asked eagerly.

'No, he won't have come down to Lower Milfrey by tomorrow. But I'm sure he'll be at the Parson Woodforde dinner. In fact, I think Brian told me he would be.'

'Oh, I do hope the Waldrons invite me to it,' Eleanor said. 'If they don't think of it themselves, perhaps you or Mollie could drop them a gentle hint that they should. Of course it's very ill-bred of me to suggest it, but I should so love to meet Luke again, and perhaps get him to let me do a portrait of him. Which reminds me, Professor, we haven't actually fixed the time you're coming along to me. How about tomorrow morning, say about eleven o'clock?'

'If you really think it's worth your while,' Andrew said reluctantly. He had not really been aware that he had committed himself so definitely.

'Thank you, thank you! Now I must be going.' She sprang up from her chair. 'I hope you enjoy the chutney, Mollie, and I'll bring you some of my raspberry jam.'

She strode from the room.

As Ian went after her to see her out, Mollie said, 'That was very nice of you, Andrew, to agree to go; I know you'll hate it, though some of those old photographs she's got are really very interesting. The truth about her is, of course, that she's really pretty lonely, so she makes a rather heavy-handed grab at anyone she meets. And the real reason why Brian hasn't mentioned his famous brother to her is simply that he himself can't stand her and doesn't want her trying to use him to renew the acquaintance—if there ever was an acquaintance. You can't be absolutely sure with Eleanor that everything she tells you is true.'

'Yet you seem to be good friends with her,' Andrew said.

'Well, when you live in a place like this you've got to put up with what you find,' Mollie said. 'Of course, Lower Milfrey isn't a village any more, with a real life of its own. It's a suburb of Rockford. Nearly everyone we know either lives in Rockford, or works there, like Brian. There's a very nice doctor we know. Felicity Mace—you'll meet her tomorrow evening—who lives here, but who belongs to a group practice in Rockford and only runs a surgery twice a week in the village. And we've another friend, Ernest Audley, who's a solicitor in Rockford. And so on. The Waldrons, of course, really belong here, and I think he'd like to think of himself as the squire, but they bought the old manor house only about six years ago and they spend a good deal of their time travelling about. As I said, they're just back from Scotland. All the same, I love it here. I feel it's the first real home I've had. That flat in Holland Park always had a temporary sort of feeling about it, but I can almost persuade myself sometimes that I've lived here all my life.'

Ian had come back into the room and wanted more tea. Mollie refilled their three cups and Andrew asked whether the Waldrons' dinner party would involve dressing, because it had not occurred to him to bring a dinner jacket.

'No, though perhaps a wig and an embroidered waistcoat might have helped,' Ian said. 'Sam would love to achieve a true eighteenth-century atmosphere, though actually it'll be quite informal—rather amusing, probably, and you can be sure the food will be excellent.'

'Now, would you like to see your room, Andrew?' Mollie asked. 'Come along. Ian will bring your suitcase.'

The room, as Mollie had said, was small, but pleasantly simple, with pale grey walls, a divan bed under an Indian bedspread, a modern dressing table and wardrobe, and another framed embroidery, similar to those in the sitting room downstairs, hanging beside the sash window which overlooked the road and the common beyond it. A small bathroom opened out of the room.

Ian and Mollie left Andrew to settle in, telling him to come down when he felt like having some sherry, and went downstairs themselves. A few minutes later, going to one of the windows to take a look at the common and a reedy lake that he could see at the further side of it, Andrew saw Ian leave the house and set off across the common towards the lake. He was carrying a pair of binoculars. It meant, Andrew supposed, that he was going to have a last look before dusk at the birds that would be feeding and that now meant so much to him.

But what interested, and in a way curiously puzzled Andrew, was the embroidery on the bedroom wall.

Embroidery must have become Mollie's hobby, he guessed, and plainly she was very skilled at it. The design was abstract, the colours mainly various soft shades of orange and cream. But where, he wondered, had the design come from? Was it her own, or if not, what was its origin? For a curious thing was that, as he had had with those like it in the sitting room, Andrew had a feeling that he had seen it before. Had it been in the Holland Park flat? He could not remember it there, and he thought that if it or any of the others had hung on a wall there, he would certainly have noticed it. It was also a little strange that the longer he looked at it, the more the sense of familiarity faded. It seemed to have been only a matter of a first impression. By the time that he had looked at it thoughtfully for only a moment or two, he was sure that he had been mistaken.

He unpacked his suitcase, had a wash, then went back to the window, leant his elbows on the sill and gazed out at the common. The dusk was deepening now and the lake in the distance was almost invisible. But he could see Eleanor Clancy's cottage and thought with some irritation of what he had committed himself to doing next day. Mollie might have saved him from it, he thought. He had not taken a liking to Eleanor, and being photographed he thought a bore. However, he could hardly get out of it now.

He rather wished that Mollie did not insist with quite as much determination as she did that this home that she and Ian had made for themselves was so completely perfect. Her very insistence made him doubt its sincerity. If it was really so exactly what she wanted, would she have proclaimed it so vehemently? Would she not be taking it more as a matter of course, letting her obvious contentment there speak for itself?

But that feeling he had might be only because he himself would have let it speak for itself. There was no reason to assume that Mollie's mind worked like his. All the same, he was haunted by a curious sense of disquiet which amounted almost to a wish that he had not come, as presently he went downstairs for his sherry.

Chapter Two

It was a misfortune of Andrew's that when his mind was not otherwise occupied, it tended to fill itself with scraps of verse or songs that he supposed he must once have admired, but which he had long outgrown. And unfortunately once one of these usually puerile fragments had taken possession of him, it would repeat itself until it was replaced by something equally inane. It gave him no pleasure and had sometimes made him wonder if it was a symptom of a mild form of insanity.

When he woke up next morning and was waiting for his breakfast to arrive, he found himself almost immediately repeating to himself:

> *On a tree by a river a little tomtit*
> *Sang Willow, titwillow, titwillow...*

The seed of it had of course been sown in his mind the evening before, when Ian had talked with enthusiasm of the birds that he had watched in the neighbourhood. He had also talked of a trip that he hoped to make in the winter with a few other members of the Rockford branch of the RSPB to Kenya, a place to which people went for really serious bird-watching, though there was a possibility that they might decide to go to the Gambia, as it would be cheaper. But the result of this was that Gilbert and Sullivan was almost sure to pursue Andrew for at least the next few hours, perhaps even the next few days. He remembered that long ago, when he was about twelve years old, he had been taken to the theatre, in itself a great adventure, had seen *The Mikado* and the song had charmed him. But now he found it intensely irritating to be compelled to repeat it over and over again until his breakfast arrived.

Mollie brought it to him soon after eight o'clock. There was coffee, some orange juice, toast and marmalade and a small square of Cheshire cheese.

'Oh, really, Mollie, you shouldn't have bothered,' Andrew said when he saw this. 'I mean to grow out of the habit.'

'But why should you?' she said, smiling. 'It's a habit that's very little trouble to other people. Did you sleep well?'

She was again in her black jeans and scarlet shirt with the look of having slept well herself.

'Excellently,' Andrew replied, and as she placed the tray on his knees, went on, 'Mollie, there's something I must ask you. I'm so struck by it. That embroidery there, did you design it?'

She looked up at it and frowned slightly, as if she were uncertain what to say, and it intrigued Andrew to see that she blushed. At least, it seemed to him that she blushed, though the normal colour in her cheeks was bright enough for him not to be sure of it.

'Not exactly,' she said. 'No, really not at all, except for the colours. The design itself came from a photograph from an electron miscroscope, and was black and white, of course. It's interesting that it caught your eye, because you know so much more about that sort of thing than I do.'

Talking to Mollie had successfully driven the tomtit back into Andrew's unconscious.

'But how do you get hold of photographs from an electron microscope?' he asked. 'You're neither of you scientists.'

'No, but a friend of ours is,' she said. 'I think we talked about him yesterday evening. Brian Singleton. Didn't we tell you he was a biochemist who works at the Rockford Agricultural Institute? It was his idea. I'd been trying my hand at watercolours soon after we came here, but I'd absolutely no real talent for that and got bored with it, and then a woman I'd met here suggested I should try my hand at embroidery. But I didn't care for the designs she suggested. They were quite nice, but mostly traditional, and I wanted to do something original. And Brian suggested I ought to look at these photographs he had, that they might give me some ideas, and they seemed to me exactly what I was looking for.'

'You must be very skilled,' Andrew said. 'They're charming.'

He was sure now of the blush on her cheeks.

'Don't let your coffee get cold,' she said, 'and come down when you feel like it. You're going to Eleanor's presently to be photographed, aren't you?'

'I'm afraid I said I would,' Andrew answered. He poured out some coffee. 'Of course, if you could think of some really good excuse to get me out of it, I'd be grateful.'

'Oh, it won't be as bad as all that,' she said. 'But if you like, I could ring up and say you've woken up with a terrible headache and have got to lie down.'

'She'd only ask me to come tomorrow, wouldn't she? I can hardly spend all my time here with a terrible headache. I'll just have to face it.'

He sipped some orange juice. Mollie laughed.

'Actually, you'll probably find some of her old photographs quite interesting, and you'll get to like her better when you've seen a bit more of her.'

Andrew doubted this. However, as Mollie left him, he found himself wondering at her blushing so easily when her work was praised. It seemed to him that there was something a little pathetic about it, as if she was not normally appreciated as she longed to be. He wondered what she thought of Ian's bird-watching. But that brought back the wretched tomtit.

Willow, titwillow…

He did his best to drown it in orange juice and coffee, ate his cheese and his toast and marmalade, then got up, shaved and had a shower, and as by then it was only half past nine, decided to go for a walk before he was due at Eleanor Clancy's. Ian was in the garden, mowing the lawn, and from sounds in the kitchen it seemed probable that Mollie was occupied already with cooking. Looking into the kitchen, he told her that he was going out, then set off across the common.

The morning was one of the delightful kind that sometimes comes in early September. The sky was a pale but radiant blue, and a slight breeze ruffled the leaves of the trees that edged the common. It was warm but not at all oppressive. Some young children with an older girl watching them were playing on the swings and slides of the playground. Passing it, Andrew walked on across the rather dusty turf towards the lake that he had seen from his window. The activity of walking kept his mind pleasantly free of songs and rhymes, but allowed him to think with some seriousness of Malpighi. Should he embark on another biography? And unlike its predecessor, would it not in truth probably never be finished? Even if he did not actually die before he had come to the end of it, would his mind maintain sufficient clarity to make steady work possible?

These thoughts were interrupted by the fact that a man was approaching him from the direction of the lake. He was carrying a fishing rod, a basket, and two fairly large fish strung on a line.

Coming level with Andrew, he observed, 'Two fine tench.'

'Yes, indeed,' Andrew agreed, thinking that he had misheard what the man had said and that actually he had remarked on it being a fine day.

'Tench,' the man said. He had stood still and was looking at Andrew with some interest. 'Plenty in the lake. Plenty in all the inland waterways in this country. Generally underrated, like carp. The thing is to know how to cook them. Coarse fish, of course, but if you soak them for three or four hours in slightly acidulated water—if you don't do that they just taste of mud—then cook them according to Mrs Beeton, you'll find they're delicious. Our forefathers knew all about that, but naturally they depended on lakes and rivers for their fish. In the days before trains and lorries you didn't eat fish if you lived inland. Well, good day.'

He strode on, leaving Andrew wondering if he had just had a brief conversation with Mr Samuel Waldron. He was a tall man and walked with long strides. He looked about fifty, and was wearing a white sweater, brown corduroy trousers and gumboots.

That gumboots would have been necessary if he had been fishing in the lake Andrew recognized as soon as he reached it himself, for its banks were muddy and its edges reedy. But the water was clear and the faint ripples raised by the breeze sparkled in the sunshine. Andrew walked all the way round it, at one point crossing a small bridge which he realized was over a narrow stream that flowed out of the lake, a placid stream in which there was hardly any movement. There were trees on its banks, not yet even faintly touched by the copper tints of autumn. And yet it seemed to him that there was a scent of autumn in the air, or at least of the ending of summer.

He enjoyed his walk and because he was returning from it too early for his appointment with Eleanor Clancy, he sat down for a while on a bench that overlooked the children's playground and watched them on the swings and slides, occasionally fighting with one another, with a good deal of shouting and hitting and kicking, to be separated by the girl who was in charge of them, only to revert, as soon as her back was turned, to this occupation which they seemed to enjoy most among those that were available. Violence shows itself early in the human creature, Andrew thought. But at times the combatants strolled about with their arms round one another, their warfare forgotten. He waited until a few minutes to eleven, then strolled down to the Clancy cottage.

Eleanor must have seen him coming, for the door opened a moment before he reached it and she welcomed him in. She took him into a small, square room with one casement window that overlooked the road and a glass door of more recent construction that opened into the garden. Outside it, on a small patio, were a couple of garden chairs and a low round table. The garden was packed in a disorganized way, but very richly, mostly with herbaceous plants, not many of which were still in flower. There was a big cluster of black-eyed susan in bloom, and some tall marguerites, a few snapdragons and geraniums, as well as roses and clumps of greenery that Andrew could not identify. There was also a splendid vine growing against the fence that enclosed the garden. It looked as if it might have been there as long as the cottage.

'You'd like some coffee, wouldn't you?' Eleanor said. 'Shall we have it in the garden? It's such a lovely morning.'

Andrew said that he would enjoy coffee and that it would be delightful to have it in the garden, and after seeing him installed in one of the chairs outside, she disappeared to make the coffee. Coming back soon with a tray, she settled down in the second chair and poured out the coffee. She was wearing the same jeans as the day before, but a frilly pale blue blouse which did not suit her angular build or her tanned colouring. It was made of silk, however, and looked as if it might have been put on in honour of her visitor.

'Ah, you're looking at my vine,' she said and as she said it she picked up a small camera that Andrew had noticed lying with some books on the table and began to fiddle with it. 'I don't know how old it is. At least a hundred years or more, I should think. I believe I'm going to have a good crop off it this year, and I'm going to try my hand at making wine. I've never done it before, but I think it should be rather exciting. I've quite a good cellar under the cottage, so I mean to make plenty. I'll take you down there presently, if you'd care to see some of the old photographic equipment I inherited from my father. It actually dates from my great-grandfather's time, and my father and his father never took any interest in it, but they treasured it—great box things, you know, that stood on tripods, and the photographer had to put a black thing over his head when he was taking the photograph, and the model had to sit absolutely motionless for some minutes while he was doing it. Is that what you were expecting today? Is that why you were so nervous of coming?—there!' She had lifted the camera while she had been talking and it had just gone click. 'That didn't hurt, did it?' She gave a giggle. 'And I'm sure it'll be very nice. Of course I want to take a few more and I'll send you proofs to choose among for the ones you like best. I can get your address from the Davidges, can't I? Or are you staying here long?'

'About a week, I think,' Andrew replied.

'Then I expect I can get them ready for you to look at before you go.'

She chatted on about her photography, and wanted to know about the book that she had been told Andrew had been writing, and although the camera went click from time to time, Andrew did not find it as disagreeable as he had expected.

'Now, come inside and look at some of my pictures,' she said, when the coffee was finished. 'I'd like you to see some of the ones I took while I was still teaching. Did you know I'd been a teacher? Games mistress at a place called St Hilda's in Hampshire, till I got too old to keep on with that kind of job. Very rewarding, except financially.' She giggled again. 'But I thoroughly enjoyed it. I've had a very satisfying life. Now look at that!'

They had gone into the little sitting room and she was pointing at a framed photograph on a wall. It was of a group of girls in dark red sweaters and short grey skirts holding cricket bats.

'Our first eleven, the year they beat Etchingham—that was another school they played matches against regularly—and there am I beside them. A bit younger than now! You needn't say it doesn't show.'

Andrew had not thought of saying that it did not show, though as a matter of fact the high, bony shoulders, the long neck, the strong, bony features and the hair cut like a cap had not changed so very much. But the grace of youth had been lost.

'Who was taking the photograph?' he asked. 'It couldn't have been yourself, since you're in the picture.'

'Oh, I forget. One of the other mistresses. It was an honour that the girls wanted me to be included. It showed gratitude, didn't it, for all the coaching I'd given them? And that—' she put a finger on one of the girls in the photograph—'is the Waldron girl. I remember her very well. A natural athlete, and a sweet personality, though very quiet. I wonder if she's any connection of the Waldrons here, or even if she's Mrs Waldron. I mean, if she'd married a cousin, she might not have changed her name. But I suppose it isn't such an uncommon one. But hearing it made me think of how much I'd like to see her again. Some of the girls, of course, used to visit the school after they'd left, and so one kept in touch with them, but I don't think Suzie ever did. Suzie Waldron, that was her name, it's just come back to me.'

'And how long ago was this photograph taken?'

The girls all being in school uniform, their clothes did not tell him anything about the date of the picture.

'Oh, twenty years at least,' she answered. 'Yes, I'd have been about thirty. I hadn't been at the school very long. But I stayed there until I retired and they gave me a most magnificent present when I left, a tea set of lovely Copenhagen china. Of course I never use it, because my dishwasher would ruin it. Now, would you like to see some of my great-grandfather's work? Only wait a minute—I think I'd like to take just one more of you, in here, with that background of books. That would be appropriate for a professor, wouldn't it?' She gave her little giggle once more.

It would also be one of the real clichés of photography, Andrew thought, remembering all the portraits of politicians, of writers, of people being interviewed on television, that he had seen against a background of books. In television the books were only too often the same ones, which did not say anything special about the subject's erudition. However, he obediently subsided into the chair that Eleanor pointed out to him and let her do her worst.

Afterwards they went down into her cellar, which he realized was used not only for storing the old cameras, jars of unknown chemicals, and some racks of glass quarter-plate negatives, but also as her own dark room. She pointed out the negatives to him.

'I wish we had time for you to see more,' she said. 'I've a lantern and a screen on which I could show them to you, but it's a bit of trouble to set up.'

Instead, taking him upstairs again, and opening a drawer in an old bureau in a corner of the room, she showed him a box full of prints, most of them sepia, and most of them of scenes taken in the Far East, many of them of delightfully pretty ladies in lungis and with parasols held over their heads and flowers in their dark hair. A few were of white ladies in what must have been an almost intolerable quantity of clothing, considering the climate, and of white gentlemen with beards and straw hats. She picked out one photograph of a young girl in a high-necked lacey blouse, gloves to her elbows and a skirt which she was saucily holding in such a way that it showed the frills of the petticoat she was wearing under it. She looked about twenty.

'Isn't she sweet?' she said. 'She's my great-grandmother. She died of malaria when she was twenty-five. There's a lot about her in the letters my great-grandfather wrote home to his parents. Of course they took weeks and weeks to arrive, but they were all treasured and they're very interesting. I really think I must make them into a book, with illustrations. Do you think any publisher would look at it?'

'I think I should attempt it,' Andrew said. 'As you said yesterday, it's history.'

He did not add that it to some extent depended on her ability to make a good job of it.

She looked pleased.

'I think I really will have a go at it, though I've never tried writing anything before,' she said. 'Not that I'd have to write much. It would be mostly a case of editing. Do you think you could take a look at it from time to time as I go along and give me advice? It would be such a help to have someone experienced to give me an opinion.'

'Experienced! My dear Miss Clancy, I've written only one book in my life which took me several years to get into a form that any publisher would look at. I'm sure you could find someone better suited for your needs. You might think about Mr Waldron. It sounds as if he's a bit of a historian.'

'Do call me Eleanor,' she said, 'and thank you so much for coming this morning.'

❊ ❊ ❊

The first guest to arrive at the small party that Ian and Mollie were giving that evening came punctually at six o'clock, and struck Andrew as someone who would always arrive at the exact time of any appointment. He was introduced to Andrew as Ernest Audley, who, he remembered from what Mollie had told him the day before about the guests they expected, was a solicitor, who lived in Lower Milfrey but worked in Rockford. He was a tall, gangling man, with sandy red hair that stood straight up from a high, narrow forehead, a thin nervous face which except for some noticeably red blotches on his cheekbones was unusually pale, light blue eyes with thick, sandy lashes, and a small mouth that seemed to have some difficulty in smiling. There was something about his whole personality that expressed a kind of detachment, even when what he was saying was friendly. He told Andrew that he had heard about him from the Davidges and had been looking forward to meeting him, yet the look with which he was regarding him might have been as fittingly fixed upon one of the pieces of furniture in the room.

However, Mollie had greeted him with a warm kiss, which as the evening progressed Andrew saw was how she greeted everybody, and Audley had returned the kiss with a certain warmth which suggested that there might be feelings in him which could be worth reaching if only one knew the trick of doing so.

The next to arrive was Brian Singleton, the biochemist who worked in the Rockford Agricultural Institute and who was the brother of the noted writer. He looked about thirty-five and was tall, broad-shouldered and strongly-built, with a square, bronzed face, big, wide-spaced grey eyes, a wide, well-shaped mouth and the sort of short nose that it is easy not to notice. His hair was fair and curly. He was carrying a basket of nectarines which he presented to Mollie after receiving the kiss of greeting, a somewhat warmer kiss than had been awarded to Ernest Audley. She said that it was sweet of him to bring them and that he ought really not to have troubled, then introduced him to Andrew, whom he said that he was delighted to meet because he had once been a student of his, though no doubt Andrew would not remember him.

A faint recollection stirred in Andrew's mind.

'I'm sorry, my memory for names and faces is terrible nowadays,' he said, 'but I believe I remember you.'

'Not for any distinction in my work,' Brian Singleton said cheerfully. 'I was lucky to get a Second, and then to get the job I've got. I'd sooner have got into a university, but I'm afraid I haven't quite got what it takes. Having one brilliant member in the family seems to be as much as one can expect.'

'Oh, you're referring to your brother,' Andrew said. 'Luke Singleton. He is your brother, isn't he?'

'Yes. And that's what everyone says to me these days,' Singleton answered, smiling. 'I've got used to it.'

'Then I hope you don't mind it.'

'Oh no, I'm even moderately proud of it. It's a pity he isn't here this evening, but he's not arriving till tomorrow. He'll be in time for the Waldrons' shindig on Saturday. You're going to that, of course.'

Audley interrupted them. He had been talking, with a glass of wine in his hand, to Ian, but now turned to Singleton.

'Did I hear you say that your brother's coming down, Brian?' he asked, and his voice had a rasp in it.

Singleton looked curiously embarrassed by the question.

'Well, yes, as a matter of fact, you did,' he answered.

'And going to the Waldrons' dinner?' Audley went on.

'I assume so, unless he takes it into his head not to go.'

'I see.' There was a chilly finality in the way that it was said.

Mollie heard it and put a hand on Audley's arm.

'Ernest, you won't mind about that, will you?' she said. 'There are things one's got to put behind one.'

'On what compulsion must I, tell me that?' he rasped at her.

'For your own sake, Ernest. Please. Start trying to forgive and forget.'

'I've no intention of doing either. I'm sorry, Brian, but if your brother's going to that dinner, I shan't be there. Perhaps you'll ring me before then and let me know just what he's planning to do.'

Brian Singleton had flushed a dark red, but unlike Mollie, he did not try to make Audley change his mind.

'All right, Ernest. Understood. But I'm sorry about it.'

'I'll count on you, then.'

Audley turned away to resume his conversation with Ian, and at just that moment the doorbell rang again, and Mollie went to let in a young woman who nodded a greeting to the people in the room, then was introduced to Andrew as Dr Felicity Mace.

She looked as if she was in her early thirties, a slim, vital young woman, with an oval face, a fine complexion, grey eyes and straight dark brown hair that she wore combed back from her forehead in a casual sweep. She was wearing a neat, loose-fitting dress, coral earrings and white shoes. It managed to look both practical and fairly elegant.

Soon after her, Eleanor Clancy arrived, her jeans changed for a full, flowery-patterned skirt, but her frilly blouse was the same one that she had been wearing in the morning, and Andrew was inclined to think that jeans and a shirt suited her better. Nothing that she could do, he thought, would make her look feminine. The Waldrons were only just behind her, which Andrew gathered made the party complete.

He had been right that the fisherman with whom he had exchanged a few words that morning was Sam Waldron, changed from his sweater and corduroys into a dark blue blazer with brass buttons and twill trousers. His hair was grey, his features aquiline, and Andrew reflected that he had been right in thinking that he was about fifty, though somehow he looked older than he had out on the common. Anna Waldron was a small woman at least ten years younger than her husband and with a look of diffidence about her, almost as if she feared that it would be inappropriate for her to compete for notice with her husband. But she was pretty in a quiet way, with pleasant grace in her movements. Her hair, tied back from her face with a small knot of scarlet ribbon, was dark and curly, her eyes were dark and bright and innocent, her dress was pale grey and although it was only of cotton managed to have a look of having been expensive. Her pearls might be genuine.

As soon as Eleanor Clancy saw her, she gave a little cry and called out, 'Suzie—it *is* Suzie, isn't it?'

Anna Waldron started and spilled a little of the wine that Ian had just given her, and instead of answering Eleanor, exclaimed, 'Oh dear, how clumsy of me! Oh dear, I shouldn't have done that.'

Eleanor advanced towards her across the room.

'It is Suzie Waldron, isn't it?' she said. 'Of St Hilda's. I dare say you don't remember me, Eleanor Clancy, but I'd have known you anywhere.'

The woman who had just been introduced to Andrew as Anna Waldron looked bewildered, and seemed to find it difficult to look the other woman in the face.

Her husband answered for her. 'Yes, you'd have known her as Suzie, but since she grew up she's preferred to be called

Anna. Her actual name is Suzanna. She's often spoken of you, Miss Clancy. She tells me she was very fond of games when she was a child. Sad to say, that's one of the things one has to leave behind as one grows older.'

'As I know only too well,' Eleanor said, looking at him with a puzzled sort of thoughtfulness, then again at his wife, in the way she had of looking as if she were committing them to memory. 'Are you cousins, perhaps?' she asked. 'I mean, because she hasn't changed her name.'

'Yes, first cousins,' he answered, 'but we haven't any children, so you needn't be afraid we've been producing dotty offspring. Not that they mightn't just as likely have been geniuses. Professor, I'm sure you could put it more scientifically, but all I can say about it is that I believe a marriage between cousins simply exaggerates what's inherited from their family. And we both had a grandfather who was a popular comedian in his time and made a fortune, and a grandmother who was a quite successful actress.' He chuckled. 'Well, if they weren't exactly geniuses, either of them, they had talent of a sort, but we've neither of us inherited it from them.'

As if she felt that she had just been given permission to do it, Anna Waldron suddenly walked up to Eleanor Clancy and kissed her on the cheek.

'Of course I remember you, dear Miss Clancy,' she said. 'You know I used to hero-worship you. I wanted to be a games mistress just like you.'

'Didn't you live with your grandparents?' Eleanor asked. 'I seem to remember we were all so sorry for you because your parents were dead.'

Anna nodded. 'They were killed in a plane crash. But I was very happy with my grandparents.'

'She'd never have been any good as a schoolmistress,' her husband said. 'Not nearly tough enough with anyone, and much too shy. Now, Miss Clancy, if we'd met sooner I'd have asked you before, but is it too late to invite you to a dinner we're giving on Saturday? A slightly odd dinner, I ought to warn you, because I'm basing it as nearly as I can on a dinner given in the eighteenth century by a certain Parson Woodforde. The good parson is rather a hobby of mine. I've the sort of feeling for him that I have for some of my old friends. He'd immense good-nature. For instance, he'd a manservant called Will who had an unfortunate habit of coming home in the evenings, "disguised in drink", as the parson put it. He was always doing it and it worried the good man, and he kept on trying to make up his mind to sack Will, as he wasn't exactly the sort of servant a parson should have. But nine years later Will is still coming home, disguised. Now you've been warned. Will you come?'

Eleanor Clancy's small, deep-set eyes sparkled.

'Thank you so much. It will give me the greatest pleasure.'

'But which of your servants, Sam, will be coming in disguised, as you call it?' Ian asked. 'I thought you had the two Bartlett sisters, sober characters if ever there were any.'

'Ah yes,' Sam Waldron said, 'I'm afraid I can't produce the whole atmosphere correctly. I've never seen either of the Bartletts touch liquor, as they call it. But they've entered into the spirit of the thing and are being most helpful. There's a good deal of work involved, of course, but I'm determined to make a success of it.'

'Just one moment, Sam,' Ernest Audley said, moving from the side of the young doctor, with whom he had been having a quiet conversation. 'I've been told that one of your guests will be that man Luke Singleton. Is that true?'

'Ah yes, he's our celebrity for the evening,' Sam Waldron answered enthusiastically. 'Brian's bringing him along. That may get our dinner at least in the local paper.'

'Then I hope you'll forgive me,' Audley said, his pale, blotchy face stern, 'but I'm afraid I must withdraw my acceptance of your invitation. I'm not going to spend an evening in the company of that bastard.'

'Oh, Ernest!' Anna said with a little gasp.

'Now, now, Ernest,' Sam said, 'you don't mean that. Why, it was all years ago.'

'I certainly mean it,' Audley said.

'No, you don't. You'll come. Do you want him to think he's somehow permanently defeated you?'

Andrew turned to Felicity Mace, who had just moved to his elbow.

'Would it be very tactless of me to inquire,' he asked, 'just what Mr Audley has against Luke Singleton?'

She smiled. She had a very pleasant, friendly smile.

'Not seriously,' she said, 'since it's common knowledge. Jane Audley left Ernest for Luke Singleton. There was a divorce, a very gory one, because with Luke being as well-known as he is, the popular press had a field day. And then when it was through, instead of marrying Jane, he deserted her. Just which part of the story really hurts him most I don't know, her leaving him, or the horrible publicity, or Luke ditching her when it was over. I think he was very angry for her.'

'And how long ago did it happen?'

'About five years.'

'That isn't so very long.' The years, for Andrew, were passing faster and faster and five years did not strike him as amounting to much. He thought it might well have taken him more than five years to get over something as traumatic as the breakdown of Ernest Audley's marriage, if such a thing had ever happened to him. It was more than ten years since Nell had died and he had never wholly got over it.

'And you didn't read anything about it when it happened?' Felicity Mace asked. 'But I suppose you don't patronize the popular press. *The Times* probably had only a small paragraph about it.'

The attempt to persuade Ernest Audley to attend the Waldrons' dinner, even if Luke Singleton was there, was continuing. Eleanor and Ian had joined in, and so after a few minutes did Dr Mace. In fact, the only people who did not seem concerned by the matter were Mollie and Brian Singleton who were sitting side by side on a sofa and talking together in low voices. About another photograph from the electron microscope, Andrew wondered. There was an air of intimacy about them and almost of withdrawal from the other people in the room, until all of a sudden Brian astonished Andrew by apparently extracting a golf ball from Mollie's ear. She gave a little squeal, then burst out laughing.

'Oh, Brian, you fool! That's a new trick, isn't it? When did you learn it?' She looked up at Andrew and explained, 'Brian's a quite expert magician. But that's a new trick. It startled me, Brian. Why don't you show Andrew a few more tricks?'

He laughed too and shook his head. 'I haven't brought the necessary apparatus, no magic jugs that disgorge yards of silk scarves, or hats with rabbits in them. Actually I don't do the trick with a rabbit, because I shouldn't be able to look after the poor creature properly. But I'm coming along quite nicely. Strictly as an amateur, but I believe I could keep a children's party entertained, at least if the children were very young.'

Eleanor was saying, 'I used to know Luke years ago, before he became successful. Such an unassuming, modest young man he used to be, but very reserved. I suppose all the ideas he had were already beginning to go round in his head, but he never talked about them.'

Mollie stood up and started handing round a plate of canapés that she had made, and Ian brought round more wine. The party broke up about eight o'clock, with the Waldrons leaving first, having extracted a half-promise from Audley that he would at least think about attending their dinner, though they were by no means to expect him. Audley himself left soon after them, then Eleanor and Brian. Felicity Mace was last.

Standing in the doorway, just about to leave, she said, 'Of course, Ernest will go to the dinner, but don't be surprised if he manages to make some sort of scene. He may even be working out now just what kind of scene to make.'

'I didn't know solicitors made scenes,' Andrew said. 'I thought they left that to barristers.'

'But solicitors are said to be human,' Felicity said. 'Of course, his scene might simply consist of refusing to notice Luke

Singleton's existence. Cleverly done, it could make all of us feel very uncomfortable. Good night now, my dears, and thank you for the party.'

'I'll come with you,' Ian said, and went to see her home.

She evidently lived quite near, for he was back in a few minutes. In the quiet that came to the room when all the guests had gone, Ian poured out one more drink for the three of them who were left, which they drank almost in silence, pleasantly relieved of the necessity to talk, then Mollie went out to the kitchen to heat some Cornish pasties in the microwave, put the nectarines that Brian had brought her out in a bowl on the table there, and made some coffee.

Andrew went to bed early, claiming to be very tired. At least, he said that he was going to bed, and it was true he felt very tired. The day seemed to have been a very full one, and nowadays he was finding that even a quiet little party of the kind that he had been at that evening seemed to fret his nerves in a way that made him feel an acute desire for peace. But once in his room and in his pyjamas, he did not get into bed, but put on his dressing gown and sat down in a chair by the open window.

The night sky was starry and there was a soft scent in the air of green things that were just beginning to feel the breath of autumn and yield a little to the first touch of decay. He had an Agatha Christie with him, one that he knew he had read at least once before, but which he was fairly sure he had managed to forget. One of the things for which he admired her was the number of times that he could read one of her books as if it was for the first time. He was most unlikely, even at a second or third reading, to remember who had done the murder. Most of his reading nowadays tended to be re-reading. He seemed almost to be on the defensive against new writers. Those who were recommended, or even lent to him by his friends had a way of remaining unread. He told himself frequently to resist this failing, but in the end he generally fell back on old friends.

But this evening, even Agatha Christie did not engross him fully. He found himself thinking with some apprehension of the Waldrons' dinner party. The idea of it, based on the menu of an eighteenth-century parson, sounded amusing, but he was sure that he would find it a great strain, even if nothing dramatic happened in the way of a quarrel between Ernest Audley and Luke Singleton. He hoped that Ernest Audley would stick to what he had proclaimed and stay away. Andrew had never been an aggressive man, and he shrank with great distaste from aggression in others. The often reasonless aggression to be encountered in the academic world, the jostling for position, for power, had always bewildered him. The escape from it had been one of the compensations for retirement. But now it sounded as if on the visit to old friends in the quiet of the countryside he was to be embroiled in it. He did not like the thought of it. He did not like it at all.

Chapter Three

Ernest Audley went to the Waldrons' dinner party. In fact, with his habit of punctuality he was the first guest to arrive. Andrew had met him once between the evening of the Davidges' little party and the night of the dinner. He had been strolling back from the village one day about five o'clock after posting some letters at the nearest letter box when a car had stopped beside him and Audley had leant out. They were, it appeared, just at the gate of Audley's house, and he had invited Andrew in for a drink.

The house, it had seemed to Andrew, was large for a man to live in by himself. It stood some way back from the road, with a stretch of well-tended garden in front of it. It had gables, a green pantile roof, picture windows, and had probably been built between the wars. Inside it felt cold, as if it suffered from not being fully inhabited. The room into which Audley took Andrew was of medium size, had a fitted dark brown carpet and was furnished with tall, wing-backed chairs covered in stiff blue linen, some reproduction chests and cabinets, a small bookcase filled with uniform editions of classics that looked as if they were seldom handled, and something that caught Andrew's eye at once: a row, hanging on the wall, of three glass-fronted cases containing butterflies. They had plainly been skilfully pinned and set, and under each specimen was a minute label.

Standing looking at them as Audley brought sherry from a corner cupboard, Andrew asked, 'Your hobby?'

'My father's,' Audley replied. 'And it's one that isn't too well regarded now when we're trying to preserve the sort of species that he has there. But I must admit that I used to go out with him when I was a child, and enjoyed chasing the things, and I wouldn't be parted from his collection for anything.' He poured out sherry. 'You've been retired for some time, I believe.'

'About ten years,' Andrew replied.

'I often wonder how I shall occupy myself when I retire,' Audley said as they both sat down. 'Have you found it a problem?'

'Not so far,' Andrew said. 'It's taken me all that time to get a book written. Not that I ever worked at it very consistently. I've travelled a good deal, and besides, the book required a good deal of research. But now it's in the hands of the publishers, I can't say I've made any very definite plans for myself.'

'You aren't married, I believe.'

'My wife died shortly before I retired.'

'Ah, I'm sorry. You'll have been told I and mine are separated. In fact, divorced. You could hardly help knowing that after what I said the other evening about that fellow Singleton. Curious how different those two brothers are. Brian's a very good friend of mine.'

'In any case, you've a good many years ahead of you before you need worry about retirement,' Andrew said. 'Do you see yourself staying in Lower Milfrey indefinitely?'

'That's something I ask myself pretty frequently. A flat in Rockford would save me a lot of trouble. But I dislike the idea of a move, probably having to sell off half my furniture because the flat would be very much smaller than this house, and undoubtedly I'd get cheated in the process, because I know nothing about the value of what I've got. I dislike the idea of being cheated. And I've some good friends here. Yes, probably I shall stay here for the foreseeable future.'

They chatted for a while longer, then Andrew made his way back to the Davidges' house, where he explained why it had taken him so long to post his letters and where he was given more sherry.

'I always think there's something pathetic about Ernest living on in that house by himself,' Mollie said. 'I think it's a kind of act of defiance. Luke Singleton got his wife, but he isn't to be allowed to feel he drove Ernest out of his home as well. Absurd, really, because he'd be far better off in Rockford, near to his office. But at least he's got a very good daily woman here, Mrs Crewe, a widow. I sometimes think he'll end up marrying her. They're about the same age and it would really suit them very well.'

'You see marriages everywhere,' Ian said. 'Why don't you try to marry him to Eleanor?'

'I don't think she'd be in the least interested,' Mollie answered. 'Anyway, she's too old for him. Of course, she might do it for the money. He's pretty well fixed, and my impression is that she finds things a bit difficult. I think she might set up as a professional photographer in Rockford, because she's really very good. But when I suggested it to her once she said the endless passport photographs and wedding groups would bore her to death and I suppose it would be pretty frightful. Even children, if you had to make them the smiling cherubs their parents wanted, would be a bit awful.'

'I'm not really sorry for Ernest,' Ian said. 'Life with him can't have been very exciting, and he'd have made very sure that it wasn't.'

Andrew had been out with Ian early that morning, and to Ian's delight they had seen a flock of what he told Andrew were lapwings arrive. They came down from the north, he said, to winter in the temperate climate of England. They came every year to Lower Milfrey, to the muddy verges of the lake on the common. They were big, greenish-black birds, with a strange, distinctive voice that seemed to be saying, 'kee-wi, kee-wi'. For a short while the sky was almost black with them and Ian was entranced and for a few minutes Andrew felt the thrill of it too. But on their way back to breakfast he found to his great annoyance that the rhyme which by now he intensely disliked was going round and round in his head.

And now I'm as sure as I'm sure that my name
Is not Willow, titwillow, titwillow,
That 'twas blighted affection that made him exclaim,
Oh, Willow...

No! He was not going to let it drive out of his mind the real pleasure that he had felt in watching the great flock of birds descending, handsome creatures with their tall, wispy crests and white breasts. Perhaps it was a pity that in St John's Wood there were seldom any birds to be seen but sparrows and the occasional pigeon. However, the place had other attractions and when he had been away from it for only a short while he generally found himself glad, as he was beginning to feel at the present moment and in spite of all the friendliness of the Davidges, that he would fairly soon be returning to it.

On the evening of the dinner party they set out in the Davidges' Ford Escort at seven o'clock to the Waldrons' house which was beyond the far end of the village. Lower Milfrey was one of the villages that are built along a road, which once might have been considered a main road but now was little more than a country lane, and which bent more than once, with a church at one bend and a public house at the other. The church was built of stone, with a square tower and an arched Norman doorway, the pub was white and thatched, with some dark beams, small windows and a fairly freshly painted sign which gave its name as the Black Horse. Most of the houses along the road were old, though here and there a modern bungalow had been jammed in where there was some room to spare. There was a post office which sold most essential groceries, a village hall and a garage. Behind the houses were mostly fields and a little woodland.

They had left the village behind by about a quarter of a mile before they reached the gate that opened on to the drive that led up to the Waldrons' house. The gate was standing open now and they could see that several cars had arrived before them. The house was a modest example of a Queen Anne manor. It was built of a soft golden-coloured brick, had tall sash windows and a portico of great dignity. The house stood on a slight rise so that it overlooked the village, seeming to dominate it. A park which stretched away into darkness surrounded it.

This evening all the windows of the house were alight and a light shone over the front door, which stood open. When Ian had parked the car in the wide gravelled court in front of the house, he and Mollie and Andrew walked in at the door, knowing from the noise that was coming from one of the doors inside where they were expected to go. But an elderly woman emerged from a passage that led out of the hall and greeted them and took their coats. Perhaps in honour of the peculiar nature of the occasion she was wearing a long white apron over a black dress and a mob cap. The Davidges evidently knew her, for they exchanged a few words with her as she led them to the door from which the sound of voices came, then turned and disappeared once more down the passage.

There were about fifteen people in the room, one of whom was Ernest Audley. He was in a corner of the room, with a drink in his hand but a look of having withdrawn as far as he could from the other guests. He was in a dark suit, as Ian was too, but there was great variety in what the people there were wearing. Some of the men were in gaudy pullovers, one in a crimson velvet jacket with a white frilly cravat spilling out at the neck, one or two in dinner jackets. Some of the women were in long skirts and well decorated with jewellery. One or two were in tight skirts that reached only halfway down their thighs, with brightly coloured blouses and shoes with very high heels. Mollie had come in probably the best dress she had in a fairly scanty wardrobe, for clothes had never been one of her interests. It was of ivory-coloured silk, simple and close-fitting. Anna Waldron, who came to meet the Davidges and Andrew as they came into the room, was in a plain black velvet dress, cut low at the neck, low-heeled black shoes with silver buckles and a collar of pearls. The hand that she held out to each of them was loaded with ancient-looking rings.

'You must forgive Sam for not being here to welcome you,' she said, as she had no doubt said to everyone else who had arrived. 'He's busy in the kitchen. He and I won't actually be dining with you tonight. When Parson Woodforde entertained or was entertained by his friends there was probably a whole staff of servants to cook and serve the wonderful meals they had, we've only got our two dear Bartletts. They've been splendid, entering into the spirit of the thing in the most delightful way, but of course Sam's the cook and he needs me to help him.'

As soon as she had seen that they were supplied with drinks, she turned away to make her prepared little speech to the next guest who had just come into the room. Andrew could see what an effort it was to her to conceal her shyness. There was no ease or spontaneity in her welcome, only a forced sweetness. The evening, he thought, would be an ordeal rather than a pleasure for her.

The next guest happened to be Felicity Mace. She was in a black jersey and a full flowered skirt and looked neat and pretty and practical. As soon as Anna had turned away from her, she remarked, 'The Singletons haven't come yet.'

Andrew had noticed that too.

She went on, 'But Ernest's here, trying to hide in that corner. I think I must go and do my best to get him out of it. Since he actually decided to come half the battle's over.'

'Or hasn't begun yet,' Ian said.

'Oh no,' she said with her pleasant, good-natured smile. 'He's got perfectly good manners. I don't really think there's any risk of his making a scene.'

'Perhaps Luke Singleton won't come,' Mollie said. 'If Brian's told him that Ernest's going to be here, he might have the sense to keep out of sight.'

'But think what a disappointment that would be for everyone,' Felicity said. 'We don't often have celebrities in Lower Milfrey.'

She moved through the throng towards the corner where Ernest Audley stood. At the same time a tall man entered the room, to be greeted by Anna with her little speech, the same as she had made to the Davidges and to Felicity, except that for a moment she sounded spontaneous, as she exclaimed, 'Oh, how good of you to come, Inspector! Of course you know we'd have understood perfectly if you'd been far too busy.'

He answered, 'I'd no intention of missing the evening if I could possibly manage it, Mrs Waldron. Your husband told me there's venison tonight. Not many people know how to cook venison and it's not much good if you don't know how. But I know I can trust him to go about it the right way, and that's a treat I wouldn't miss for anything.'

He was a broad-shouldered man, heavy in his build, and though he did not look much more than forty, his short, rough hair was already turning grey. His face was square, with wide-spaced, heavy-lidded eyes. He was in a dark suit that did not fit him very well. It did not actually look too tight for him, but as if perhaps it had been made for him when his muscles had somehow been differently developed from their present condition.

As he came further into the room, his eyes fell on Andrew. He stood still for a moment, looking at him. Then he suddenly came forward, his hand outstretched.

'Professor Basnett,' he said. 'I wonder if you remember me.'

'Inspector Roland,' Andrew answered. 'I certainly do.'

'We meet in pleasanter circumstances than last time,' the detective said. 'You were of great help to us, as I remember it, over that very unpleasant affair at Upper Cullonden. But you may not care to have it recalled.'

'It isn't a pleasant memory,' Andrew admitted, 'but I'm glad if you think I was of help.' He turned to Ian and Mollie. 'Let me introduce an old acquaintance of mine, Inspector Roland, who had to handle the affair of the bomb that killed Sir Lucas Dearden. Inspector, these are old friends of mine with whom I'm staying at the moment, Mr and Mrs Davidge.'

'And are you particularly interested in Parson Woodforde?' the Inspector asked. 'This dinner seems to be held in honour of him.'

'I've heard of him, but never read his diary,' Andrew said.

'You should, you should,' Roland said. 'Mr Waldron introduced me to him. He's the only man I know of who actually let his pigs get drunk. As I remember it, he gave his pigs some beer grounds taken out of a barrel he had and they got so drunk that they couldn't stand up. He says he never saw pigs so drunk in his life.'

'I must certainly read him,' Andrew said. 'I've never seen a drunk pig.'

'I wonder if it improved the flavour of the pork,' Ian said. 'I'll ask Singleton if they've ever made any experiments of the kind at the Rockford Agricultural Institute.'

'Talking of Singleton,' Roland said, looking round the room, 'has our celebrity arrived? I know his brother, but I don't see him.'

'No, they aren't here yet,' Ian answered.

'I think I've read everything he's written,' Roland went on. 'Hopelessly inaccurate—his police procedure, you know—but such good reading. I can almost believe in the world he's created, it's so alive. I'll be interested to see what he's like.'

But the next to arrive were not the Singleton brothers, but Eleanor Clancy. She was in a short, sleeveless dress of vivid green, which somehow made her look even bonier and gawkier than she had when Andrew had seen her last. She gave a little crow of pleasure on seeing Ian and Mollie, and clutched Mollie by the arm.

'Oh, my dears, I'm so glad you're here before me, because of course I don't know a soul,' she said, 'and really I feel I've no right to be here. I mean, I only met Mr and Mrs Waldron that once in your house. Of course it was very interesting to meet them, very interesting. It was so strange recognizing her after all these years. But I still have a sort of feeling I'm imposing on them by coming. I very nearly changed my mind at the last minute and didn't come. But then I'm so anxious to meet Luke again. I told you I used to know him slightly in the days before he got famous, didn't I? I wonder if I'll recognize him as I did Suzie—I mean Anna. I think I'm rather clever at recognizing people. Oh—there he is!' As she broke off Brian Singleton came into the room, followed by another man.

It struck Andrew that the brothers bore no resemblance to one another. Whereas Brian was tall and broad-shouldered, muscular and ruddy, Luke Singleton was several inches the shorter, slender, sharp-featured and pallid. He held himself with a rigid uprightness, almost as if he was on parade, and his face was bleakly expressionless. It gave no sign of the colourful and violent imagination that must churn within him. When Anna Waldron hurried to greet him he responded with a small smile and a stiff little bow that was almost Germanic. When Brian introduced him to the Davidges and Andrew, he repeated the bow, accepted a drink and then was led by Brian to meet other people.

'You see, he didn't know me!' Eleanor exclaimed, but she said it almost as if this pleased her, rather than otherwise. She gave a little giggle. 'But I'd have known him anywhere, although he's really changed a great deal. He used to look much friendlier, and that stiff way of holding himself, as if he'd like you to think he's in the army, that's new. But I suppose he has to keep people at arm's length or they'd trample all over him. I believe in his way he's really very shy—oh!' She broke off again as Sam Waldron appeared in the doorway.

He was wearing a long white apron and a cook's white hat. As he appeared he clapped his hands, and at once there was silence in the room.

'Ladies and gentlemen,' he said, 'may I have your attention for a moment?'

❀ ❀ ❀

He beamed at the company in the room.

'First of all,' he said, as the company waited, 'I want to bid you welcome and to thank you for coming here tonight to help me indulge this whim of mine. It is my desire to give you the kind of meal that the people who lived in this house over two hundred years ago, but who I can't pretend, as you know, were kin of mine, would have given you as a matter of course on a festive occasion. But you needn't be frightened. I don't want to chase you away by making you fear for your digestions. I am not going to give you the actual meal that they would have had, but I will read you a menu of such a meal, then tell you what items I have selected from it, I hope for your pleasure.'

He paused for a moment, took a piece of paper from a pocket in his great white apron, and went on.

'This was a dinner given by a bishop in his palace to twenty guests. You are about twenty this evening, I believe, but alas, I am no bishop and this is not a palace, and this is not the year 1783, but is near the end of the twentieth century. Had these things been otherwise, however, you would have had two dishes of prodigious fine stewed carp and tench, a fine haunch of venison, a fine turkey poult, partridges, pigeons and sweetmeats, followed by mulberries, melon, currants, peaches, nectarines and grapes. And do you know, as I read it now, that doesn't seem such an outrageously great meal as it did when I read it first. All the same, I'm not about to inflict it on you. There are tench, caught in our own pond on the common, but no carp, and I hope, after the way in which I have cooked them you will not find they taste of mud. There is a fine haunch of venison. Anna and I brought it back with us from Scotland, and it has been marinading in red wine with herbs and garlic for two days. I hope you will enjoy it. Then there are partridges and pigeons if you can face them, but I have omitted the turkey, and for sweetmeats I have made raspberry tarts, as these seem to have been a particular favourite of our friend Woodforde. For dessert I have omitted the melon and currants, but am proud that I managed to obtain some mulberries. And of course there are Madeira and red and white wines. I'm sorry that Anna and I will not be with you when you sit down to this meal, as we shall be needed in the kitchen, but we hope to join you for coffee. Two excellent ladies, the Bartlett sisters, will wait on you. Now please make your way to the dining room.'

A burst of clapping followed the end of the speech. Sam Waldron bowed, then disappeared as suddenly as he had come. Anna remained to usher the guests into the dining room, then disappeared also.

They filed from one room into the other, finding that they were expected to choose seats for themselves. The room was a long one, with a long, narrow table down the middle of it, and a magnificent arrangement of flowers down its centre. It was set with fine silver, probably Georgian, and glittering glass and was covered with a delicately embroidered cloth which had surely been preserved with loving care in some chest or cupboard for all of two hundred years and was probably a thing of great value. To Andrew, the scene seemed so perfect in its way that it was a pity that anything should be done to disturb it.

Brian Singleton guided his brother to a seat about half way down the table and he himself took one opposite him on the other side of it. Andrew found himself somehow near one end, with the vicar on one side of him and a small dumpling of a woman on the other, who introduced herself as Mrs Delano and who had a rosy, wrinkled face and very short grey hair. He guessed that she was well over eighty, but to judge by all that she told him about herself as they sat side by side, she was involved in all the activities of the village, more often than not as chairman and was taking all those accumulated years in her stride. The vicar startled a good many people by loudly clearing his throat to catch their attention, then saying grace, a

ritual to which many of them were not accustomed. But all that
he wanted to talk about to Andrew was cricket, about which
Andrew happened to know even less than he did about the
church, which he had seldom attended except for the marriages
or funerals of friends. However, the vicar was a friendly, good-
humoured man who found Andrew's ignorance amusing but
forgivable.

The Davidges had separated. Ian was at the far end of
the table, Mollie about half way down it, sitting next to Brian
Singleton. Inspector Roland had managed to secure a place on
the left hand of Luke Singleton. Felicity Mace was on his right.
Eleanor Clancy was beside the Inspector. When Andrew first
glanced round the table he thought that Ernest Audley after all
had decided not to attend the dinner, but then he saw him only
a few places from himself, but with a singularly massive man
between them, who nearly concealed him. There was no one
else at the table whom Andrew had met before, but he noticed
that almost everyone was middle-aged to elderly. It was clear
that the Waldrons had felt that the kind of entertainment that
they were offering would not appeal to the young.

Andrew found the entertainment, when it came, formi-
dable. Served with skill and efficiency by two women, one of
whom had met them when they arrived and both of whom wore
long aprons, starched cuffs and mob caps, it was still extremely
solid and as course followed course he found himself leaving at
least half of each untouched. For a few years now he had almost
given up eating a heavy meal in the evening. A sandwich, some
fruit and a cup of coffee was what suited him best. Yet he found
the tench excellent, the venison, not one of his favourite dishes,
more appetizing than he had expected, and a minute portion
of partridge just manageable. He skipped the raspberry tarts
and waited for the fruit, the fine selection of which looked very
tempting. He drank Madeira, something he seldom did, but
which he found that in the circumstances he quite enjoyed, and
with some curiosity he watched the other people at the table to
see how they were faring. Most of them were managing rather

better than he was, the vicar, in fact, made a very hearty meal of it, and perhaps, Andrew thought, might have been happier in the eighteenth century than most of the other people there.

He saw that Luke Singleton was very quiet. He talked only a little to either of his neighbours. Yet when he talked to Felicity a sudden smile of great charm would light up his pale, stern face. Talking to the Inspector it was more likely to remain tight and expressionless. Andrew recognized that when he chose, he could become surprisingly handsome. His features, in their sharp way, were good and all that they needed was some animation to make him no doubt attractive to women. He had at least been able to take Ernest Audley's wife away from him. As far as Andrew had seen, neither he nor Audley had taken any notice of one another. He had either recognized Eleanor Clancy or had been introduced to her, for occasionally he responded when she talked to him with determination across the Inspector, nodding at what she said if he did not go quite so far as to answer it, and once or twice giving her the benefit of his charming smile.

Brian Singleton appeared to be in extremely good spirits, chatting mostly to Mollie and ignoring a small, fidgety man who was on the other side of him. It was as he watched Brian and Mollie that what was surely an absurd yet still a disturbing thought came into Andrew's mind. It was simply that they always seemed so relaxed, so contented, one might almost say so happy in one another's company. Thinking back, he realized that it had always been so when he had seen them together, though at the time he had paid it no attention. And probably there was no reason why he should do so now. Yet all of a sudden he remembered with a slight shock how strangely Mollie had blushed when he had praised her embroidery.

He had taken it at the time as merely a sign that perhaps she did not get as much praise for her work as was due to her from Ian, whose interests were all outdoor ones, and who perhaps thought embroidery an uninteresting, female sort of occupation. But later Andrew had heard that all Mollie's designs had been supplied by Brian, taken from photographs from the electron microscope at the Institute. It had not meant anything to Andrew at the time, but now the memory of the strange brightness of her face when he spoke of her designs thrust itself into his mind and in spite of himself took on a possibly distressing meaning. For it would distress him if it should turn out that her marriage to Ian was not a satisfactory one. Andrew liked people to be happily married.

But how stupid he was being, perhaps just because of the Madeira and the heavy food and the noise that engulfed him in the room, and a story that Mrs Delano was telling him about the pregnancy of her cleaning woman, such a nice, quiet respectable young woman, who would shortly have to give up her work, leaving Mrs Delano with no help in the house.

'And that, at my age, is a serious matter,' she said. 'I've very kind neighbours who I'm sure will help me, but I don't like to impose on people, just because I'm old. Already my shopping is often done for me. Do you know Mr Singleton? Brian Singleton, the brother of the author. He generally drives me once a week into Rockford to the supermarket and pushes my trolley round for me inside and brings me home again. He's so kind and good-natured. I often wonder why he's never got married. But for all one knows these days he's got a girlfriend, who's got a job of her own, and they just don't bother about marriage. I sometimes wonder what I'd have done myself if things had been different when I was young. I married at nineteen. My husband was a young surgeon, who became very successful and who was ten years older than me. I had a voice, you know, I might have done something with it. But during the war years we saw so little of one another that I sometimes wondered if being married was really such an advantage. He died of a stroke, poor man, fifteen years ago, working to the end...'

Her talk drifted away from the subject of marriage to the activities of an amateur operatic society in the village and Andrew stopped worrying about Mollie and Brian, except to wonder a little at himself for ever asking himself the question he had about their relationship.

Coffee came at last. A good deal of the food that had been brought into the dining room had been taken back to the kitchen, but still it had been an outstanding meal, one to remember. When the remnants of it had been cleared away the Bartlett sisters came round with coffee cups, and with the coffee which they poured into them. Cream and sugar were put on the table.

In a low tone, the vicar said to Andrew, 'When Sam and Anna appear, one of us ought to give a vote of thanks. If no one else has been appointed to do it, I'll take it on myself. Do you think that would be appropriate?'

'I'm sure it would,' Andrew replied. 'And I quite agree with you that someone should do it.'

'They must have worked for days, you know, to give us this extraordinary feast. Not that I'm not certain they've enjoyed every minute of it. I know that Sam was planning something of the sort at some time and only delayed it as long as he did because he didn't feel sure of the reception of something which, of course, is a little eccentric. But I wouldn't have missed it for worlds—'

He broke off as an extraordinary noise came from further down the table. It began as a kind of cry, then came a choking sound, then a coffee cup fell on the table and coffee splashed over the beautifully embroidered cloth. Then a chair fell over backwards with someone in it who went into violent convulsive seizures. It was Luke Singleton.

Nearly everyone at the table pushed their chairs back, standing up to try to discover what was happening, but Inspector Roland and Felicity Mace had immediately knelt down on either side of the fallen man, who appeared to be unconscious, whose jaws were clenched and who had some fine foam coming out from between his lips.

'A fit,' the vicar murmured in Andrew's ear. 'Poor chap. I'd never heard he was epileptic.'

Felicity was feeling Luke Singleton's pulse, the Inspector was lifting one of his eyelids; Eleanor Clancy reached out to set the spilled coffee cup the right way up.

Seeing what she was about to do, Roland shouted at her, 'Don't touch it!'

She drew her hand sharply back, frightened at his tone.

Brian Singleton had raced round the table and stooped, white-faced, over his brother, but most people drew a little back, making a circle round the group on the floor. The Bartlett sisters fled together to the kitchen, to tell Sam and Anna how their party had ended.

The Inspector gave a deep sigh and stood up. He bent over the table where the coffee had been spilled and sniffed it.

'Cyanide, Doctor, you agree?' he said to Felicity.

'No doubt of it at all,' she answered.

At that moment Sam Waldron came running into the room. He looked wild with anxiety. Anna was a little way behind him. She looked strangely calm, which might be how she would always react to disaster, but was very pale.

'What's happened?' Sam cried out. 'Those Bartlett women talked about someone being taken ill—oh God!' He had seen Luke Singleton on the floor, still now, the seizures having come to an end. 'What's the matter with him, Roland?'

'Death,' the Inspector said. 'That's what's the matter with him.'

Sam strode forward. 'You don't mean it!' But he stood still a yard or two away from the terribly still figure and drew a few deep breaths, trying to gain control of himself. 'But how? When?'

'I'm not making any official statement,' the Inspector said, 'but my guess is that he was poisoned a few minutes ago with cyanide, which somehow got into the coffee he drank. You can smell the bitter almond smell, and his symptoms are typical, rapid loss of consciousness, dilated pupils non-reactive to light, an irregular pulse, jaws tightly clenched and froth at the mouth, convulsive seizures, and death following almost immediately.'

'He's dead. You're really sure he's dead?' Sam demanded.

Roland gave a grave glance at Felicity, who nodded.

'Here—poisoned—after my dinner!'

The habit of quotation that had such power over Andrew's consciousness asserted itself now, bringing to his mind the reaction of Lady Macbeth, when she hears from Macduff that Duncan has been murdered, and cries out, 'What, in our house!'

But Sam seemed to recognize immediately how inappropriate his cry had been, for he laid a hand on Brian's shoulder and said, 'Brian, I'm sorry—damnably sorry! I don't begin to understand what can have happened. No one else has suffered. But that this should have happened to your brother, of all people, your gifted brother... Roland, what do you want us to do? You're in charge here.'

'I think it would help if everyone would go into the other room, where we were before coming in here for dinner,' Roland replied. 'And then I would like the use of a telephone.'

'Certainly, certainly!' Sam said. He turned to the people grouped near the dead man and those still at the table. 'Did you all hear that? Inspector Roland would like us all to go into the room across the hall.'

'And I would be grateful if no one leaves the house for the moment,' Roland added. 'I'm sorry if it's an inconvenience for you.'

'No one could think it an inconvenience at such a time,' the vicar said. 'We'll of course do what you ask.'

Sam seemed suddenly to lose his self-control again. 'But it isn't possible, it simply isn't possible! How could he be given cyanide at my table?'

No one tried to answer him, and the move towards the other room began. People trod slowly and quietly on the soft, deep carpet, as if they felt that unless they took due care they could disturb the man they had left behind them. Mostly they avoided meeting each other's eyes, looking down at the floor. But for a moment Andrew met the eyes of Ernest Audley. It was only for a moment, and afterwards Andrew would not have been ready to swear that he had seen what he thought that he had, but very briefly it seemed to him that there was a smile on the man's face.

Chapter Four

It was half past one before the Davidges and Andrew got home. A lot had happened in the Waldrons' house before, one by one, having been briefly questioned by Inspector Roland, with a young sergeant present in the room, the guests had been allowed to leave. The questioning took place in a small room beside the dining room. It had little in it but a big desk, a table, some bookcases and a few chairs. Andrew supposed, when he saw it, that Sam Waldron must use it as a study. But before Andrew's turn there came, the house seemed to have filled with busy, often loud-voiced men, tramping about, some with cameras, some presently with a stretcher, and it sounded as if there was a frequent coming and going of cars in the courtyard in front of the house.

As they waited in the room where they had had drinks before the dinner, Sam pressed his guests to have brandy, but very few accepted the offer. Perhaps there was something not very inviting about the thought of drinking in a house where poisoning by cyanide had just taken place. Sam himself, divested of his apron and hat, was the first to be called to his study. He was gone some time, and while he was gone there was almost silence in the room that he had left. Then, when he returned, there was a long pause before anyone else was asked to follow him.

He explained it. 'They're questioning the Bartlett sisters. That seems crazy, doesn't it, two innocent souls like them, but really it makes quite good sense. They were serving the coffee. If anyone had a chance of seeing how this impossible thing was done, it might be them. It is just possible, I suppose, that they could have seen something that didn't strike them as meaning anything at the time, but which will mean something to that policeman. No, I don't believe it. I don't believe it really happened at all, unless, of course, it was suicide. That's the only explanation that makes sense.'

No one made any response to this suggestion, and after a while Brian Singleton was called out of the room.

He did not return to it, so it seemed likely that he had either been allowed to return to his home, or perhaps had left in the ambulance that had taken away his brother's body, though there would have been nothing that he could have done for him, and seeing him settled into the morgue would not have been anything but a very distressing experience.

After him, Felicity Mace had been questioned. She had come into the room where all the other guests were waiting some time later than any of them, for she had been kept in the dining room until the police surgeon from Rockford had arrived. Then it was Eleanor Clancy's turn. Then, strangely enough, it was Mollie's. But the reason for this was quite simple. She had been sitting almost opposite Luke Singleton and although the elaborate flower arrangement with which the table was decorated had been between them, she was one of the people who might have seen anything strange that had happened about the way that the coffee was served to him, or that had been done to it immediately afterwards. When she came back and sat down beside Ian she was very white and as he was the next to be called away she turned to Andrew.

'I didn't see anything,' she murmured. 'I wasn't even looking at him. Brian had just picked a carnation out of those flowers on the table and given it to me, and I was telling him he ought not to have done such a thing, but he insisted on my slipping it in behind this brooch I'm wearing, and then that awful noise began…' She gave a gulp to stop herself sobbing.

Andrew noticed that the carnation was gone.

'What have you done with the flower?' he asked.

'The police kept it,' she answered, 'I don't know why. And they kept on and on asking me if I hadn't seen anything that could explain how the cyanide got into the coffee, but I hadn't, I really hadn't. Oh, Andrew, how awful to have brought you down here for this.'

'That's a fairly minor part of the trouble,' he assured her. 'But I think you can be glad that Roland's in charge. He's an intelligent man.'

Andrew's own interrogation came some time later. As he entered Sam Waldron's office, the Inspector gave him a grim sort of smile and as he invited him to take one of the chairs at the table he observed, 'It seems to be our lot, Professor, to meet under distressing circumstances. Sometimes I think we should make an arrangement to meet where crime really cannot occur, such as the middle of a Highland moor or in a boat on some very quiet lake somewhere or other.'

'The Highlands have seen plenty of crime in their day,' Andrew answered, 'and we might find a body or two in the lake. But perhaps we might one day meet, say, for tea at the Ritz. I have a feeling we could safely develop our relationship there in peace and quiet.'

'You're probably right,' Roland said. 'And I'm sure we should find we had a good deal of interest to tell one another. Meantime, however, we have work to do. We'll begin, I think, with my asking you what brought you to Lower Milfrey at just this time?'

'I came because I'd been invited to come by my old friends, the Davidges. I'd known them for years when they lived in London. Ian Davidge was my accountant long ago, while his first wife was still alive, and mine too. I think it was partly because the two women met and became very good friends that Davidge and I drifted into friendship. My visit had no special purpose except to spend a pleasant week with him and Mollie Davidge. The time we chose for it had no special significance.'

Roland nodded, and the sergeant who was sitting in a corner of the room jotted something down in his notebook.

'Is this your first visit here, then?' Roland asked.

'Yes,' Andrew answered.

'Had you ever met any of the other people here before this evening?'

'Before this visit? No. But I met several of them a few evenings ago at a small party the Davidges gave. And I spent most of the morning with Miss Clancy, being photographed.'

'Ah, you've had that experience. Do you know, she asked me this evening if I'd allow her to photograph me. She said I had a splendid head. However, we settled nothing, and I have a feeling she may not be as anxious to pursue the matter now—though you never know. What's happened this evening, and the fact that I was sitting next to the victim, might add a special sense of excitement to the experience. You never know where you are with these enthusiasts. But do I understand that you know very little about the relationships among the people you met?'

'Very little indeed.'

'Do you know anything, for instance, about Luke Singleton's relationship with a former Mrs Audley?'

'Only what I've heard by way of gossip,' Andrew said. 'I've been told that she left her husband for Singleton, that there was a divorce, and that after it he deserted her. But I never met the lady, and I met Audley for the first time at the Davidges' party the other evening. I've been into his home once since then for a drink, and seen his very interesting collection of butterflies, and that's really all I know about him.'

'Butterflies? He collects butterflies, does he?' The Inspector seemed unexpectedly interested.

'I don't think so,' Andrew replied. 'I think he told me the collection was made by his father. It's a hobby that isn't too well regarded these days, when there's a feeling that we ought to protect the lovely things instead of catching and killing them. But they made a very fine show on his wall.'

Roland gave a shake of his head. 'A pity.' But it was not pity for the butterflies that made him say it. 'Here's someone with a really sound motive for wanting Singleton dead, and he was at the far end of the table. Unless he managed to bribe one of those worthy women who were waiting on us to drop some cyanide in Singleton's coffee, or perhaps put it in his cup before it was actually put down before him and filled, I can't think of any possible way that he could have administered the poison. Now can you tell me if you yourself observed anything that could be useful to us that happened after Singleton had been served? I realize, of course, that I myself must be one of the chief suspects, sitting next to him as I was, and if you wish to question me, please do so. But I know you're an observant man, and though you were sitting some way away from Singleton, it seems to me just possible you may have noticed if anything odd happened near him.'

'The only slightly odd thing I saw is something I believe you've been told about already,' Andrew said. 'Just before Singleton gave that awful cry, I saw Brian Singleton, who was sitting opposite him, reach out and pluck a flower out of that elaborate affair on the table and turn to Mrs Davidge and persuade her to wear it. But I don't see how that can have anything to do with putting poison in his brother's coffee. It isn't as if he'd reached far across the table.'

Roland nodded. 'Yes, that agrees with what Mrs Davidge told us. There's just a possibility, I suppose, that when he reached out, for the flower, he did it to hide the fact that he was throwing a capsule of the poison into the coffee cup opposite. But he'd have been taking a fearful risk of being observed. I myself might have looked at him at just the wrong moment. However, he'd a motive, or probably he had. Luke Singleton was a rich man, and his brother very likely inherits what he had to leave. We shan't know that till tomorrow, when we've had a chance to talk to his solicitor, but it's at least worth investigating. Then Miss Clancy told me she'd known Singleton slightly a number of years ago. She'd told me that at the dinner, before the murder happened. She seemed very proud of it, but when she talked to him across me, he seemed very vague about recognizing her. He didn't quite say that he hadn't the least idea who she was, but he gave the impression of simply being too polite to say that, though it was the fact.'

'You're sure it was murder, not suicide?' Andrew asked.

'Don't you think so yourself?'

'Well, yes, I do. It would have been a singularly exhibitionist way of committing suicide. But if you rule that out, you're back to the problem of how the cyanide got into Singleton's coffee, and nobody else's.'

'Of course, it might have been to some extent a mistake. I mean, that it was given to the wrong man. It just possibly might have been meant for me. There I was, right beside him, and there are plenty of people, I think, who wouldn't mind seeing the last of me.'

'But even then, you'd still be left with the problem of how the poison got into just that one cup of coffee.'

'Yes, and I've a feeling that when we've found that out, we'll know who did it. Good night, Professor. Thank you for your help.'

That was the end of the questioning of Andrew, and he was told that if he and the Davidges wanted to go home, they were free to do so.

He joined them in the room where they were waiting for him and the three of them went out to the Davidges' car. When they arrived home, Mollie said that she was going to make some cocoa, but Ian and Andrew both said that they would prefer the brandy that they had refused in the Waldrons' house. They were all very tired, and though they remained in the sitting room for some time, they spoke very little. All of them, Andrew thought, were almost afraid of going to bed, because they would only have to face the torment of sleeplessness.

However, all of a sudden Ian exclaimed, 'Of course it's impossible! It couldn't have happened.'

'But it did,' Mollie muttered. 'It did.'

'But the only people who could have done it are the Bartlett sisters, and that's nonsense.'

'I wonder if it *is* such nonsense,' Mollie said.

'What d'you mean?' he asked sharply.

'Well, what do we really know about them?' she asked.

'That they're two very respectable women who've lived in Lower Milfrey all their lives, and have worked for the Waldrons ever since they came here, about six years ago.'

'I wonder who they worked for before that. Why were they free to go to the Waldrons? Were there any mysterious deaths in the family who employed them?'

'Mollie, I think it's time we went to bed. You're beginning to wander in your mind.'

'Not really,' she insisted. 'Actually I'm only trying to eliminate the Bartletts. At the same time, I think we should face facts. They *could* have done the murder.'

'Thank God it isn't our job to face facts,' Ian said. 'We can leave that to the estimable Inspector Roland.'

'He had a rather interesting idea,' Andrew said. 'It was that the poison was intended for him and not for Luke Singleton and that it was put in the coffee cup in front of Singleton by mistake.'

'There you are!' Mollie exclaimed. 'The Bartletts may never have met Luke Singleton in their lives and so just couldn't have had any reason to kill him. But it isn't at all unlikely that they've sometime encountered Roland. Perhaps one of them had a lover once and Roland got him put in gaol, and that dinner was the first opportunity they've had since then to have their revenge. They'd have known he was coming to it and could have laid in the cyanide somehow, in preparation for it, and simply relied on their reputation for virtue not to be suspected.'

'How did they get the cyanide?' Ian asked.

'Oh, I'm sure there are all sorts of ways of getting it, if you're determined enough. And knowing who was coming to the dinner, they'd have had time to do it.'

'You don't actually believe a word you're saying, do you?'

She sighed. 'I suppose I don't. But there's one thing I'm sure of and that is that the Inspector isn't going to take their innocence for granted. He'll have thought of all the things I've just been saying to you and he'll investigate those two good women very thoroughly, just as he's going to investigate all of us, and Felicity too, who was sitting beside Luke, and Eleanor, who was sitting beside Roland. After all, when Roland was talking to Luke, with his head turned away from Eleanor, she might have reached out and slipped something into Luke's cup. And she used to know Luke, when they were both teachers.'

'Do you think she'd really have paraded that, as she did, if she'd been intending to kill him?'

'And how could she know beforehand that she'd be sitting near him?' Andrew asked. 'We all sat down pretty much at random, and she might easily have found herself with a helping of cyanide in her handbag, but no chance of getting near him.'

'I wonder if Felicity ever had an affair with Luke,' Mollie said thoughtfully.

That seemed to bring the discussion to a close. For a little while they remained there, silent, Ian helping himself to more brandy, but both Mollie and Andrew refusing it, and Andrew then standing up and saying that he was going to bed.

'We're going to be so tired of the whole subject before we're finished,' he said. 'There's no point in exhausting all its possibilities now. Good night. Sleep well.' He left them and went up to his room.

In bed, he turned out the light on his bedside table, but as he had expected, sleep did not come with the darkness. But it was restful to be stretched out and still. It was strange that he did not find himself thinking much of the scene in the Waldrons' dining room. It was as if a curtain had come down in his mind, concealing it from him. Instead he began to think of other occasions when he had been away from home, on holidays with Nell. There was one that he remembered which they had spent in a small fishing village near Marseilles, almost as soon as it had been possible to go abroad after the end of the war. The amount of foreign currency they had been allowed to take with them had been minute, and they had had to consider carefully the cost of every cup of coffee that they had, every bottle of the cheap *vin du pays*.

But they had been young, the weather had been perfect, the swimming in the little bay delightful, and Nell's excellent French had made a firm friend of their landlady who had had a way of slipping little delicacies to them that did not appear on the bill. Andrew remembered that there had been a small Greek staying in the village, who went about naked except for a faded and tattered pair of shorts, and who had tried very hard, though without success, to persuade them to buy a variety of goods from him on the black market. He was ready to let them take the goods home with them without payment, if they would agree to deposit a cheque for what they owed him in a certain London bank. 'I trust you, you see,' he said. 'I do business like an Englishman.'

Then the following year they had gone to Italy. The amount of foreign currency they had been able to take with them was twenty-five pounds each, but on that they had managed to stay in a little hotel near Sorrento, swimming and revelling in sunshine for three weeks, counting every lira that they spent and refusing to be tempted into buying any of the pretty things they saw in the way of corals and inlaid boxes.

But that in its way had been a mistake, though they had learnt something from it, for on returning home and having their luggage examined at Customs, their statement that they had nothing to declare had simply not been believed, and their suitcases had been searched from top to bottom. His inability to discover anything on which duty would have to be paid had intensely irritated the Customs officer who was dealing with them and he had looked at them with deepening dislike and suspicion, until at the bottom of Nell's suitcase he had at last found a paper bag containing something that he instantly found suspicious. He had glanced at her with an air of triumph. But all the paper bag had contained was some knitting wool that she had taken abroad with her but had never got around to using. The official's look at her had been venomous. And ever after that, when they went abroad, they had always made a point of buying and declaring something, a thing that became easier to do as currency restrictions were relaxed, and which had generally led to their suitcases being passed through Customs without being opened. Innocence, they had realized, was a very suspicious thing. People found it very hard to believe in it. And there he was, after all, back to what had happened at the Waldrons', because soon, like Mollie, people were going to start questioning the innocence of the Bartlett sisters. They might even start questioning the innocence of Sam and Anna Waldron, though both had been in the kitchen and could not possibly have had anything to do with giving Luke Singleton poisoned coffee unless they had somehow used the Bartletts to do it for them. Knowingly or unknowingly.

By the time that he had reached that point, drowsiness had descended on Andrew and with a confused conviction in his mind that Sam, Anna and the Bartletts might soon be in need of protection, he drifted into sleep.

❀ ❀ ❀

Next morning Mollie brought him his breakfast tray as she had every morning since his arrival, though rather later than she had done it before. He wondered, looking at her, if she had had any sleep at all. There were blue shadows under her eyes and they had the reddened look of weariness. But the coffee, the orange juice, the cornflakes, the toast and marmalade and the cube of cheese were all as usual. She asked him if he had slept well, but did not seem to listen for his answer, and left him quickly, as if there were things that she had to see to. But when he went downstairs presently he found her sitting idly in the sitting room with the Sunday paper open on her knees, but her gaze fixed absently on the window. Ian was at a table, mounting photographs of birds in an album.

When Andrew came into the room, Mollie gave a deep sigh, as if his presence was one thing more than she could bear and which made him feel that if only the police would agree to his going home, it would be an excellent thing for him to do. Actually, that was something about which he had been thinking while he had been getting shaved and dressed. It would be so very pleasant to return to his flat in St John's Wood, to be alone there, quiet and free from the sense of violence near him. But until he had had a chance to discuss this with Inspector Roland, he could hardly raise it with Ian and Mollie.

She held the newspaper out to him.

'They've got it here already,' she said, 'and it was on the news at nine—only a brief item as something that had just come in, but of course the press will be down in hordes now. It'll be frightful.'

'There's no special reason why they should bother us,' Ian said, looking up from what he was doing. 'We're not involved with any of the people concerned. Look at that.' He held out a photograph to Andrew. 'Isn't it a beauty? It's a golden plover. I took it last year, but I never seem to have had time to cope with the job of mounting these things.'

Andrew glanced at it, but was more anxious to read what was in the newspaper that Mollie was holding out to him. He found that there was only a brief paragraph about the sudden death of a famous writer, but it did not call it murder. All the same, it implied that there was certainly more to come, that the death was suspicious and that the police were on the scene.

While he was reading, the doorbell rang.

Ian went to answer it and brought in the Inspector. He also had the look of having had a sleepless night, but of being better able to bear it than any of the others in the room. He must have to face them more often than they did, Andrew guessed. He refused the coffee that Mollie offered him, but was ready to drop wearily into a chair by the empty fireplace and cover his mouth with his hand as he gave a great yawn.

'I'm sorry to bother you at this time of day,' he said, 'but there's something I want to ask you. A small thing. I believe you're fairly close friends of Brian Singleton.'

Ian looked at Mollie as if he expected her to answer, and she said shortly, 'Yes.'

'Then can you confirm something that I've been told,' Roland went on. 'I've been told he's an expert conjuror.'

'Magicians, they seem to like to call themselves nowadays,' Ian said. 'It's a bit of a hobby of Singleton's, but I don't think he's very expert. He only took it up a year or two ago.'

'Expert enough though, perhaps, for a little sleight of hand?' Roland suggested.

Mollie jumped up from her chair. Her blue eyes were blazing.

'I know what you mean, I know what you're going to say!' she cried. 'You're going to say that when Brian reached out to get that flower for me, he was really doing it to cover his somehow putting the cyanide into Luke's coffee. Isn't that it?'

'It's something we've got to consider,' Roland said.

'Well, it's nonsense, utter nonsense!' she went on vehemently. 'If he'd done anything like that I'd have seen it. Of course I would. Or do you think I did see it and that I'm in it with him? That's possible, isn't it? We're very good friends, and of course, if I'd seen anything like that I'd keep quiet about it, wouldn't I?'

'Mollie, shut up,' Ian said quietly. 'Let the Inspector do the talking.'

'Thank you, Mr Davidge,' Roland said, 'but there's really not much else I want to say at the moment. There's the question, of course, of where the cyanide came from. Have you any useful ideas about that?'

No one answered him.

He went on, 'I'm not sure if it's still in use, I've an idea that it isn't, but it was once used in all photographic work, and Miss

Clancy, I've learned, is a very keen photographer, with a special interest in the kind of work that was done in her grandfather's, or was it her great-grandfather's day? She might have a supply of the stuff. Then Mr Audley has a collection of butterflies in his house, made by his father, and in his day killing bottles containing cyanide were a normal part of any entomologist's equipment. Surprisingly easy they were to get, too, at least if your chemist happened to know you and just let you sign his poison register and get away with enough cyanide to kill a regiment. Then Mr Singleton works in a scientific institute, and I'm sure cyanide's likely to be available there—'

'I knew it, I knew it!' Mollie broke in. 'I knew you'd get around to him sooner or later. You've made up your mind he's guilty.'

'My dear Mrs Davidge,' Roland said peaceably, 'I hadn't even got to the end of the possible sources of cyanide that I was going to mention. For one more than I have already, there's Dr Mace. I don't know if the people who supply her with drugs would be a little surprised if she ordered cyanide, but no doubt they'd assume she had a good use for it and would send it to her. And altogether there were about twenty people at the dinner party. So far we've been concentrating on the people who live in Lower Milfrey, we've even been questioning the vicar, to find out if he has any hobby that requires a supply of cyanide, but he seems to need all his time for his job. But we'll be going on to the people who came out from Rockford next. And I assure you we haven't made up our minds about anything. In fact, I can't remember a case of murder in which I've been involved—luckily there haven't been many—in which my mind has so completely failed to be made up about any aspect of it this number of hours after it happened. And with me sitting next to the victim! By the way, have you been troubled by the press yet?'

'No,' Ian replied.

'You will be, if I'm not mistaken. Everyone who was at that dinner is likely to be approached, and some of them will actually enjoy it. Now, good morning, and thank you for your help.'

He turned to the door and Ian went with him to show him out of the house.

Coming back, Ian said, 'I'm going for a walk.'

What struck Andrew as strange about him was that he looked astonishingly angry. There was almost a scowl on his face. He did not invite either Mollie or Andrew to accompany him, but without giving either of them a direct look, went out after the detective. When he closed the front door it was with a slight slam.

Looking at Mollie to see what she made of this, Andrew saw to his surprise that she was crying. She was trying to control her sobs, but tears were streaming down her cheeks.

When she saw Andrew looking at her, she simply muttered, 'Hell!' gulped, and started to rub fiercely at her eyes with her handkerchief.

Andrew sat down and waited.

After a minute or two, she said huskily, 'It's obvious to everyone, isn't it?'

'That you and Brian are in love with each other?' he said. 'Yes.'

'If you wanted to conceal it, you could have made a better job of it.'

'I don't know what I want. I don't know what Brian wants.'

'Do you want to leave Ian?'

'I don't know. I'm awfully fond of him, you see, and I hate to hurt him. But I don't think I was ever in love with anyone till I met Brian. And yet I was perfectly happy, isn't that strange?'

'You rather force that happiness of yours down one's throat, you know. From the first I found it a bit unconvincing.'

She was silent for a moment, then said, 'I wonder why I'm talking to you like this. I've never talked about it to anyone.'

'Not even to Brian?' he asked.

'Oh yes, to Brian, but we always end up with everything undecided. We've never been lovers, you know. I mean, we haven't slept together.'

'Perhaps you need that to clear the atmosphere.'

She gave him a look of surprise. 'I'd never have expected you to say that.'

'I'm not sure that I expected it of myself. How much does Ian know?'

'Everything, I think, though he's never said a word about it. But you saw how angry he got when I defended Brian to that policeman, and now going out for a walk by himself is just the sort of thing he always does when the truth looks like coming out.'

'He probably thinks that if he gives you time, you'll get over it. He must be very afraid of losing you. He may feel he'd never get over it.'

'But I'm a second wife and he got over losing his first wife, didn't he?'

'Perhaps he never has, and that's the trouble.'

This seemed to be a new thought for her and she sat staring before her, giving it some consideration. Then she shook her head.

'If I left him,' she said, 'he'd be very angry, and I suppose very hurt, but he wouldn't live alone for long. He might take up with Felicity. I've often wished he would, because that would solve everything.'

'Have there ever been any signs that he might do such a thing?'

She gave a troubled little laugh. 'None that I've ever noticed. It's just wish fulfilment on my part. Meanwhile, his bird-watching keeps him busy. But what do you think I ought to do, Andrew? Now that I've told you so much, can't you give me some advice?'

He shook his head. 'That's something I'd never dream of doing.'

'Do you think I ought to talk to Ian about it, bring it all out into the open, so to speak?'

'If that's what you want to do. All I can say is that I feel very sorry for all of you. Somebody's got to be hurt, whichever one of you it is. You'll have to face that. There are no magic remedies for this kind of thing. Now I think I'm going to go for a walk myself. Do you mind?'

'Not so long as it isn't because I'm driving you out by this outpouring of my emotions. I really don't know why it happened.'

'You had to talk to someone after you'd been so scared by Roland. But I shouldn't brood too much on that, Mollie. Brian would have to be a very brilliant magician to be able to lob poison across the table into his brother's cup without anyone seeing him.'

'But did that man believe I didn't see him?' She had been growing calmer, which was partly what had made Andrew decide to leave her, but now a note of hysteria was back in her voice. 'And anyway, if Brian didn't do it, who could have? Who did?'

'Mollie, you aren't implying that you yourself believe he did it, are you?' Andrew demanded, more deeply worried now than he had been by anything that had gone before.

'No, no, of course not. And go off for your walk, and try to forget everything I've been saying to you!'

She ran out of the room and Andrew heard her dart into the kitchen and start banging crockery and saucepans about with an unnecessary amount of noise. Reflecting sadly that he had not done her much good, and that no one would recommend him as a marriage counsellor, he started out on his walk.

In the road he hesitated, uncertain whether to go towards the village, or in the opposite direction, and his hesitation, in the mood that he was in at the moment, was fatal, for at that moment Eleanor Clancy came out of her cottage, saw him standing there and descended on him.

'Oh, Professor, just the person I want to see!' she cried, hurrying up to him. 'I was thinking of calling in at the Davidges', hoping I'd have a chance to talk to you, but this is ever so much better. You'll come in for a cup of coffee, won't you?'

'Are the photographs ready then?' he asked, finding himself walking towards her cottage with her.

'No, I'm afraid I haven't even started on them,' she answered. 'I was hoping, you see, that I might get a few of Luke Singleton—oh, doesn't that sound awful now?—and I was going to have a big day, working on them all. But I'll let you have proofs in a day or two. You'll still be here, won't you, you aren't thinking of going home because of what's happened?'

'I'm afraid, even if I wanted to, Inspector Roland might be against it,' Andrew said.

'But he's got no right to keep you here, if you want to leave, has he?'

'Technically, I believe not, but I don't want to make myself too unpopular.'

They had reached the cottage and gone in. Eleanor did not suggest that they have their coffee in the garden this morning, for the sky was overcast and there was a chilly little breeze blowing. She saw Andrew settled in an easy chair, thrust a Sunday paper at him and asked him if he had seen the notice in it of the murder, then went out to her kitchen to make the coffee. The paper was a different one from the Davidges', but the paragraph in it about the murder was more or less the same as the one that he had already read. There would be more than a paragraph tomorrow, he thought, and when Eleanor came in with the coffee tray he asked her if she had yet been troubled by the press.

'I've had one or two telephone calls,' she said, pouring out the coffee and sitting down. 'And that's one of the things I wanted your advice about. You see, someone's told them that I used to know Luke Singleton in the old days, and they wanted me to tell them about our relationship. Our relationship—I ask you! I simply told them there wasn't one, but I don't think they believed me, and I think they'll be round presently, badgering me about it. Well, what do you think I ought to do? I mean, do I stick to it that I didn't know him, or that I only knew him a little, or do I simply refuse to say anything at all? I've never had any dealing with the press and I'm rather scared of them in case they get me to say something wholly inappropriate. That's one thing I thought you might be able to advise me about.'

Andrew shook his head. 'I've had occasional dealings with them, but not enough to be able to advise you. And unless you've a strong feeling that you don't want to say anything at all, I'm inclined to think the only thing for you to do is to stick very carefully to the truth and to tell exactly the same story to all of them. Don't let any of them put words in your mouth. But you did know Singleton, didn't you? I remember hearing you say something of the kind.'

She gave an uneasy little smile.

'I did, yes, but I may have—well, exaggerated a little how well we knew each other. We belonged to the same tennis club, and sometimes after a game we'd have a drink together. But we never even went out together, and I can't remember a single thing we ever talked about. I think we used to discuss the game, and criticize one or two other players, and perhaps arrange to play again sometime, but you couldn't call that a relationship, now could you?'

Andrew remembered that Ian had said that you could not always believe what Eleanor said and he wondered now if what she was telling him was the truth, or whether what she had implied before was the more accurate.

'You recognized him when you saw him yesterday evening, didn't you?' he said.

'Oh yes, immediately!' she exclaimed. 'He'd changed very little. Those sharp features, and the thin cheeks—I'd have known them anywhere. But then I've rather a trick of recognizing people. Look at the way I knew Suzie at once.'

'I've noticed that you seem very observant,' Andrew said. 'You've a way of looking at people as if you were really working at committing them to memory.'

'Have I? I didn't realize...' She paused and her expression changed. A curiously wary look came over it, as if she suddenly felt that she should be careful what she said. But then, as if with an effort, she smiled again. 'I remember when I was a child people used to tell me not to stare at them so. Of course I only did it because I was interested in them, but people sometimes didn't like it. But I've always been very interested in people. That's a good thing for a teacher, of course.'

'You retired rather early, didn't you?' Andrew said.

'Well, a games mistress can't keep going too long,' she answered. 'And then I came into a little inheritance from an aunt, so I thought I'd go while I was still young enough to start a new life. Now may I ask you something more?'

'If you think I can help you.'

'Oh, it isn't a case of helping *me*, it's someone else. Someone I've grown very fond of in the short time I've been here. Do you think Mollie's in love with Brian Singleton?'

Of all the questions that she could have thought of asking him, it was the one that he would least have wanted to have to answer. But he knew that he must answer quickly, or she would become suspicious.

'That's an extraordinary question,' he said. 'Whatever made you think it?'

'Perhaps just that observant way I have of looking at people,' she said, and there was irony in her tone, as if she recognized that he had dodged her question.

He left as soon after that as he could and set out on the walk that she had interrupted.

He had gone only a little way along the pleasant country road, noticing that here and there among the trees the first copper tints of autumn were beginning to appear, when the verse that he had been keeping at bay all the morning gained possession of his mind and insisted on filling it.

And now I'm as sure as I'm sure that my name
Is not Willow, titwillow, titwillow,
That 'twas blighted affection that made him exclaim
Oh Willow, titwillow, titwillow...

He strode faster, hoping to defeat the rhyme by action. But apart from the lines, the thought of blighted affection was strongly present in his mind. But whose? Mollie's? Brian's? Or most all, perhaps, Ian's?

Then a quite different thought, without his even noticing that it had happened, took over his attention. It was the question of why, momentarily, Eleanor Clancy had seemed to be almost frightened when he told her that she had a way of looking at people as if she were committing them to memory. Why should she have minded it? She must know that she did it. There was something odd about the way that she had looked at him. Something rather odd too about the woman herself, though he did not know why he felt this.

Chapter Five

When Andrew returned to the Davidges' house he found that Ian had returned before him, and that he had Sam Waldron with him in the sitting room. Mollie was in the kitchen, busy with the lunch. Sam Waldron had the tiredness in his face that afflicted everyone whom Andrew had seen that morning. He thought it likely that neither of the Waldrons had been to bed at all the night before. The police had probably been in their home all night.

Sitting down, more tired himself than he had realized that he would be when he set out, he asked, 'Has anything at all been discovered yet about what happened last night?'

Sam made a grimace in answer.

'I think they've come to the conclusion that neither of the Bartletts had anything to do with it. And I think they believe the Bartletts that neither Mollie nor I gave them any special instructions about putting any particular cup down in front of Singleton. That was one of the bright ideas they had, you see—that we put cyanide into a cup in the kitchen, then instructed one of the Bartletts that that cup was to be given to Singleton. That would have made things nice and simple, wouldn't it? I think they've given it up now. They've found nothing useful in the way of fingerprints on Singleton's cup, or anywhere else, and all they've got is a small crop of motives, of which, of course, Audley's is the best. Only they don't pretend to be able to guess how someone sitting at the far end of the table, as Audley was, could have dropped anything into Singleton's coffee. It would have had to be done by magic. And talking of magic, they're fairly interested in Brian, because they know in a small way he's a so-called magician, and he did reach out across the table, I'm told, to pick a flower out of that arrangement on it, and might have done something tricky in the way of sleight of hand. If Brian had known the hours Anna took creating that arrangement, he might not have done anything so thoughtless, and would be saving himself some trouble now. But what I'd particularly like to know about that is whether Miss Clancy saw anything. If she did, she's keeping very quiet about it.'

'You know where she was sitting, then,' Ian said.

'Oh yes, the police have made a map of where everyone was sitting and I was given a copy of it, to see if it stimulated any ideas in my head. But I've really only one idea, you know, and that is that I'll never be able to look Parson Woodforde in the face again. To have tried to lay on a dinner in his honour, and have it turn out as it did! I think his diary will go back on to my bookshelf and stay there for a long time to come.'

Andrew was wondering if anything special had brought Sam Waldron to visit the Davidges that morning, or if it was something that might happen at any time without any special reason.

'I'm interested in why you should particularly want to know what Miss Clancy may have seen,' he said, 'rather than Dr Mace. She was actually sitting next to Singleton, Miss Clancy had the Inspector between her and him.'

Sam Waldron nodded, looking thoughtful.

'You're quite right, of course,' he said, 'and I suppose the only reason why I'm a bit suspicious of Miss Clancy is that I don't know her. I've known Felicity Mace for several years and I feel she's a person of complete integrity. But except that Miss Clancy once taught my wife lacrosse and cricket, and how to vault over horses in the gym and do clever things on horizontal bars, I don't know a thing about her. I think Anna once had a bit of a crush on her, but that doesn't mean she had the least understanding of her. What do you actually know about her, Ian?'

'Very little,' Ian answered. 'We put an advertisement in the local paper that we'd a cottage to let, and she answered it, then came to look it over and said she'd take it. She didn't argue about the rent or make trouble of any kind. She gave the headmistress at the school where she used to teach as a reference and moved in, and she's been a very good neighbour. She brings us homemade chutney and jam and she's taken our photographs and she gives me advice about the garden. Mollie likes her.'

'But you don't,' Sam said.

'Oh, I wouldn't say that,' Ian replied. 'We've nothing much in common, but I should say she's an admirable person.'

Sam nodded again, as if Ian's answer only confirmed what he had just said. He turned to Andrew.

'You haven't been very fortunate in the time of your visit,' he said. 'I assure you we haven't had another murder here in living memory. I'd like to invite you up to our house for a quiet drink, but I don't see much hope of quiet for the present.'

'Thank you,' Andrew said. 'You'll have plenty of visitors shortly, I imagine, without having me there to complicate things. Haven't the press descended on you yet?'

'By telephone, and that's partly why I came out. They were threatening to appear in person. Tell me, Professor, what's your impression of Eleanor Clancy?'

Andrew gave a shrug of uncertainty.

'I can't say why it is,' he said, 'but I've a feeling that there's something odd about her, apart, I mean, from her obvious eccentricities, which she rather likes to show off. Actually, I find myself in agreement with you that she may have seen something last night about which she's chosen to keep quiet. A dangerous thing to do. But I really don't know why I feel it. I may be totally wrong.'

'Yes, we may both be wrong,' Sam said, 'but I'm interested that you should have the same feeling as I have. Ian, do you know if she's wealthy?'

'Far from it, I should say,' Ian replied.

'I only thought...' Sam began, then stopped himself.

'Were you wondering if she might make use of her knowledge?' Andrew asked.

'What, blackmail, d'you mean?' Ian looked extremely startled.

'I only thought it might be what Waldron had in mind,' Andrew said.

'Well, for a moment I did think...' But Sam paused again. 'No, on our almost non-existent knowledge, it's outrageous to make such a suggestion. I'm sorry if I gave that impression. Ian, I'll be going now. I left Anna in bed, with her door locked against possible intruders, and the Bartletts to protect her, but I'd better see how she is. She got no sleep at all and she's not very strong. I'm worried about her. We'll see each other again soon, I expect.'

Ian saw him to the door.

Returning, he said, 'I think we'll have some sherry. Mollie—' He went to the hall and called, 'Mollie, we're going to have some sherry. D'you want to join us?'

There was no suggestion in his voice that he and Mollie had been close to a quarrel earlier, which had been avoided only by his deciding to go out for a walk. If he guessed what Mollie might have said to Andrew while he was gone, he gave no sign of it.

But that might be because he did not dream that Mollie would talk about her private feelings to Andrew. In answer to his call she came into the room and Ian poured out sherry for the three of them. She was looking her normal self, with no trace of tears on her face.

'What did Sam want?' she asked. 'I'm sorry I disappeared, but I felt I couldn't stand another dose of hashing up this murder. I suppose it was what he wanted to talk about.'

'What I thought he seemed to want,' Ian said, 'was to put it into our heads that Eleanor saw how Singleton was poisoned and is keeping her knowledge to herself in order to be able to blackmail whoever it was who did it. You know her a great deal better than I do. Would you say that's possible?'

'Eleanor?' Mollie gasped. 'Blackmail!' She began to laugh. 'Oh, she isn't that sort of person at all.'

'You think you know what sort of person a blackmailer is?'

'I don't think I've ever actually met one,' she said. 'Anyway, what was there for Eleanor to see? No one's come up yet with a reasonable suggestion about that. I'm beginning to think that after all, Luke Singleton committed suicide, and deliberately did it in a way that would get his death maximum coverage in the press. I wonder what his religious beliefs were. He may have thought he'd a chance of looking on while that was happening.'

'I doubt if anyone's ever committed suicide with that in view,' Andrew said. 'But he may have had reasons we know nothing about for doing it. Suppose he'd discovered he'd got an incurable illness. AIDS, for instance.'

'Or finally failed with some woman with whom for once he was really in love, and felt he couldn't face the humiliation,' Mollie suggested. 'Oh, it isn't difficult to find motives for suicide, any more than it is to find motives for his murder among the people who were in the room that evening. But the question remains, *how* was it done, unless it was done by one of the Bartletts.'

Ian nodded thoughtfully. 'I doubt if the police have really made up their minds about them yet, whatever they may be saying about them. Andrew, have some more sherry.'

'Thank you.' Andrew held out his glass. 'Now I want to ask you something, and I want you, please, to be absolutely honest in your answer. If the police don't want me to stay around, would you sooner I went home? It's a very disastrous thing that's happened to you, and you might feel better if you didn't feel you had to bother about me.'

'Oh no!' Mollie cried with a note of shrill alarm in her voice. 'I mean, unless you want to. If you do, of course, you must go home. But really it feels so helpful to have you around. You keep your head so well, you're a tremendous help.'

It was Mollie's view of the matter that Andrew had really wanted to know, for there was more than a possibility, he had thought, that by now she might be sorely regretting her confidence to him earlier in the morning. But he noticed that Ian had not answered.

'Are you sure?' Andrew said. 'You aren't going to hurt my feelings if you say you'd sooner be alone.'

Ian answered then with a kind of reluctance. 'You'd hardly be human if you didn't want to go, but Mollie's right, having you here is helpful.'

'If you're sure then...' Andrew said.

'Oh, we are,' Ian replied.

Andrew left it at that. It was more or less what he had expected, in spite of his uncertainty about Mollie, and he did his best to tuck away to the back of his mind a slight regret that he had not been given leave of absence.

What he himself would have felt in their position he did not know. Probably, he thought, he would have eagerly seized the opportunity of not having to cope with a visitor, but then he had become so used to solitude that it seemed to him a normal thing to desire. However, his real use at the moment to the Davidges, he thought, in spite of what he had thought Mollie's feelings might be, was as a sort of buffer between them, because the problem of Brian Singleton was coming to a head. Ian, he thought, knew all about it and was deeply depressed. Mollie was almost desperate, scared and insecure in the grip of stronger emotions than she had ever felt before. What Brian felt was something that Andrew knew nothing about, and he did not much want to know any more about it. He reflected that in the afternoon he might call on Eleanor Clancy and ask her to show him some of her great-grandfather's photographs.

But after lunch he decided to lie down for a little while before setting out, and he had no sooner lain down than he fell sound asleep. The lack of sleep in the night had really caught up with him, and it held him now, deep and dreamless, and when he woke he had to spend a little while trying to remember where he was. There seemed to be no reason for a window to be where it was, or a dressing table to be in the corner of the room, or for its walls to be pale grey. Then memory returned with a jerk and he sat up hurriedly, thinking of his intention of visiting Eleanor Clancy. But looking at his watch, he saw that it was half past five. He had slept for about three and a half hours, and a visit at this time seemed inappropriate. He got up, combed his hair and went downstairs.

He was only half way down them when he became aware, from voices in the sitting room, that the Davidges had a visitor. It was a man's voice he heard, and thinking that it might be Brian, he considered returning to his room and taking refuge in Agatha Christie. But something about the voice convinced him that it was not Brian, and he continued downstairs. The visitor was Ernest Audley.

It sounded as if he had only just arrived, for he was explaining to the Davidges why he had come.

'I thought to myself, I'll call in on the Davidges,' he was saying. 'I'll find out if they've been badgered by the police as much as I have. To the best of my belief you don't keep a supply of cyanide on the premises, as I do.' He saw Andrew at the door and immediately stood up. 'Good afternoon, Professor,' he said. 'I was just telling Ian and Mollie that I've been most infernally troubled by the police today, and all because I still happened to have kept one or two of the killing bottles my father used to use when he went out after his butterflies. They insisted on removing them, I can only assume to check whether there were any signs of some of the stuff having been abstracted. Would they be able to find that out, do you think? And you're a scientist. Can you tell me if the stuff would have retained its potency, or by this time have become innocuous?'

'I rather think it would still be pretty poisonous,' Andrew replied, 'but I can't speak with any authority. It's a matter I never had any reason to investigate.'

They had both sat down. Mollie was in a chair by the window, where the remaining light of the early evening fell on some embroidery in a frame, on which she was working. Ian was standing with his back to the empty fireplace, his hands in his pockets.

84 E. X. Ferrars

'I'm the prime suspect, of course,' Audley went on. 'I hated the bastard from the bottom of my heart and if I were to meet the murderer I'd shake him by the hand. But motive and means aren't sufficient for an arrest. There's got to be opportunity too. And even our brilliant Inspector Roland hasn't managed to come up yet with any theory as to how I could have lobbed cyanide from where I was sitting near the bottom of the table to where Singleton was sitting. Have you any theories of your own, Professor, as to how it could have been done?'

'None,' Andrew said.

'My own view is the simplest one,' Audley said. 'Generally the simpler a theory is, the more convincing it is. It's that the Bartlett sisters aren't what they seem. I doubt if any motive they might have had for killing Singleton would have been sexual. Wide-ranging as his tastes were, I doubt if those worthy elderly sisters would have appealed to him. But he might have damaged someone to whom they were devoted and who was more his type. That seems to me quite probable. The damage might have been emotional, physical, economic, social. The police will certainly be looking into all that. Because it stares one in the face, doesn't it, that it would have been the easiest thing in the world for one of the sisters to drop a little poison into Singleton's cup while she was serving him? How she acquired any cyanide I don't presume to guess, though I'm certain it wasn't from me. Concerning that, however, I've wondered about our dear Miss Clancy. You know she photographed the sisters, don't you? She thought the two of them, side by side, so dignified, so precise and decorous, made a splendid subject. And she had cyanide connected with her ancestor's photographic work and they might have had a chance to help themselves to some while they were in the cottage. So there you are, a solution to the whole mystery.'

Andrew had not remembered, from his previous meetings with Audley, that he spoke with such pomposity, but a good geal of it now was assumed, Andrew thought, with a note of irony in it. Audley really made very little effort to conceal the fact that he felt a certain pleasure in the murder, and it amused him to blame the least likely persons for having committed it. There was an animation in his pale, blotchy face that was not usually there. His light blue eyes under their thick lashes gleamed.

'I know you aren't taking me seriously,' he said, 'but can any of you come up with a better solution?'

'I don't think you want us to,' Ian said. 'I think you'll be very pleased if this murder is filed away among unsolved crimes.'

'Perhaps, perhaps,' Audley agreed. 'I don't see why anyone should be too concerned if it is, except for his publishers. They'll be the only people I know of who'll have a truly sincere regret for Singleton's death. My ex-wife will probably cry a little about it. Even after he deserted her she nursed an absurd amount of affection for him.'

'Have you and she ever thought of joining up again?' Ian asked. 'Will Singleton's death make any difference to that?'

'Most unlikely, I should say.' Audley said it emphatically and quickly; a little too quickly, Andrew thought, for it to sound entirely convincing. Was it possible, he wondered, that Audley's satisfaction at Luke Singleton's death was not wholly due to his simple hatred of the man, but had in it an element of hope that if the man was finally lost to her, his wife might return to him?

When Audley had left, which he did a few minutes later, Andrew asked Ian if he knew what sort of woman Mrs Audley had been.

'We never met her,' Ian said. 'The whole affair happened before we came to live here, but I know she was a friend of Felicity's and I think she sometimes hears from her.'

'I wish we could work out a way Ernest could have done the murder,' Mollie said. 'He's got such an excellent motive for it, and he actually likes to parade it. He's very sure, isn't he, that he simply can't be suspected—' She broke off as the telephone rang.

Ian went into the hall to answer it. The call was brief and when he came back into the room there was a very strange expression of bewilderment on his face.

'That was Sam,' he said. 'Of all crazy things to happen, the Bartletts have disappeared.'

❀ ❀ ❀

It was not until next morning that the Davidges and Andrew heard how the disappearance of the sisters had happened. They heard it from Inspector Roland, who called in on them at about ten o'clock, accompanied by a young man whom he introduced as Sergeant Giles. Mollie once more offered them coffee, but it was again refused. The two men did not even sit down. They seemed in a hurry.

'I don't expect you to be able to help us,' Roland said, 'but we're asking everyone along this road, as it's the road to London, if they saw anything of the two women in an old red Mini drive past some time between two and four yesterday afternoon. That's when they must have left the Waldrons' house. Mrs Waldron had been in bed all day, and only saw Enid Bartlett, the older of the two sisters, when she brought up a tray with her lunch. Mr Waldron had his lunch served to him in the dining room, then went to lie down for a rest, and says he heard the sisters moving about—there was a lot of clearing up to do after the trouble the night before—until he fell asleep, which he thinks happened about two o'clock. He woke up about four and presently went downstairs to make sure some tea would be taken up to his wife, but there was no sign of the Bartletts. He was surprised, because it was unlike them simply to go out without making sure beforehand that it was convenient, and even though it was a Sunday, and their usual afternoon off, he'd assumed that after the events the night before they wouldn't have gone. However, he didn't worry much about it until about six o'clock when a married sister of theirs who lives in the village rang up to ask if they were all right, because they hadn't gone to see her as they usually did on their Sundays off. She'd heard about the murder, of course—who hasn't?—and she thought their not coming to her must have something to do with that. But they didn't come back to the Waldrons at all that evening, and about eleven o'clock Mr Waldron got in touch with us about it. And they still haven't appeared. We're to blame, of course, for having made it possible for the women to have got away like that without being stopped, but it's too late now to worry about that, the main thing is to find them.'

'Why do you think they went to London?' Ian asked.

'Their sister seemed to think it was probable,' Roland replied. 'They've another sister there, a widow, who runs a boarding house in Finchley, and she thought that they might have gone to her. But inquiries in London haven't led to anything. Apparently they haven't been in touch with that sister, or she swears they haven't. However, London's an obvious place to go to if you want to disappear.'

'But why should they want to disappear?' Mollie asked.

'I think they must have been scared that they'd come under suspicion,' Roland answered. 'They must have realized they were the only people who could easily have given the poison to Singleton.'

'But did you suspect them?'

Roland gave a slight shrug. 'We couldn't say it wasn't possible they'd done it, could we? As long as we can't find any other way that the poison could have been administered to Singleton, we've got to think about them.'

'But if you do,' Andrew observed, 'then isn't Mr Waldron the most likely person to have arranged for them to do it?'

'And no one is more aware of that than he is himself,' Roland said. 'He's very anxious for us to find them.'

'The red Mini's their own, is it?' Andrew asked.

Roland nodded and told them the number of the car.

'Well, I'm sorry, but we've seen nothing of them,' Ian said. 'But we were all sleeping it off ourselves yesterday afternoon, and wouldn't have seen them even if they'd passed.'

'Well, no doubt they'll be found soon enough,' Roland said. 'I doubt if women like that will really know how to conceal themselves, even in London. They may even have second thoughts and come home of their own accord. Meanwhile, it's just making a bit of extra trouble for us.' He gave Andrew a long look. 'You haven't had any special ideas about what's happened, have you, Professor?'

Andrew shook his head.

'You had some good ideas the last time we met,' Roland persisted.

'If I have any this time, you shall be the first to hear them,' Andrew promised.

'Good. Well, good morning. Sorry to have troubled you.'

Roland and the sergeant took their leave.

When they had gone, Ian said that he felt like making some of that coffee that the detectives had refused and went out to the kitchen to do it. Mollie sat down at her embroidery frame.

'You've really met that man before, have you, Andrew?' she asked.

'Yes, I was on the spot when an unfortunate man called Sir Lucas Dearden was blown up by a bomb,' Andrew answered, 'and I think Roland rather overestimates the help I gave him. That's a very lovely piece of embroidery you're doing, Mollie.'

'Would you like it?' she said. 'I could get it framed for you or made into a cushion.'

'Would you really do that?'

'Of course, if you truly like it. Which shall it be?'

Andrew thought of his sitting room and of how the embroidery would look in it.

'A cushion, I think,' he said.

'You shall have it. But, Andrew...'

'Yes?'

'This isn't your first experience of murder?'

'Not quite.'

'And do you believe either of the Bartletts could have done it?'

'Not really.'

'Have you any suspicions of anyone who was at that dinner?'

'Probably no more than you have. Do you suspect anyone in particular?'

'I do, as a matter of fact, only it doesn't make sense.'

'Ernest Audley?'

'No.'

'Then who?'

She bent her head over her work, apparently concentrating on it and thinking of nothing else. Then after a moment she said, 'No, I don't think I'll say. It isn't really serious, and it might just make trouble.'

'You're probably wise.'

That seemed to spur her into wanting to tell him more.

'All the same, if the Bartletts had anything to do with it, then that makes it possible, doesn't it, that just about anyone who was at that dinner might have been at the back of it? As you said, it's Sam who looks the most probable, but what about Eleanor, for instance? She's admitted she used to know Luke Singleton, and whether that was just a bit of boasting and exaggerating, or whether she really knew him very well and was playing it down, we don't know, do we? And she probably had cyanide and might have arranged to pay a Bartlett to do the job for her. Then there's Felicity.'

'Is she the person you really suspect?' Andrew asked.

But before she answered, Ian came in with coffee for the three of them and as he poured it out, silence fell on them. Mollie resumed her embroidery and except for muttering something about it being impossible that the Bartletts could have had anything to do with it, Ian withdrew into himself, looking ill-tempered, as if he found the events of the morning particularly outrageous.

Andrew was grateful not to be expected to talk. He had an uneasy feeling that Mollie at least might have started to think of him as an expert on murder, when he happened for the present to be feeling entirely uninspired. Wondering what to do, he thought of making the call that he had abandoned the evening before on Eleanor Clancy, asking to be shown some of her treasured old photographs, because an idea concerning them had begun to form in his mind. He needed an occupation, now that his work on Robert Hooke was done. As his nephew, Peter Dilly, had said, he needed a hobby. And might it not be possible, if Eleanor would give him access to the letters and the negatives that her great-grandfather had left behind him, to write his life? Might it not be quite interesting? It was true that she had seemed to be thinking of doing this herself, but Andrew felt that this was one of the projects that was unlikely ever to be more than a project. Yes, he thought, he would call on her.

Without telling the Davidges what he actually had in mind, but only saying that he was going out for a breath of air, he let himself out into the road and started along it.

But he did not stop at Eleanor Clancy's cottage. The fresh, bright morning gave him the feeling that what he needed was simply a walk, and passing the cottage, he went straight on. His idea of writing the life of a long ago Clancy began to feel quite unrealistic. For one thing, it would almost certainly mean having to have a fair amount of contact with Eleanor herself, and he had not really taken much of a liking to her. It would also mean spending a good deal of time in Lower Milfrey, and that was a thing he thought that he would never be able to contemplate with pleasure. Quite apart from the murder and its consequences, his relationship with the Davidges had been most unhappily damaged; Mollie's confidences to him about her feelings for Brian Singleton had made it almost impossible for him to maintain his old relationship with Ian. He did not know whether to be sorry for him, or critical of him, or even contemptuous of him. The one thing that seemed impossible, unless Ian should choose to confide in him too, was to be simple and honest with him.

Just then, perhaps because he had been thinking of Ian, he noticed that the sky seemed to be full of swallows. They were swooping in every direction in swift, beautiful curves. Were they preparing for their journey south, he wondered? He stood still, watching them, and as he did so a car that had been coming towards him stopped near him and Felicity Mace leant out.

'Good morning, Professor,' she called out. 'Are you going anywhere special? Can I give you a lift?'

He was about to reply that he was merely out for a short walk, when a sudden idea occurred to him.

'I was thinking of a walk,' he said, 'but if you feel like driving me to the nearest pleasant pub and coming in for a drink with me, I'd very happily give up the idea of the walk.'

'Let me think,' she said. 'The nicest pub, I think, is the Wheatsheaf, and it won't take us more than a few minutes to get there. Get in.' She leant across the car and opened the door for Andrew to climb into the seat beside her. She then turned the car and drove off in the direction from which she had come. 'I've just been to see a patient out this way,' she said, 'and was going home for my lunch, but that can wait for a little while.'

'I'd like to suggest we have lunch in the Wheatsheaf,' Andrew said, 'but Mollie and Ian will be expecting me.'

'It's all right, I've an excellent Marks & Spencer lunch waiting to go into my microwave,' she said. She had a friendly smile on her lively oval face and seemed really glad to have met him. 'My microwave has revolutionized my life. It's the perfect answer for busy people who live alone. Have you got one?'

'No, but then I'm not a truly busy person,' Andrew answered.

'All the same, you should try it.'

They chatted about microwaves and the problems of cooking for yourself if you lived alone until they came to a building that stood by itself at a crossroads which turned out to be the Wheatsheaf. It was a solid-looking, square brick building with a slate roof and a large car park beside it, in which there were a surprising number of cars, considering that the pub appeared to have no village near it. It was plainly popular enough for people to come to it from some distance away. Inside, it was cheerfully comfortable in an unpretentious way, and had a fair number of customers in it already. Felicity and Andrew went to a small table by the window and Andrew went to the bar to order their drinks. They each had a half pint of lager.

As he sat down at the table facing her, she gave him her friendly smile again and said, 'Well, what is it you really want to ask me?'

'It's as obvious as that, is it?' he asked.

'It certainly seemed probable. Not that I don't enjoy being picked up by distinguished visitors. But I thought there might be strings attached to it.'

'You make me wish there weren't,' he said. 'I'd really like you to talk about things like the holiday you had this year, and the one you're planning for next year, and anything that has nothing to do with the murder. I keep telling myself that the one thing I want is to stop thinking about it, but of course, that isn't true. It's going to obsess me until it's solved.'

'Perhaps I can help you more than you'd expect,' she said. 'That's to say, I can tell you a little about my summer holiday, and just connect it up a little with our murder. My holiday was in Russia, a trip by ship on the inland waterways from Moscow to St Petersburg, and very wonderful it was, and I'd love to go on talking about it. But what you'll want to hear, I think, is a little about the friend I went with. It was Jane Audley.'

He showed his surprise. 'Ernest Audley's wife?'

'His ex-wife.'

'Yes, yes, of course. And actually, she was one of the people I wanted to ask you about. Someone told me you'd known her.'

'We're very close friends. We met when I first settled here and we've kept in touch ever since she left. We generally go on holiday together.'

'So you'd have some idea if there's any possibility, now that Luke Singleton's dead, that she'd return to Audley. I know Singleton deserted her after the divorce, but it seemed to me possible that she might have nursed a hope that he'd come back to her in the end, and now that that most certainly can't happen, she might see if she could return to Audley.'

She shook her head. 'Not a chance of it. The marriage was pretty well on the rocks before Luke showed up. If it hadn't been Luke, it'd have been someone else. She told me once she regarded the years she'd spent with Ernest as utterly wasted. He's a terrible old bore, you know, and very demanding, and she married him for all the wrong reasons. She was very young for one thing, and very eager to get married and have a home of her own and a position in our society here. And then, of course, children. Having lived nearly all her life in Lower Milfrey, she thought of him as a man of distinction and consequence, you see, and it took her a little while to find out that he isn't exactly either. And the children didn't come. So Luke was the escape she'd been looking for, and I'm not sure that she was passionately devoted to him or that it mattered to her too much when he left her. There've been one or two other men in her life since he did, but what really keeps her going is a job she's got as assistant editor on a women's magazine. She's very talented in her way and very hard-working.'

'So even if Audley had an idea that with Singleton dead she might come back to him, you'd say he was quite wrong.'

'Oh, utterly.'

'But do you think he might have such an idea himself?'

She gave him a quizzical look, then drank some of her lager.

'So you want to make out that he's the murderer, even though it's completely impossible that he could have done it, sitting where he was?'

'You've heard, of course, that the Bartlett sisters have disappeared?'

She nodded. 'And if they were the instrument that administered the poison, then Ernest, or almost anyone in that room could have been the real culprit. As a matter of fact, it doesn't even have to have been someone in that room. It could have been pretty well anyone in the wide world. That's an idea that ought to keep you occupied for a nice long time.'

But it did not keep Andrew occupied for very long, for that evening the Bartletts were discovered. They were staying with their widowed sister in Finchley after all. They had been there when the police had gone to her house to inquire for them, but had insisted on remaining in hiding, and she had denied that they were with her when they were upstairs in her attic. But not long afterwards their red Mini had been discovered in a car park only a few streets away from her home, and the police had then returned to it and been a good deal more insistent in their questioning. The widowed sister by then had been working on the two Bartletts to let the police know their whereabouts. With a houseful of lodgers it was hardly practical for her to keep a couple of strange women concealed from them all, particularly as the newspapers had made a good deal of their disappearance, even hinting that a reward might be given for information leading to their discovery. However, they did not return to Lower Milfrey, but for the time being remained in Finchley. They would have to return for the inquest, they were told, but for the moment were left in peace. Inspector Roland, who told all this to the Davidges and Andrew, whom he called in on again later that evening, said that the women had truly been afraid that they were suspected of the poisoning of Luke Singleton and had had a wild idea of borrowing money from their sister and escaping to South America. They had very little knowledge of such matters as passports and visas and had simply been in a state of hopeless panic.

Nevertheless, their attempt at escape did them good service. The next morning, when without any doubt they were in a room that happened to be vacant in a boarding house in Finchley, Ian, as he so often did, set out in the early morning with his binoculars to see if anything interesting in the way of waders recently arrived from the north had appeared in the mud around the lake on the common, but what he saw for once put all thoughts of birds out of his mind. For tucked among the reeds near the little bridge that crossed the stream that made its placid way out of the lake, he happened to catch sight of a pair of shoes. And the shoes were on a pair of feet. And the feet were those of Eleanor Clancy, floating in deathly stillness in the water.

Chapter Six

Ian came running across the common, through the turnstile and into the house where Mollie was just taking Andrew's breakfast tray in to him. Andrew heard Ian shouting for Mollie. She dumped the tray on his knees more abruptly than usual, went out on to the landing and called, 'What is it?'

Andrew heard Ian call back, 'The police! I've got to phone them! I found—I found—'

But there he seemed to gag. There was silence for a moment, then there came the tinkle of the bell on the telephone as it was lifted. Andrew put his tray aside, got out of bed, put on his dressing gown and went out on to the landing.

He overheard Ian say, 'Yes, by the bridge... Oh yes, dead, no question of it. I wouldn't have left her if there'd been any doubt, would I?... Yes, straight away, and you'll meet me there... Yes, I understand... In the reeds by the bridge, you're sure you know where I mean?... All right, but come as quickly as you can.'

He slammed the telephone down and seemed about to go straight out of the front door again when Andrew called out, 'What's happened, Ian?'

Ian paused in the doorway, looking up at him on the stairs.

'It's Eleanor,' he said. 'Lying in the lake, dead. Drowned, I suppose. I was out early, looking for some waders, but what I saw was Eleanor. I don't know how long she's been there, but I'm going straight back. The police are coming. Will you come with me?'

'I will, if you'll wait a moment till I get into some clothes,' Andrew answered.

That morning the coffee on his tray, the toast and marmalade and the cheese were left untouched. It was only a few minutes before he was downstairs with Ian, unwashed, unshaved, but at least decent in trousers, a shirt and a pullover. They went out together while Mollie stayed in the doorway, watching them go.

They strode across the common towards the lake as fast as they could. There was no one else about. The morning felt colder than the day before, and there were low-hanging dark clouds in the sky, as if it might rain soon. Ian began to mutter something about the bridge and the reeds, but then gave up the attempt to speak, and led the way up to the little hump-backed bridge and pointed down.

There, almost under it, with reeds bowing over her, was the still body of Eleanor Clancy. She was on her back, with her small deep-set eyes staring strangely at the sky. Her clothes were only a sodden shroud, but it looked as if she was wearing her black jeans and tartan shirt. Her cap of brown hair swam in the water like a dark halo round her head. Her face was blue-white. Ian had certainly been right. She was dead and probably had been dead for hours.

Andrew wondered if the cold of the morning came from those threatening clouds and a feeling of moisture in the air, or mostly from the stiff figure below them. He looked around him. He looked at the narrow lane that curved off to the right on the far side of the bridge. There were hedges on either side of the lane, so that he could not see where it led, but he thought that it ran about parallel to the main road behind most of the houses of the village. On the morning when he had walked as far as the bridge, then round the lake and back to the children's playground, he had not paid much attention to the lane, but now he found himself gazing up it, wondering if it had been along it that death had come.

Ian was leaning on the brick coping of the bridge.

'Could it have been an accident?' he asked, not sounding hopeful.

'I suppose it's possible,' Andrew said. 'Accidents have a queer way of happening. But she was athletic. She's certain to have been a good swimmer. If she'd somehow fallen into the water she'd surely have been able to save herself. Anyway, the water doesn't look very deep.'

Though there was mud along the rim of the lake, where the stream flowed out the water was so clear that he could see pebbles on the bottom of it.

'So she was unconscious when she fell in,' Ian said.

'Or dead already.'

'You've made up your mind it was murder?'

'Thank God, it isn't for me to do that. That's a job for Inspector Roland.'

'But it is what you think, isn't it, Andrew?'

Andrew did not reply immediately. He stood gazing down with a horrified kind of interest at the figure in the water below them.

Then he said, 'Why did she come here? To meet somebody? And why here?'

'Couldn't it have been by chance? I mean, suppose she was out jogging, which was the sort of thing she used to do, and just happened to meet someone who—well, who wanted her dead?'

'Why should anyone want that? Of course, I know what you're going to say. Someone she saw give the cyanide to Singleton. Or someone she knew had arranged it somehow. But wasn't meeting her just a too lucky chance for whoever it was? I think it's more likely she met someone by appointment.'

'But whom would she have agreed to meet in a lonely spot like this when she knew she was a fearful danger to that person? Wouldn't she have been too afraid of him?'

'Or her.'

'Could a woman have done it?'

'I don't know. We don't know yet what they did, do we?'

'I still think it's extraordinary she should have agreed to meet whoever it was, if she really knew something about the murder of Luke.'

'It is extraordinary. Perhaps a little too extraordinary to have happened just like that.'

Ian gave Andrew a puzzled look. 'You seem to think they didn't meet by chance, but not by appointment either. Then how did they meet?'

'Oh, by one or the other,' Andrew said. 'But perhaps not for the reason we've been talking about.'

'What other reason could there be?'

'I know too little about her to do any guessing. Perhaps her chutney gave someone indigestion. Or perhaps one of her photographs displeased someone… Sorry, Ian, I'm not really being flippant, I'm just stressing the fact that she'd led a life before the dinner in honour of Parson Woodforde.'

They were interrupted then by voices on the common and saw several men coming towards them, with Inspector Roland at the head of them.

Andrew and Ian came down from the bridge to make room for Roland to go up on to it. He stood staring down.

'Christ!' was all he said for a moment.

Then he came down and spoke to Ian. 'It was you who found her, was it?'

'Yes,' Ian said.

'How did that happen?'

'I came out to take a look at the birds round here, and what I found was…' He gestured at the reeds.

'You often come out as early as this?' Roland asked.

'Pretty often,' Ian replied.

'Did you see anyone else around here?'

'No.'

'I'm not thinking of someone who might have done this thing, but another witness.'

'No, there was no one else about.'

'You assume it was murder, do you, Inspector?' Andrew asked.

'We'll know more about that later,' Roland said. 'But there's something about her neck, the angle of her head, that suggests...Well, we'll leave that to the experts. Meanwhile, Professor, I think you and Mr Davidge might go home and I'll come in to see you later. I don't think you can give us any help here now.'

Andrew was very glad to be sent away. He and Ian walked down to the turnstile in silence and crossed the road to the house, the door of which still stood open. Two police cars were parked in the road, and as they crossed it an ambulance drew up there.

As soon as she heard them on the path leading up to the door, Mollie came out of the kitchen and stood still in the middle of the hall with a look of horrified questioning on her face.

'It's really Eleanor, is it?' she said in a whispering voice.

'Yes,' Ian said.

'And she's dead?'

'Yes.'

'Drowned?'

'I thought so,' Ian replied, 'but Roland seems to have his doubts. I got the impression he thinks she may have been dead already when she went into the water. Didn't you, Andrew?'

'He was considering it, certainly,' Andrew said.

'You mean it was murder, not an accident or suicide? Who would want to murder Eleanor?' Mollie's white face was taut with shock.

'The person whom she knew murdered Luke,' Ian said.

'But how could she know that? I know she was sitting near him, but all the same...' She stopped, still staring at them incredulously, then suddenly she said, 'You haven't had any breakfast. Andrew, you didn't touch yours. I'll make some more coffee.'

She turned and went hurriedly back into the kitchen, moving as swiftly as if she was running away from them and their information.

While she was making the second pot of coffee, Andrew went upstairs, had a quick, casual wash and shaved, and seeing the breakfast tray that he had ignored on the bed, picked the portion of cheese off it and, chewing it, went downstairs again. Mollie had brought coffee and toast and marmalade on a tray into the sitting room where the electric fire was alight.

'I thought we could do with a bit of warmth this morning,' she said. 'It's turned quite cold, hasn't it?'

Her voice was back to normal and her face, though a little pale, had lost its look of horrified blankness. She appeared merely thoughtful.

'You must be right,' she said, 'but I still can't make any sense of it.'

Andrew was very grateful for the hot coffee. Having finished his cheese, he helped himself to toast and marmalade and presently to a second cup of coffee. None of them talked much, though once or twice Mollie started what sounded as if it was going to be a question, but which she did not finish. Andrew thought that they were all waiting for something to happen, probably the arrival of the police, though it might be of one of the Davidges' neighbours, who would have seen the police cars arriving and parking outside their house. Meanwhile, all three of them wanted to ask the same questions to which none of them could give any answers. It had become almost impossible to talk.

It was over an hour before they heard footsteps on the paved path outside the door and Ian, going quickly to it, brought in Inspector Roland and the young sergeant. Roland expressed satisfaction on seeing the glowing red bars of the electric fire, went up to it and held out his hands to the warmth. If he had had anything to do with moving the body in the water, they might well be chilled.

Rubbing them against one another, he remarked, 'Soon be Christmas.'

'Good heavens, Inspector!' Mollie exclaimed. 'This is only September.'

'Yes, but time flies,' he said. 'Flies faster and faster the older you get. I get the feeling that chap Singleton has been dead for a week or two, but it was only a couple of days ago that it happened. It may interest you to know, by the way, that the Bartlett sisters have been traced in London. They'd gone, as we thought they might, to the house of their widowed sister, and were simply hiding when the first inquiries were made there. But they showed up yesterday evening.'

'Are you telling us that that gives them an alibi for this murder this morning?' Ian asked.

'Absolutely watertight,' Roland answered. 'But though we haven't any definite facts yet, our impression is that the murder wasn't done this morning, but at least twelve hours before you found her. We'll know more about that later when the forensic people have had time to do their stuff. That twelve hours is only a rough guess.'

'But have you found how she died?' Andrew asked. 'You presumably got her out of the water pretty quickly.'

'Again, we've nothing official,' Roland said. 'Our surgeon is there, and he agrees with me that probably she was throttled from behind by a strong pair of hands, then tipped off the bridge into the water.' At a gesture of invitation from Mollie, he had sat down, and all the others except Ian, who remained standing at the window, watching what might be happening in the road, had found chairs. 'It looks as if her neck's broken.'

'But twelve hours ago,' Andrew said, 'that makes it seven o'clock or so, and it's dark by then. What was she doing out there on the common in the dark with someone who she knew had committed a murder?'

'It isn't really dark by seven,' Roland said. 'It's dusk. If you turn on the lights indoors it looks dark outside, but if you're out, it's still almost daylight.'

'All the same, it's a bit strange to go out for a walk in semi-darkness to meet a murderer,' Andrew said. 'Why did she trust him?'

'She might have met him by chance,' Roland said. 'It was a fine evening, and even murderers may sometimes feel like a breath of fresh air.'

'That's what I suggested to Professor Basnett,' Ian said, 'but he thought it was more likely she'd met someone by appointment.'

'Any reason for that, Professor?' Roland asked.

Andrew considered it. 'Not really. Just that I find it unlikely that our murderer should be so lucky as to meet his second victim, who happened to be threatening him, when he was out all by himself on a lonely common. I know it could happen, but it doesn't feel likely.'

'It might not have happened quite like that,' Roland said. 'She might have gone off for a short walk across the common just before it got dark—she was the sort of person who might do that, mightn't she?—and the murderer was coming along this road here when he saw her start off and quietly followed her. I was going to ask you if you'd seen anyone pass the house, going in either direction about that time. Anyone of any kind. It doesn't necessarily have to have been someone who was at that dinner. It's natural to think it probably was, but that could be a mistake. It could be a mistake to assume that the two murders have any connection. She could have been killed by the sort of pervert who happens to like killing lonely women. There were a couple of murders of that kind in Rockford a year or two ago, and we thought we'd got the killer, but we could have been wrong and he's still about, or there could be another.'

'Was she raped?' Mollie breathed.

'No,' he answered. 'That's to say, her clothing wasn't disarranged. We haven't been able to examine her yet.'

'But it's true the two crimes are remarkably unlike,' Andrew said. 'The one's extremely subtle and complicated, the other's straightforward and brutal. It could be two different minds at work.'

'Meanwhile, you haven't answered my question,' Roland said. 'Did you happen to see anyone at all going along this road towards evening? Someone walking or someone in a car?'

Ian turned from the window. 'We couldn't have seen anyone, I'm afraid, because by then we'd have drawn the curtains. But even if no one walked past, I should say it's certain that a number of cars went by. There isn't much traffic on this road, but sooner or later something comes along.'

'And were you in this room at that time?'

'Ah, you're asking us for our alibis,' Ian said. 'Yes, we were all in this room, drinking sherry. Then about eight o'clock we went into the kitchen for supper. And earlier than that time we were together here, watching the television news. Is that sufficient?'

'Inspector, if you're right that Eleanor Clancy's murder might have been some random pervert,' Andrew said, 'doesn't that destroy the Bartletts' alibis for Luke Singleton's murder? Not that they actually have alibis for that. However, if Miss Clancy was killed because she knew who'd done that murder, then their alibi for yesterday evening makes it fairly impossible that they could have had anything to do with poisoning Singleton. You needn't look for someone who used them to do the killing, which would have meant it could have been someone anywhere in Lower Milfrey or Rockford or London, or anywhere you choose. You're back to looking for someone who was in that room at that dinner. And why need this second murderer of yours have come along this road? Isn't it a good deal more likely that he came along the lane that comes down to the bridge?'

'Of course, of course, Professor,' Roland said, giving a sardonic little smile. 'You're right on all points. And you've probably made up your mind that I haven't much faith in the existence of this second killer. I only consider that he has to be borne in mind. But I might have guessed you'd see through me. I think the Bartletts are blameless, and God knows how, we've got to find Singleton's killer in that dining room.'

'Miss Clancy made a curious remark the last time I saw her,' Andrew said. 'I can't remember her exact words, but what she meant was that she had quite a bit of a gift for recognizing people. Or that's how I took it. And of course, she did recognize Mrs Waldron, although it was years since they'd met.

And she recognized Luke Singleton immediately. But what perhaps makes that unimportant is that in both cases she knew the person's name in advance. She knew whom she was going to meet. All the same, there may have been someone else in that room whom she recognized, someone she knew a little too much about for that person's comfort, and whom she could envisage committing a very complicated murder.'

'And that suggests someone who came from Rockford,' Roland said. 'She'd probably have met all the Lower Milfrey guests already and they'd have known that she'd recognized them and wouldn't have taken risks with her there. Of course we're questioning all the Rockford people, but we haven't got anywhere so far.'

'Have you tried the Lady Mayoress? She was there that evening,' Ian remarked. 'She quite often gets her picture in the local paper. Eleanor would have recognized her.'

'Mr Davidge, this is a serious matter,' Roland said reprovingly. 'This matter of recognition may turn out to be important.'

Ian went abruptly into one of his sullen moods. 'Any bloody thing that happened during the last three days may turn out to be important, mayn't it? It's a whole waste-bag of events. And everything you pull out seems to have something against it. And probably there's something that's been staring us in the face all the time that would solve the whole business—Oh God, what's this now?'

He has been interrupted by the sound of running footsteps on the path up from the road.

The doorbell was strenuously rung.

❊ ❊ ❊

Ian went to answer it. A young uniformed constable came bounding into the room. He was carrying a package of some sort, wrapped in transparent plastic. He thrust it out to Roland.

'One of the divers found this,' he said. 'Sergeant Merryweather told me to bring it straight to you, sir.' He added warningly, 'It's wet.'

Roland took it, but he held it between his hands, touching it as little as possible.

Looking at it through the plastic, he stated, 'It looks like a handbag.'

'And it's got money in it,' the constable said.

'I suppose you've all been handling it,' Roland said. 'Any fingerprints on it won't mean a thing.'

'Sergeant Merryweather looked inside it, sir,' the constable said, 'then put it in this sheeting. But he said there wouldn't be any prints left after the soaking it's had.'

'You found it in the lake, did you?'

'One of the divers found it, just about a yard or so from where the body was lying. And it's got a thousand pounds in it, and a cheque-book with Miss Clancy's name on it, and a purse with some change in it, and a comb, and a diary, and a hand-kerchief and a latchkey and a car key.'

'And a thousand pounds?'

'Yes, sir.'

'In what form?'

'Fifty-pound notes, just in a bundle with a rubber band round them.'

'You're sure about that cheque-book?'

'So Sergeant Merryweather said, sir.'

'So the handbag is Miss Clancy's.'

Ian had drawn near enough to Roland to be taking a look at the package on his knee.

'It's Eleanor's all right,' he said. 'I've seen her carrying it.'

Roland handed the package back to the constable.

'You'd better take this in to the station. Hand it over to the forensic people and tell them how it was found. Try not to handle it more than you can help, though the sergeant's probably right, with the soaking it's had there won't be any prints left on it.'

The young man took it and left as speedily as he had come.

'Now why should anyone throw a handbag with a thousand pounds in it into the lake?' Roland demanded.

'An accident,' Andrew suggested. 'She was carrying it when she was attacked and simply had it jerked out of her hand and let it go and it fell in the water.'

'That thousand pounds has the smell of blackmail to me,' Roland said.

'But who was blackmailing who?' Andrew asked.

'Had she just been paid it by her attacker, or was she going to pay it to him?'

'But it isn't blackmail!' Mollie said angrily. 'I'm sure Eleanor'd never done anything in her life for which anyone could blackmail her, and she wouldn't try to blackmail anybody. I believe, if she really had that sort of money in her handbag and went up on the bridge to meet someone, then she was taking the money to help them in some way.'

'And so he killed her,' Roland observed drily.

'Anyway, I don't believe she'd have been able to scrape together a thousand pounds just like that,' Mollie said. 'She was pretty hard up.'

'But one can be so wrong about people,' Andrew murmured.

'Who's being wrong now?' she asked.

'I've a feeling it's you, my dear,' he said. 'I don't see Eleanor Clancy as an example of all the virtues. She may have been a fairly worthy woman, but if the possession of some dangerous knowledge came her way, and as you say, she really was hard up, then I don't think it's impossible she might try to use it.'

'And she was fool enough to go up to a lonely spot like that bridge at twilight to meet this person she was blackmailing and so just happened to get murdered.' Mollie was scornful. 'Why didn't she get them to come to her cottage?'

'I believe that's a rather important question,' Andrew said.

'And it makes me think,' Roland said, 'that my next step will be to go to that cottage and take a look round. Her latchkey was in that handbag they found in the lake.' He looked at Ian. 'Have you by any chance got a spare? You're her landlord, aren't you?'

'Yes, we've a spare set of keys to her front door, her back door and her garage. Wait a moment, I'll get them.'

He left the room and was back almost at once with some keys on a ring.

Standing up, as did the sergeant, Roland looked suddenly at Andrew and said, 'Care to come with us?'

That the invitation was meant for Andrew only and not for Ian or Mollie was very clear. He looked at them questioningly, feeling that as their guest it was only courteous to obtain their permission for his suddenly leaving them, but as he had expected, both nodded at him, sending him off. He followed the Inspector out of the house and started along the road with them to what had been Eleanor Clancy's cottage.

But before they reached it the Inspector paused, looking towards the common. A small procession of men was coming towards them, and between them they were carrying something. It was a stretcher covered with what looked like a blanket. It was loaded on to the waiting ambulance, which was then driven away. Most of the men who had accompanied the stretcher then got into the police cars parked in the road, though two or three paused at the turnstile, then returned the way they had come.

Roland leant his elbows on the fence, peering up musingly across the common.

'How long have the Davidges been living here?' he asked after a moment.

'I think it's about two years,' Andrew answered.

'And before that?'

'In a flat in Holland Park.'

'Holland Park—that's an expensive area, isn't it?'

'I believe so.'

'And their car's a BMW.'

'Yes.'

'So they aren't what Mrs Davidge called hard up.'

'Oh no.'

'Nor really wealthy?'

'No.'

'How long have you known them?'

'Oh, I can't remember. I've known Davidge twenty or twenty-five years.'

'But his wife not so long?'

'She's his second wife, you know. His first wife died some years ago, and about three years after it happened he married Mollie. She was his secretary.'

'Happy marriage?'

Only a few days ago Andrew would have answered, 'Very.' Now he hesitated, and having hesitated, did not know in the least how to go on. His pause would inevitably have been noticed by Roland, so it hardly seemed worthwhile to say anything.

'Not so very, then,' Roland said; a statement, not a question.

'Is it relevant?' Andrew asked.

'Maybe, maybe not. Just something in that rag-bag of events your friend was talking about. They hadn't known the Clancy woman long, had they?'

'No.'

'But some of the things Mrs Davidge was saying about her made sense.'

'I suppose they did.'

'For instance, why did this victim of her blackmail, if that was what he was, want to meet her up there by the bridge and not come to her cottage? Of course, the answer's pretty obvious. He didn't want to risk being seen going past your house about the time he meant to kill the woman in case you recognized him and remembered it later. And it needn't have been only passing your home that he was afraid of. Just being seen walking through the village might seem suspicious. So he agreed to meet her, but insisted it should be on the common, which he reached by that lane on the far side of the lake. A very quiet lane. It's not much used. But he may have been unlucky and met someone, and this, naturally, is the first thing we're going to try to find out. We'll be working on that in the lane itself this afternoon. If anyone passed that way they may have left some traces of themselves. Meantime, we'll want a lot of alibis. But at least the Bartletts are off our list.'

'You're sure of that?'

'For tonight, of course. And as I see it, that crosses them off too for Singleton's murder. I don't really believe we've two murderers on the loose. We haven't the beginnings of an answer to that. Now let's go in the cottage.'

They turned towards the cottage.

There was no need for a key to get into it. They discovered that the lock was broken. Inside it was dark, for the curtains were drawn. It took Roland a moment to find the light-switch as they entered. When he did and the light came on in the little hall, both men stood still, staring incredulously at what they saw. A small bookcase had had all the books that had been on it thrown to the floor. A rug had been kicked to one side. A candle-shaped light bracket on the wall had been twisted round and now hung down by its flex. It was the same in the sitting room. Pictures, including the photograph of the girls' cricket eleven at St Hilda's School that had beaten the girls from Etchingham, had been torn down. Cushions had been ripped open. What books there were had been scattered on the floor. A few small china ornaments had been thrown down and looked as if they had been ground to fragments underfoot. A television had had its screen smashed. A telephone had been pulled away from the wall and lay on its side on the floor. A bowl that had had flowers in it, that stood on a little round table, had been over-turned, and the flowers and the water that had been in the bowl lay in a damp puddle on the carpet. The table was on its side.

The two men stood silently taking it in. Roland was the first to speak.

'Curtains drawn,' he observed.

'That doesn't tell us much,' Andrew said.

'No, but it must have happened after Miss Clancy left the house, so it was probably dark by then and they needed light to do the job. But it's true it could have happened at any time during the night. Looks as if someone was searching for something.'

'It was a bit more than that, wasn't it?' Andrew said. 'Vandals at work, or else someone simply in a blind rage. The sort of rage that perhaps killed Eleanor Clancy. Who's going to find anything in a bowl of flowers? Shall we look at the rest of the house?'

'Yes, but don't touch anything. We've got to get the photograph and the fingerprint people in on this.'

Andrew did not need to be told not to touch anything, yet he was almost automatically about to lay a hand on the banister rail, mounting stairs having been something he had become cautious about during the last year or two, when he recollected himself and went up with his hands hanging by his sides.

The scene of destruction upstairs was the same as it was below. There were two small bedrooms with sloping ceilings and one small window each and a small bathroom. In the two bedrooms mirrors had been smashed, mattresses rolled back and slashed, pillows ripped, with their feathery contents scattered everywhere, drawers pulled out and their contents spilled on the floor. In the room that Eleanor Clancy herself had obviously used, clothes had been torn off their hangers and dropped on the floor. In the bathroom the mirror on a cabinet on the wall above the handbasin had been smashed and the contents of the cabinet, packets of aspirin, laxatives, rolls of sticking-plaster and a bottle of disinfectant, all tumbled in the basin. The odour of the disinfectant was strong in the air.

Except for muttering to himself as they went along what sounded like a long stream of disgusted obscenities, Roland said nothing, and Andrew also was silent, though from time to time, his breath caught. Going downstairs again, they explored the kitchen. It was in the same state as the rest of the cottage. Flour and sugar had been spilled on the floor and the table, coffee beans mixed up in them, what had been a saucepan full of stew overturned on the electric stove, making a foul greasy-looking pool over the top of it, the refrigerator yawned open with its light on inside but its contents in a heap in front of it.

'Someone must have felt tired when they got to the end of doing all this,' Roland observed.

'What did he use?' Andrew asked.

'To smash the mirror and things?' Roland turned back into the sitting room. He pointed at a poker lying by the great old empty hearth. 'Could have been that. But it could have been something he took away with him.'

'We still haven't looked in the cellar,' Andrew said.

'The cellar? There's a cellar, is there? Yes, let's get it over, then we'll send for the other chaps to do their stuff. I'll phone from my car. Better not touch that phone there.'

He followed Andrew down into the cellar.

The first thing that caught Andrew's eye was that all Eleanor Clancy's carefully hoarded photographic equipment, which by now might almost have had antique value, had been destroyed. What gave him a feeling of blind horror was that the precious negatives, which when he had seen them last had been in neat rows on a rack, and which had probably given a rare glimpse of a period that was long passed and of a country that had totally altered, had been ground into fragments that were now entirely meaningless. They had been precious to Eleanor Clancy and were irreplaceable. Andrew remembered the thought that he had had of discussing with her whether it might not be possible for him, using her photographs and the letters that had come down to her from her great-grandfather, forest officer in Burma in the mid-nineteenth-century, unknown, obscure, but leaving a piece of history behind him, to write the story of his life. But after all, he would have to stick to Malpighi.

'I've never seen anything like it,' Roland said. 'Vandals, yes, plenty of them about. Telephone boxes, shop windows and all that. But this systematic destruction of a person's whole home—that's something new to me.'

There was a sound of bitter, though carefully subdued anger in his voice.

'There has to be a reason for it,' Andrew said.

'Looks to me like the work of a madman.'

'Suppose it was someone who was looking for something and lost his temper because he couldn't find it.'

Roland gave him a sardonic look.

'You've some idea about it, Professor. Go on and tell me what it is.'

'It just struck me…' Andrew began, then paused.

'Yes?' Roland prompted him.

'Well, we've been wondering what could have taken Miss Clancy up on to the common at dusk to meet someone she was blackmailing, haven't we? A dangerous thing to do, as it turned out. But suppose she thought she'd protected herself. Suppose she told her victim that she'd left a full account of how he'd managed to murder Luke Singleton in her home, and that if anything happened to her, that account would be found and he'd be exposed. Only she'd misunderstood the man she was dealing with, someone quite ruthless and very bold. The way he handled the situation was first to murder her, then sometime in the night to come here and search the place from top to bottom for that account she'd said she'd left here. And he didn't find it and all the violence in him exploded in a fit of blind rage and he started smashing everything he could find. Rage fuelled by fear, because that account may still be somewhere.'

'Here in this cottage, after he'd searched it as he did?'

'Perhaps. Or perhaps with her solicitor, or in her bank. Or perhaps it never existed.'

'She merely said it did when she began to understand the danger she was in?'

'That's possible.' Andrew had managed to withdraw his gaze from the shattered negatives and was looking around the cellar. On a shelf he saw a row of neatly labelled bottles of jam and chutney. He remembered that Eleanor Clancy had said she was going to try making wine from the grapes on her own vine.

'A woman of many hobbies,' he observed. 'Everyone I've met here seems to have a hobby. And now it looks as if someone may be making a hobby of murder.'

Chapter Seven

When Andrew returned to the Davidges' house he found that Mollie had gone out. Ian said she had gone shopping. He was alone in the sitting room with a glass of whisky at his elbow. He offered some to Andrew, who accepted it gladly. He told Ian what he and the Inspector had found in Eleanor Clancy's cottage, but Ian seemed less interested than he would have expected. He nodded his head from time to time, but asked hardly any questions. It was as if his mind was on something else. He helped himself to more whisky before he gave any indication that this indeed was so, and had drunk half of it before he undertook to tell Andrew what it was.

It came abruptly after a short silence.

'Mollie's leaving me,' Ian said.

There did not seem to Andrew to be any answer to that, so he said nothing.

'You don't seem surprised,' Ian said after a moment.

'Well, yes and no,' Andrew said. 'I'm surprised that she's actually made up her mind to do it, but she confided in me a certain amount about her feelings for Brian, and I realized it was possible. You don't seem surprised yourself.'

'No, I've seen it coming for some time,' Ian said. Except that his large, dark eyes looked very tired and his round face which was normally a cheerful one had a kind of expressionless emptiness about it, he showed no signs of emotional disturbance.

'Are you sure about it?' Andrew asked.

'Yes, I think it's final this time,' Ian said.

'Oh, then you've talked about it before, have you?'

'God knows how often.'

'She didn't tell me that,' Andrew said. 'She gave me the impression you didn't know much about it.'

Ian gave a slight shake of his head. 'Mollie's never been able to keep anything to herself. Almost as soon as she and Brian met I could see there was something between them, and just in the way she assured me there was nothing, it was obvious that there was. It's been like the way she's talked as if this house is perfection and the house she's always wanted, I could tell she was overdoing it and was longing to get away.'

'That struck me too,' Andrew said.

'The only perfection about it was that by coming here she met Brian.' For the first time there was some bitterness in Ian's voice. 'But she tried hard to make it work, I'll give her that.'

'You've been trying, too.'

'Well, I suppose I've felt responsible for things going wrong. I ought never to have married her. I didn't give her the kind of love she wanted. I'm too old for her, for one thing.'

'She didn't have to marry you.'

'I think she felt she did. She'd seen what I went through when Vera died, how lonely and helpless I was, and I think she felt she'd got to look after me. And she wanted to be married to someone. She wasn't young any more, and though she'd had her affairs before, they'd none of them lasted and I was offering her security and a change in her whole way of living. Must be pretty boring, being a secretary in an accountant's office. She didn't think about the fact that there are all sorts of ways of being bored. As she didn't think that after she was safely married she might meet with Brian Singleton.'

'Ian, I've got a feeling that you're experiencing a kind of relief at what's happened this morning,' Andrew said.

Ian swirled round the remains of the whisky in his glass, looking into it as if he might find some truth lurking in its depths.

'Well, perhaps I do,' he said. 'It's as if I've shed a load I didn't even know I was carrying. We're very fond of each other, you see. We've a lot of real affection for one another. And we've neither of us wanted to hurt the other. Now I can stop trying to have feelings I haven't got. I expect I sound a pretty cold-blooded fish to you.'

'No, only someone who set himself standards he couldn't possibly live up to. This not wanting to hurt each other, the truth is it's probably what you've both been wanting to do more than anything else ever since the affair with Brian started. The affection may be real, but so's a lot of hate and anger.'

'I don't hate Brian,' Ian said. 'I'm not even angry with him.'

Andrew looked sceptical.

'I'm quite glad he's going to take Mollie off my hands,' Ian insisted.

'You're sure he will?'

'Oh yes.'

'When she spoke to me about it, she didn't seem really certain what his feelings were.'

'I don't think she need have any worries about it now that he's going to have plenty of money.'

'I'd never have thought she was mercenary.'

'I don't think she is. But Brian wouldn't care for going through with a divorce, however peaceful, while he's in his present job, and Mollie might not like going on living here through it and remarrying and trying to fit in with the wives of his colleagues. Not that they'd have much difficulty about all that nowadays, but they'd probably prefer to get away. It isn't as if the job's anything specially distinguished or that Brian's particularly talented. I don't believe he is. My guess is they'll look for something abroad. Anyway, money always makes everything easier.'

'You're lucky you haven't any children.'

'Thank God, yes!'

'She told me she wished you'd find another woman for yourself.'

'I think that's something I can do without.'

'What will you do? Stay on here?'

Ian looked vacantly at the empty fireplace. 'I don't know. I haven't thought. I haven't even begun to think what it's going to mean. I've just got this feeling something's settled and on the whole I'm thankful for it. You never went through anything like this, did you, Andrew?'

'No.'

'I've a feeling you think my attitude's all wrong. I oughtn't to be taking it all so calmly.'

'Indeed I don't, Ian. I think it's very fortunate you can feel as you do. Whether you'll still be feeling quite so calm when the shock's worn off I wouldn't like to prophesy.'

'I think I'll probably move back to London,' Ian said. 'I might find something in your neighbourhood. Have you anything against that?'

'Of course not. But you'll find it pretty expensive these days. When Nell and I bought our flat there it was going for a song, but prices have gone as mad there as everywhere else.'

'Luckily, money isn't one of the things I've got to worry about.'

'But what about your birds? You won't be able to do much bird-watching in London.'

Ian gave a little sigh. 'I'll miss it, but recently, you know, it's become a bit of a substitute for marriage. And I can still go to Kenya or the Gambia with the RSPB chaps, not only this year, but as long as I feel up to going. For some years, I hope. But I'll have to find something to occupy me in between whiles. Have you any suggestions?'

Andrew shook his head. 'It's hard enough for me to find the right thing to do myself, now that Robert Hooke's off my hands. I ought never to have finished that book, you know.

Working on it kept me pretty contented. But the idea of seeing it in print became a fatal temptation. I had an absurd sort of idea after meeting Eleanor Clancy that I might settle down to writing a life of her great-grandfather. I was going to ask her to let me take a look at his letters, to see if there was enough in them for me to be able to make something interesting of them. The illustrations, I thought, were all to be found in those quarter-plate negatives she'd kept so carefully. Beautiful things, I was ready to believe. But now just a heap of broken glass. There's a madman loose in this village, Ian, or else someone exceptionally cunning.'

'What could be cunning about smashing those negatives?' Ian asked.

'Perhaps to make us say what I've just said, that there's a madman on the loose.'

'You don't believe there is?'

'Oh, I don't know. Isn't there always an element of madness in murder? And with two murders that's something to think about.'

'Do you think Eleanor really knew who killed Luke Singleton and was blackmailing him for it, and that's why she was killed?'

'That's how it looks, doesn't it?'

Andrew leant back in his chair, stretching his long legs out before him. He wished that he knew what Ian really wanted now, to have someone to talk to, or to be left to himself, to brood on his own personal problems in quiet. Andrew felt fairly sure that he himself would have wanted to be alone. Not that he had ever experienced anything remotely like what Ian was having to face now. Particularly in Andrew's early days with Nell, he and she had quarrelled from time to time. Not very often and not at all fiercely. The deeper things in their marriage had never felt threatened. But he had other friends whose marriages, for one reason or another, had gone on the rocks and he had several times found himself the recipient of confidences which embarrassed him because he felt so little able to help. All he could do was listen, something at which he was fairly accomplished, and wait for some sign that would give him a hint of what he ought to do. For the moment he felt that talk of murder and blackmail was a fairly useful distraction.

'She went out on to the common to meet someone who gave her a thousand pounds and then killed her,' he said. 'And someone must be feeling very annoyed with himself that in the struggle that I suppose there was, she flung her handbag out into the lake. He's a thousand pounds the poorer. Why he gave her the money in the first place, I don't pretend to understand.'

'What strikes me about that thousand pounds,' Ian said, 'is that it's really rather a small sum to find you've got to pay if you've been detected in a murder. I'd have expected it to be twenty or thirty times that amount at least.'

'It might have been just a first instalment,' Andrew said. 'As much as the victim could lay his hands on in a hurry.'

'Or perhaps Eleanor wasn't a very experienced blackmailer and didn't know the value of her knowledge,' Ian suggested.

'Mollie didn't believe she was a blackmailer at all.'

'And she probably doesn't believe Brian's a murderer.'

'But you do?'

'Actually, I find it very hard to believe,' Ian said. 'Not because of his character. That's something I prefer not to think about too much at the moment. But the idea that when he pulled out that flower to give to Mollie he actually managed to flick a pellet of poison into his brother's cup across the table would mean he's a cleverer conjuror than I believe he is. But I don't say it's impossible. And the only other people who could have done it are Inspector Roland and Felicity. I believe they could have done it fairly easily, sitting either side of Singleton as they were. And Eleanor was so close to them that she might have seen one of them do it. But then there's the problem of that meeting on the common. I can't believe Eleanor would ever have gone up there all alone to meet Roland. She'd have been too scared of him. She might have agreed to meet Felicity. Eleanor was the taller and could have thought she was the stronger of the two, but Felicity could have taken her by surprise somehow. And about Eleanor having been given the thousand pounds before she was killed...' Ian paused, his forehead wrinkled in thought.

'Yes?' Andrew said.

'Suppose it *was* Felicity she met,' Ian said hesitantly. He was thinking something out as he went along. 'Eleanor wouldn't have been afraid of her and might have agreed to meet her on the common. And Felicity gave her the money as a sort of bait and then in the friendliest way possible, drew her, chatting, towards the bridge. She wanted to do the job there, because she wanted to knock her into the water, to make it harder for the exact time of the murder to be fixed. But it was Felicity's bad luck that the handbag with the money in it went into the water too. She'd have been very angry. I don't believe Felicity could spare a thousand pounds very easily.'

'But what had Felicity against Luke Singleton?' Andrew asked. 'I'll grant you all the rest is possible. But why did she do that first murder?'

Ian gave an ironic little laugh.

'I'm not serious, you know. I don't believe for a moment Felicity did it.'

'Why not?'

'Well, it's true I know very little about her private life. I'm quite sure there've been men in it, and she could probably have been married several times over if she'd wanted it. But she likes her work and I suppose she doesn't want children. You said just now how lucky Mollie and I are that we haven't got children, and I agree with you. If we had, I'd feel we'd got to make our marriage stick together somehow. But unless you want children, what's the point of marrying? Why did I marry Mollie?'

Ian's voice had changed. A harsher note had come into it. Andrew began to feel fairly sure that the time had come for him to find some reason for going up to his room. The danger that if he remained where he was he might find himself forced into taking sides seemed a very good reason for leaving. He stood up.

'Well, I'm terribly sorry things have turned out as they have,' he said, 'but I'm glad you seem to feel it'll be all for the best in the end. But I know you'll both go through a bad time before you can finally put it all behind you. I imagine you'd sooner I went home tomorrow.'

'Go or stay, as you like,' Ian answered in a tone of indifference. 'That man Roland will probably want you to stay.'

Andrew was afraid that that was probably true, though he thought that by next day Ian might be only too glad to be rid of him. However, that need not be settled now. He left the room, climbed the stairs to his bedroom, kicked off his shoes and flung himself, clothed, on the bed. All of a sudden he felt an almost unbearable sense of fatigue. That was one of the great disadvantages of being as old as he was, he thought. Fatigue could overpower you all in a moment and turn you into a useless, thoughtless hulk. It was true that he had every reason for feeling tired. The strain of the last few days might have bowled over a very much younger man. But as long as he had been talking to Ian, he had somehow managed to keep his need for rest at bay, in fact, almost to be unaware of it. Presently, to his great annoyance, his mind, which had felt quite empty, was filled with the rhyme that had troubled him off and on for the last day or two.

And now I'm as sure as I'm sure that my name
Is not Willow, titwillow, titwillow,
That 'twas blighted affection that made him exclaim…

Blighted affection! He had been hearing enough about that since coming to Lower Milfrey. Ian and Mollie. Ernest Audley and his lost wife. And possibly Felicity Mace and Luke Singleton. Not that that last had ever been stated plainly. There had merely been hints that some feeling between them might once have had some existence. Of the people whom Andrew had been meeting since arriving here only the Waldrons appeared to be a reasonably contented couple, and what did he know about them, after all?

There was a time when he thought that he heard voices downstairs, and he wondered if after all Mollie had come home. But when at last he made himself go downstairs, he found Ian alone, preparing a lunch of ham and salad.

'So she's gone, has she?' Andrew said. 'She didn't change her mind while she was out shopping?'

'No, and taken the car, says she'll bring it back when she and Brian have sorted things out, so now I've got to manage without it. The one thing I'm scared of now is that she and the car will come back together, because I don't honestly believe she'll be happy living with a murderer. And he's got to be the murderer, hasn't he? God knows how he did it, but no one else had the chance. And I think she knows it, knows how it was done and all. Well, it's her choice. If she can live with a murderer, who am I to stop her?'

❉ ❉ ❉

The rest of the day passed quietly, except for two or three visits from the press, and both Ian and Andrew went to bed early. Next morning they had a silent breakfast in the kitchen, then Ian settled down with his bird photographs, mounting them in an album, whistling under his breath while he did it. Andrew sat in a chair by the window with *The Times*. He read an account of the murder of Eleanor Clancy, and that the police were considering the possibility that it was linked to that of Luke Singleton, but that there was so far no proof of this. There was an article devoted to the work of Luke Singleton, which was somewhat patronizing in tone, though it gave full marks to him for the money that he had made. So if what everyone had been assuming was correct and all that money had been left to his brother, then Mollie Davidge had gone from mere comfort and security to riches.

It was at about ten o'clock that Ernest Audley came to the house. He came in apologizing for calling on them at such an hour, but said that he had thought that he would look in before leaving for his office in Rockford, because he wanted to know if they knew anything about the death of Eleanor Clancy. The red blotches on his cheekbones seemed to be particularly bright against the pallor of his thin face. The sandy hair that stood straight up from his narrow forehead looked a little as if he had forgotten to comb it that morning. Yet on the whole he looked cheerful.

'Of course you've heard the Bartletts have alibis for the woman's murder, haven't you?' he said. 'And that seems to clear them of poisoning Singleton. And I'd be suspect Number One for his murder if only they could tell me how I did it. You know, if I could think of a way I could have done it, I believe I'd be telling them about it, I'd be so proud of myself. And certainly I'd have sold my story to the popular press so that there'd be a nice hoard waiting for me when I came out of gaol. What d'you think I'd get? Life, of course, but that doesn't mean life nowadays. Sometimes it's a mere ten years. And I don't know that ten years in prison would be all that much worse than ten years in a solicitor's office in Rockford.'

'Don't be a fool, Ernest,' Ian muttered. 'You didn't do it, so don't give yourself airs.'

'No, and the fact is, of course, that nobody did it,' Audley said. 'It couldn't happen, so it didn't happen. By the way, where's Mollie?'

'Out shopping,' Ian lied.

'She liked that Clancy woman quite a lot, didn't she?' Audley went on. 'Is she badly upset?'

'About as much as you'd expect,' Ian answered.

His tenseness did not seem to quell Audley, who seemed to be in particularly good spirits that morning.

'D'you believe she was blackmailing someone?' he asked. 'That's what I heard.'

'How?' Ian said.

'How was she blackmailing someone? Easy enough, I suppose, if she happened to know what nobody else does.'

'I meant, how did you hear it?' Ian said.

'Oh, from my cleaning lady, whose husband's a policeman. I'm often put into possession of interesting information through her before other people get it. For instance, before this murder of Eleanor Clancy, I heard that the police were leaning to the idea that Singleton's death was suicide. I was ready to believe it myself. Choosing the most exhibitionist way possible of killing himself was quite in character.'

'So that's what you really meant when you said his murder couldn't happen, so it didn't happen.'

'No, no, I meant that we'd all been hypnotized into believing it had happened, when it simply hadn't happened at all.' Audley gave a pleased little chuckle. 'Complete illusion. You know, I thought Mollie must be taking the news of Clancy to Brian. I saw your car outside his bungalow. Tell me, won't you, if you have any bright ideas about how that Singleton murder was done?'

He gave a little wave to Andrew with one hand and let himself out.

'Bastard,' Ian muttered, not getting up to see him out and going on pasting photographs into his album.

About eleven o'clock he suddenly suggested, 'D'you feel like dropping in on the Waldrons? I'd be glad to know what Sam makes of the whole situation. After all, it was at his dinner that everything started. I shouldn't be surprised if he's got theories about it by now, and they'll be a little more soundly based than mass hypnotism. Are you coming?'

Andrew dropped *The Times* and stood up. He was glad to be able to do something active, rather than remaining in a house that seemed to have lost all that had given it life. He went with Ian out into the road.

'We'll have to walk, since Mollie's taken the car,' Ian said. They set off into the village.

That it seemed so normal, that the people they saw were going about their usual business, just as if drama and tragedy had never come near them, seemed strange, though in its way it was reassuring. The morning was a grey one, with pale, level clouds covering the sky. There was no breeze, yet it felt colder than the day before. Autumn was upon them, and soon it would be winter. Winter could come with very little warning, even if it was to make only a foray of a few days of bitter cold, then to become mild again, perhaps not returning for several weeks. But Andrew knew that some of the cold that he felt had nothing to do with the time of year, which after all was only September, but was inside himself. He was glad Ian felt inclined to walk fast. Andrew could still walk fairly fast, for which he was thankful, though catching sight of his reflection in the window of the village grocer as they passed it, it struck him that his stoop had increased markedly since he had noticed it last. Winter, his own winter, was waiting for him.

He and Ian were silent for a while, then Ian remarked, 'Audley's a queer chap, isn't he? I don't believe I could ever work up the state of hatred he seems to live in. He's really glad, you know, that Luke Singleton was murdered, and he doesn't seem much concerned that one of the results of it was that poor woman getting killed.'

'You're sorry for her even if it turns out she's a blackmailer?'

'Of course I am. I hate violence of all kinds.'

'Isn't blackmail a kind of violence?'

'You don't have to give in to it, do you?'

'It must be very difficult sometimes not to.'

'Anyway, I'm not altogether convinced she was a black-mailer. Mollie may be right about her.'

'I gather you don't have any very violent feelings against Brian.'

'No. I don't even really dislike him. What's happened isn't his fault, or Mollie's either, or even mine. It was just something that was going to happen sooner or later, and it might as well be with Brian as anyone else.'

'How long ago did you realize it was going to happen?'

'Well, it's easy to be wise after the event, but I've an idea it was about from the start. I knew quite soon, so it seems to me now, that Mollie would leave me sooner or later.'

'And I suppose that makes things easier now.'

'Oh yes, as I told you yesterday, it's a kind of relief.'

After that they were silent again for some time.

About a quarter of a mile beyond the end of the village they reached the gates that opened on to the drive that led up to the Waldrons' house. Seeing it in daylight, Andrew thought what a pleasantly dignified place it was, without any ostentation or pretension, though standing on a slight rise, as it did, it seemed to overlook the village. He could see now the park stretching around it, with some fine old chestnuts near the house, just beginning to show the first faint tints of autumn. When Ian rang the doorbell it was some time before the door was opened by Anna Waldron. Andrew was struck at once, as he had been when he saw her first, by her air of diffidence, yet at the same time by the grace of her movements. She was wearing well-cut dark blue jeans and a sweater of emerald green. Her dark hair was tied back from her face with a bright green ribbon.

'Oh, Ian, how nice to see you—and Professor, how good of you to come!' she exclaimed. 'The only other people we've seen for the last day or two have been the police. And of course, the Bartletts have left us. You know that, do you? And how we'll ever manage to replace them I don't know. How do you find people who'll come and work in a place where there's been an unsolved murder? Yet I can't possibly cope with things by myself. Of course, Sam and I can manage for the moment, but as everything begins to get dusty and horrible we'll just have to move out. Go abroad perhaps to somewhere like Portugal, where I believe you can still get servants. Oh, why am I talking like this? Do come in. Sam will be so glad to see you.'

She was chattering in the way of a shy person who is afraid that if she stops for a moment she may be quite unable to get started again, and who is really very much afraid of the people to whom she is chattering.

Sam Waldron's voice was heard coming from a room inside. 'Who's there, Anna? What are you doing out there? Bring them in, bring them in.'

Then he appeared in the doorway of the room where his guests had had drinks before his dinner. He was wearing the brown corduroy trousers and white sweater in which Andrew had seen him first, but checked bedroom slippers instead of gum boots, and if he did not look quite as impressive as he had on the night of the dinner, when he had been swathed in a long white apron and had been made to appear even taller than he was by the chef's hat that he had had on his head, he had lost none of his air of distinction.

'We aren't managing very well, I'm afraid, now that the Bartletts have left us,' he said. 'But we can offer you drinks. Come in here and please forgive the mess we're in. We've been so dependent for so long on those two good women that we hardly know how to fry bacon and eggs. We don't really know why they took off as they did. Panic, I suppose. Fear that they were going to be suspected of poisoning Singleton. Crazy, but I don't suppose they realized how utterly virtuous they appeared to other people. Of course, none of us knows how we appear to other people. Now what'll you have, whisky, vodka, sherry?'

The room into which he had taken Ian and Andrew was not really in a mess. A newspaper lay on the floor. Cushions in the easy chairs had not been plumped up. Ashes in the fireplace had not been swept up. That was all.

Ian and Andrew chose whisky, Sam Waldron vodka, and Anna sherry. She had come into the room behind the others, and now perched on the arm of an easy chair in one of the graceful poses that seemed to come to her naturally.

'You've read the papers, of course,' Sam said, when he had poured out drinks for the four of them and they were all sitting down.

'And you have too,' Ian said.

Sam gave a deep sigh. 'Yes. But it doesn't tell one much, except that the woman's dead. One supposes it's because she knew too much about Singleton's death, but it doesn't say so. D'you know any more about it?'

'A certain amount,' Ian answered. 'I found her in the lake, you know. And the police have found her handbag in the lake, with a thousand pounds in it. The theory is that she was attacked from behind and the handbag flew out of her hand and landed in the water.'

'That sounds very strange to me,' Sam said, thoughtfully rubbing a finger slowly down his aquiline nose. 'What was she doing, wandering about with a thousand pounds in her handbag? That doesn't sound like her.'

'They're considering the possibility of blackmail,' Ian said.

'That she was being blackmailed, d'you mean? No, of course you mean she was blackmailing someone and had just been paid. Well, well, what extraordinary things one learns about people—if it's true, that's to say. But it ought not to surprise me too much. Take the case of dear old Parson Woodforde. Respectability itself. Yet he took it for granted that he should buy his tea and his brandy from someone he called the Smuggler. According to his view, that was perfectly acceptable behaviour in a quiet country parson. So perhaps Miss Clancy found a touch of blackmail acceptable too. It was on a surprisingly small scale, wasn't it, if it was only a thousand pounds?'

'There's a suggestion that it was just a first instalment,' Ian said.

Sam nodded. 'That makes sense. So she knew who murdered Singleton, and how it was done. Extraordinary. She must have been a much cleverer woman in her way than I'd ever have given her credit for—oh, darling!' He had turned with a look of great distress to his wife, for her slight body had suddenly become shaken with sobs and tears were pouring down her face. 'Darling, don't cry! We couldn't have done anything to help her.'

She mopped at the tears with a handkerchief but went on shuddering. Sam sat down abruptly in the chair on the arm of which she was sitting and put his arms around her.

'Don't!' he repeated. 'I know you cared for her very much once, but that was years ago. And I know everything's horrible now, but it'll pass. They'll find out who did those things, and we'll get back to normal.'

'No, we won't!' she snuffled into her handkerchief. 'Nothing's ever going to be the same again. We were so happy and everything was going so well, but now it's all spoilt, and the only way to get over it will be to go away. And I don't want to go away. I just want none of it to have happened.'

'Well, that's something I'm afraid I can't arrange for you,' Sam said. 'I'd do anything else on earth, but putting the clock back's something I can't do.'

'If only we'd never given that awful dinner,' she moaned. 'Then if it was going to happen anyhow, it wouldn't have been here in our house. It wouldn't have been anything to do with us.'

Sam looked at Ian and Andrew.

'I'm sorry about this,' he said. 'She's usually so controlled. But she's gone to pieces since the dinner and now the news about the Clancy woman is just too much for her.'

'Andrew hasn't told you about the state of Eleanor's cottage,' Ian said. 'He was taken into it by Roland. They're old friends, you see, and Roland seems to have a great regard for Andrew's perspicacity.'

'Her cottage, you say?' Sam said. 'But I thought you said her body was found in the lake.'

'Yes, but someone got loose in her cottage after killing her. Andrew, tell Sam what you saw in the cottage.'

Andrew gave a brief description of what he had seen. Anna's sobbing gradually grew less as she listened, her reddened eyes fixed incredulously on Andrew's face. Once or twice she shook her head, as if she could not bring herself to believe what he was saying.

'And I believe the prevailing theory at the moment,' Andrew concluded, 'is that Miss Clancy thought she could protect herself from her victim by telling him that she'd written an account of what she knew which would be found if anything happened to her, but that she was killed all the same and her murderer went to the cottage to find what she'd written, and when he didn't find it smashed the place up in a rage.'

'And do you believe that?' Sam asked.

'I've no other theory to offer,' Andrew answered. 'On the whole, it seems to me quite probable.'

'I don't believe any of it,' Anna cried. 'I don't believe Luke was murdered, I think he committed suicide, and I don't think my dear Clancy was killed by someone she was blackmailing, but just by one of those horrible perverts one's always hearing about, who found a lonely woman out for an evening walk and wanted to rape her, only she fought him off and all he managed to do was kill her and throw her body in the lake. And then he went and wrecked her cottage because he was one of those awful vandals who love to smash things.'

'What about the thousand pounds in her handbag?' Ian asked. 'As Sam said, it isn't the sort of sum you'd expect her to be carrying about with her.'

'How d'you know why she had it?' Anna demanded. Her voice had risen. She was almost screaming. 'She may have got it to give to somebody next day. The bank may be able to tell whether or not she cashed it herself. I can imagine her giving it to someone who was in difficulties of some sort. She was wonderfully warm-hearted and generous, that's partly why we all loved her so at St Hilda's. You could always go to her with your troubles. This idea that she was a blackmailer—it's horrible, horrible!'

Her husband's arms held her close, but she went on crying, 'Horrible!'

That was the word that rang in Andrew's head as he and Ian presently walked home. But being horrible does not make a thing improbable. He was not sure that Anna's defence of Eleanor Clancy had not made him more inclined to think of her as someone capable of blackmail than he had been before it. Also, he thought of what Sam had said as he had seen them out of the door. He had said that he would never fish in that lake again. Andrew found that he did not believe in that, either. As soon as propriety allowed, he felt sure, Sam would be back after his tench and his carp, and he would be cooking them himself after soaking them for some hours in slightly acidulated water to get rid of the taste of mud. And Anna would calm down and life would go on for the two of them in the way that was normal for them.

Other murders in other towns and villages would fill the newspapers. Death would stalk the land as usual. Planes would crash, killing all the passengers and crew. Buses would be overturned on motorways, with a long list of casualties. Children would be indecently assaulted, would be killed crossing roads, or by their impatient parents or step-parents. And Luke Singleton's novels would go on selling as well as ever, if not better, for a considerable time after his death.

The murders in Lower Milfrey would be forgotten. What was it Ernest Audley had said that morning? 'It couldn't happen, so it didn't happen...'

The words lingered in Andrew's mind as he and Ian went back to an empty house. Was it possible that after all they meant something?

Chapter Eight

Andrew cooked the lunch of sausages, bacon and frozen chips as he was more used to cooking for himself than Ian was. After it, Andrew went upstairs to his room, kicked off his shoes and lay down on the bed. He was having some difficulty keeping the wretched tomtit at bay. *Willow, titwillow, titwillow* kept repeating itself maddeningly in his head. He felt that if only it would stop his mind might become clear, his ideas lucid, his vision of what had really happened at Sam Waldron's dinner convincing. For he found that he had a belief that he knew more about it than he was aware of knowing. That that was probably an illusion was something that he accepted, yet it would be such a relief to find that it was true, to be able to fit just a few missing pieces into the puzzle of that evening and so complete the picture. It would bring such peace of mind. Meanwhile, sleep gave it to him for a little while, but after only about half an hour he woke up to find that the tomtit was still with him.

> *But now I'm as sure as I'm sure that my name*
> *Is not Willow, titwillow, titwillow*
> *That 'twas blighted affection—*

He sat up in bed with a jerk. The jingle stopped. For suppose it was not blighted affection? Suppose blighted affection had had nothing to do either with the death of the tomtit or of Luke Singleton.

Everyone, he thought, had been taking for granted that the motive for his murder had been sexual. But suppose sex had had nothing to do with it. Did that mean automatically that the motive must be financial? Suppose it was not that either. Andrew's thoughts began to run in an entirely new direction and piece by piece fitted into the puzzle so that a strange picture began to take shape. But this could be as mistaken as the obsession with blighted affection, which he had decided was a delusion. Unless he could obtain some information he could not feel sure that the sense of inspiration which possessed him now was anything but self-deception. And how was that information to be obtained?

After a short spell of very careful thinking he got up, not troubling to put on his shoes or slippers, but moving quietly in his socks, a habit he had when he was at home, went downstairs and picked up the telephone in the hall. He did not know where Ian was, but hoped that it was in his bedroom, for he did not want what he had to say to be overheard. But even if it was, it would not make much sense to Ian.

He dialled the London number of his nephew, Peter Dilly. When he answered, Andrew said, 'Peter, there's something I'd like you to do for me. It'll mean a bit of trouble, I'm afraid, and take a bit of time, but it's urgent. Have you any time to spare?'

'I can make it,' Peter answered. 'Is it to do with that murder you've got in your neighbourhood?'

'So you've been reading about it, have you?'

'One can hardly avoid it,' Peter said.

'Well yes, it is. There's some information I want rather badly. If certain facts are what I think they may be, I believe we can clear the whole thing up, but they need to be corroborated.'

'Go ahead, then. If it's anything I can actually do, I'll do my best.'

'Get paper and pencil, then.'

'It's all right, I've got them here.'

Andrew then told Peter as briefly as he could what it was that he wanted Peter to find out for him. It was not a great deal, but Andrew had no idea how long it might take for the facts to be checked.

When he finished, Peter said, 'It sounds simple enough. I suppose you don't want to tell me what you've got on your mind.'

'Not till I'm clearer about it myself,' Andrew answered.

'All right, then. I'll set out on the job straight away, and I'll phone you as soon as I've anything to tell you.'

'Thank you. I knew I could count on you. Thank you very much, Peter.'

They both rang off and Andrew returned to his bedroom.

It was about four o'clock when he came downstairs again and now he heard voices in the sitting room. Going in, he found Ian, Mollie and Brian sitting there, with a tea tray between them. Mollie was just pouring out the tea.

Andrew was about to withdraw hurriedly, feeling that if a triangular discussion was in progress, a fourth member would hardly be helpful, but Mollie said at once, 'Oh, there you are. We couldn't decide whether to call you down for tea. I'll just get another cup.'

She put the teapot down and hurried past Andrew into the kitchen. It looked all very normally domestic.

As he still hesitated in the hall just outside the doorway, Ian said, 'It's all right, come in. We've just been settling a few things, nothing to worry you.'

Andrew would have preferred to return to his bedroom and do without the tea, but Mollie, returning from the kitchen with a fourth teacup, slid her arm through his and drew him into the room. She was smiling, but her eyelids were red and puffy, as if she had been crying.

'Yes, we've settled everything,' she said as she sat down and picked up the teapot again. 'That is, I suppose we have.' She looked at Ian. 'Haven't we?'

'There was nothing much to settle, once the two of you had made up your minds,' he said. 'You're moving out, Brian's giving up his job as soon as he's sure he's going to have an income, I get a divorce moving. I suppose that's really worthwhile, is it? The divorce, I mean.'

Brian's square, tanned face was more sombre than usual.

'Of course it is,' he said. 'I want to marry Mollie.'

'One can't help wondering why,' Ian said. 'Marriage nowadays seems so totally unnecessary.'

'What do you think, Andrew?' Mollie asked. She was trying to make it sound light, but there was a slight tremor in her voice. 'A divorce can be quite expensive. Do you think we should bother about it?'

Andrew had sat down and accepted the cup of tea that she held out to him.

'I can tell you one good reason for marrying Brian,' he said, 'if you and Ian have really decided to separate.'

'Oh, we have,' she said. 'He really wants it as much as I do.'

'What's this good reason?' Ian asked.

'I'm afraid you'll think it morbid,' Andrew said. 'It's just that I'm assuming that Brian is going to become a pretty rich man and that he'll make a will leaving all he has to Mollie.' He looked at Brian. 'Is that correct?'

Brian nodded. 'I haven't heard anything definite about Luke's will, but he told me he was leaving all he had to me. That includes his copyrights, I believe. It should amount to a good deal. And of course I'll make a will sometime and leave everything to Mollie, if she really wants to stick to me, but what's that got to do with our getting married?'

'Only that if you're married and you should happen to die before her,' Andrew said, 'she won't have to pay any death duties on what she inherits from you, whereas if you're merely living together she'd find the tax considerable.'

'Andrew!' Mollie gave a little shriek. 'Morbid—I should think so! Do you think I'm going to marry Brian and then wait for what he's going to leave me when he dies? I never knew you could say anything so outrageous.'

'I think it makes very good sense,' Brian said thoughtfully. 'Yes, suppose there's someone who's got it in for the Singletons, and I'm the next to go... No, that doesn't really sound very convincing. If that was so, I'd be liable to be finished off pretty soon, wouldn't you say? And a divorce takes ages to go through. So even if we've decided on marriage, we probably shouldn't have got married in time to dodge the death duty.'

Ian burst out laughing. It was a curious sound to hear in that room where tragedy of a kind was being enacted.

'Don't take Andrew too seriously,' he said. 'I know him in this mood. He's very embarrassed and wants to deal with that by reducing it to absurdity. But perhaps it's quite natural that early death should be on his mind. Neither Luke nor Eleanor were what one could call young, but they died before their time.'

'I haven't reduced anything to absurdity,' Andrew said. 'I've merely stated a fact. And remember, Brian, that if you make a will in the near future leaving all you have to Mollie, and then later you marry her, the marriage cancels all wills made before it, and if you don't make another, she won't inherit anything. All you meant to leave to her will go to your next of kin. Have you any next of kin?'

'A cousin or two whom I've seen about twice in my life,' Brian answered. 'Are you suggesting they might have a motive for murdering me?'

'Not so long as you make a will soon, and another as soon as you've got married,' Andrew said.

'I see,' Brian said. 'Then I'd better get ahead with that. Thank you, Professor.'

'Don't be absurd,' Mollie said to him tenderly. 'Andrew's just teasing you, because, as I said, he's embarrassed at finding himself assisting at the break-up of a marriage. But Andrew dear, there's no need to be embarrassed now. The worst is over. If you'd come downstairs a bit sooner you'd have heard Ian and Brian shouting at each other, and me in tears. We were all arguing about what was to be done about this house. It belongs to Ian and me, you see, and Ian wants to sell it and I think he ought to keep it, because it suits him so splendidly...'

'Suits me!' Ian suddenly shouted. 'You think I want to keep a place where I've been made an utter fool of! A place where I've been reduced to misery and self-pity while I was trying to convince myself that my insane behaviour was what people insist on calling civilized! I want to get rid of the damned place as soon as I can.'

'Yes, yes, I know that's how you feel now,' Mollie said, beginning to sound as if her tears might be returning. 'But I never meant to make a fool of you. I'm the one who's a fool. The trouble was I was so fond of both of you. I couldn't bear it that either of you should be hurt. But what was I to do? Well, we've settled that, haven't we? I'm going to pack a suitcase and I'll go home with Brian. But Ian, I'll always love you. You do understand that, don't you?'

'I wish to God you hated my guts!' he cried. 'Then I could hate yours and Brian's. It's an abominable frustration, not being able to hate as you want to. Some good, honest hatred is what the three of us need.'

'Oh, don't say that,' Mollie begged. 'I believe I should go out of my mind if I found that I really hated somebody. It would frighten me horribly.'

'Because you could see yourself dropping cyanide in his coffee?' Ian said.

There was suddenly silence in the room.

Then Brian stood up and put an arm round Mollie.

'Come on, we'd better go,' he said. 'Go and pack that suitcase and we'll push off. Ian knows I didn't put cyanide into Luke's coffee, and you didn't either. We'll probably never know who did. Professor, I'm sorry you've been involved in all this, but as Mollie said, the worst is over. By which she meant, I think, that we've all made up our minds and we've just got to get adjusted to the new state of affairs. None of us likes what we've been doing to one another, but it couldn't be helped. And it's got nothing to do with cyanide, or people getting murdered on the common.'

Mollie got up and shot out of the room. They could hear her running up the stairs, then the sound of footsteps in the room overhead.

Ian reached for the teapot and poured himself out a second cup of tea.

'Of course, Brian's right,' he said quite calmly. 'But we'll sell this house as soon as possible. I assume Mollie won't actually object to that—or does she want it as a bolt-hole in case things don't work out as well as she hoped?'

For the first time Andrew saw anger in Brian's eyes.

'If they don't, I don't imagine she'd want to come back here,' he said. 'But it's sometimes sensible not to make important decisions when emotions are running high. Why not wait a little before you make up your mind?'

'I'm tired of waiting,' Ian said. 'It's what I've been doing for the last couple of years. You can wait and hope, and then you wait without hoping, and then waiting itself becomes a bit too much for you. No, I'm sorry, Brian, I'm tired of bloody everything. You'd like me to take it better than I'm doing, but I can't oblige. And the sooner you and Mollie are out of the house, the better.'

They were gone in about a quarter of an hour. They left in Brian's car. Mollie had brought the BMW back. Ian put it away in the garage, then took the tea tray out to the kitchen and stacked the cups and saucers in the dishwasher, all in silence. When he returned to the sitting room he stayed silent for a while, sitting down in the chair where he had sat before and staring broodingly before him. But after a while he spoke.

'I wish I felt more certain than I do that Brian had nothing to do with Luke's murder.'

'Because you don't like the idea of handing Mollie over to a murderer?' Andrew said.

'That's it, more or less.'

'Well, I don't think you need worry about that.'

'You don't think he'd anything to do with it?'

'No.'

Ian turned his head a little to look at Andrew. 'Does that mean you think you know who did it?'

'I'm not sure, but I think so.'

'Who?'

'I don't think I'll say anything about that just yet,' Andrew answered. 'I may have gone quite off the rails. At the moment I'm waiting for some information which may help to make sense of things. Till I get it, I think I'll keep my ideas to myself.'

'Was that what you were telephoning about?'

'Yes, it was.'

'Don't worry, I didn't hear what you said. I just heard the tinkle of the telephone when you picked it up, then your voice. But I was half asleep at the time, and anyway I couldn't have heard what you were saying from my room upstairs.'

'I was telephoning my nephew, Peter Dilly. He's going to try to get me the information I want. I'm sorry, Ian, I'd rather like to talk the whole thing over with you, but if I'm quite wrong I don't want to start up crazy ideas about a quite innocent person. All the same, what I don't mind saying is that I believe someone wanted us all to think in a particular way, and that's just what we've been doing. We've been thinking exactly as he wanted us to think. And what we've got to do now is to turn the whole thing upside down and start from there. Or do I mean back to front? Anyway, get off the track he laid down for us. Try that, and see if you don't come to the same conclusion as me. You know all the facts that I know.'

'But I've never thought of myself as having half as ingenious a mind as you've got. Now what about a drink?'

'Thank you.'

'Whisky?'

'Yes, please.'

Ian went to get the drinks and while he was gone Andrew got up and went to the window. It was not yet dusk and he could see across the common, and see the children playing on their swings and slides. They would soon be fetched in, he supposed, and darkness would presently blot out what had been the scene of murder. A murder which it was generally assumed had happened because Eleanor Clancy knew who had killed Luke Singleton. But turn that upside down, or back to front, or whatever you like to call it. Anyway, get off that track that the murderer had laid for them all, and why should that be the explanation of anything? One by one, Andrew started going over the facts, or what should more properly be called the ideas, that had filled his mind for the last two or three hours, putting them in order, thinking out how he should explain them to anyone when the time came to do so.

Then the clink of bottle and glasses interrupted him and he turned away from the window. Ian poured out the drinks.

'Did I behave very badly this afternoon?' he asked. 'I mean, losing my temper suddenly. I'd absolutely made up my mind to keep it.'

'I've no standard to go by,' Andrew said. 'You had my sympathy.'

'But probably they had it too.'

'Well, yes, if you like to put it like that.'

'I'd be glad if we never had to meet again, but Mollie will have to get her things. That suitcase she took won't last long. But I can try to be out of the way when she comes to do her serious packing. And I'm inclined to think that the best thing to do about the furniture and so on is to get in one of those clearance firms and tell them to take the lot—'

He broke off as the front doorbell rang.

It was Felicity Mace. She came into the room looking strangely unlike her usual poised and practical self. Her face was white, her eyes seemed to glitter unnaturally. Ian followed her in with perplexity on his face. She had said nothing to him at the door, but had thrust straight in past him, then abruptly stood still in the middle of the room.

'You haven't heard!' she said in a shrill, sharp voice.

'I don't know,' Ian said. 'Haven't we?'

'About Anna Waldron.'

'We saw her this morning—'

'No, no,' she broke in. 'This afternoon. Only about an hour ago. She threw herself out of a top-floor window. She killed herself. She's dead.'

❊ ❊ ❊

Ian guided her to a chair. She sank into it and for a moment covered her face with her hands. When she dropped them it was as if what she had been doing was putting her normal face back in place. It was still white, but the wildness had gone. Her eyes looked dull and tired rather than glittering.

'Sam called me instead of the police,' she said in a weary voice. 'I had to tell him over and over again that he mustn't touch her and had got to get them. In the end, I phoned them myself. They're in charge there and thank God, Winslow's there.' Winslow, Andrew had gathered from Roland, was the police surgeon. 'Sam's simply sitting perfectly still in his study, staring at nothing. I thought you might go to him, Ian. He likes you.'

'We were there this morning,' Ian said. 'Anna was in a queer mood. Quite hysterical really. But I never dreamt she was anywhere near doing a thing like this. It almost seems...' He stopped.

'She talked about the murders,' Andrew explained, 'only she didn't believe, or said she didn't, that Luke Singleton's death was murder. She claimed it was suicide. And she didn't believe Eleanor Clancy was killed because she was blackmailing anyone, but by a pervert who failed to rape her and killed her instead.'

'But none of that has anything to do with her suicide,' Felicity said.

'I was going to say,' Ian said hesitantly, 'that one might take it in its way as a confession of guilt. I mean, that she'd got involved in the murders somehow and couldn't bear it, and what she said about them was what she wished had happened, not what she knew really had. Only I suppose I'm talking nonsense.'

'She couldn't have had anything to do with the murder of Luke,' Felicity said. 'She was in the kitchen, like Sam, at the time it happened. It's not so impossible that she had something to do with the murder of Eleanor, if she had any kind of motive. It's been a puzzle, hasn't it, how anyone could persuade Eleanor to meet them out there on the common at dusk and all alone. But if Anna wanted to meet her, she'd probably have gone. She'd have trusted her as a matter of course. And although Anna was small and slight, she was very strong. She was extremely athletic when she was younger. I believe she might have been able to strangle Eleanor. But what are we doing, talking like this? We've no reason to think she killed herself because she couldn't stand the burden of guilt. We're obsessed with the subject, that's the trouble.'

'Has anyone told you about the state of Eleanor's cottage?' Ian asked.

'No,' she said.

'You tell her, Andrew. You're the one who saw it.'

He described it as well as he could, ending up with what had affected him most, the destruction of the negatives. Felicity listened intently, and when he finished gave a little sigh.

'That really tells one quite a lot, doesn't it?' she said. 'Madness. It has to be madness. And I suppose that means it might have been Anna. I've heard of other cases where someone committed suicide because they realized they were going mad. It's usually happened when the person has gone through a period of insanity before and is supposed to have recovered from it, then when the symptoms start again they realize what's happening to them and they can't face it. But that's supposing it was Anna whom Eleanor went to meet on the common. If it was, it might have had nothing to do with Luke's murder, though that just might have triggered it off in some way. I mean, that happening in her home, at the dinner that was supposed to be such fun for all of us. It might have tipped her over the brink.'

Andrew was remembering how he and Ian had discussed the possibility that it had been Felicity whom Eleanor had gone to meet on the common.

'Has anyone told you about Eleanor's handbag being found in the lake, with a thousand pounds in it?' he asked.

Felicity shook her head.

'I've been thinking about that thousand pounds,' Andrew said. 'The bank that cashed them may be able to tell by whom they were cashed and when.'

She nodded this time, but there was no change on her face.

'By the way,' she said, 'where's Mollie?'

For a moment it looked as if Ian did not intend to answer, and Andrew wondered if he was expected to do it. Then Ian moved away to the window, standing with his back to the room.

'She's left me,' he said abruptly.

Felicity turned her head quickly to look at him, but she could not see his face.

After a moment she said, 'Oh.' Then after another moment she said, 'I knew it would happen sometime. I'm very sorry, Ian.'

'No need to be,' he said. 'It's painful, but I'm glad it's over. Better than the sort of pretence we've been putting on for a good while now.'

'She's gone to Brian, has she?' Felicity asked.

'Yes.'

'And if he's involved in Luke's murder?'

'Andrew and I have been discussing that,' Ian said. 'Andrew's sure that he isn't. I'm not certain myself. I wish I were. Now, about your suggestion, Felicity, that I should go along to Sam. I think I'll go. No...' He had turned and seen that she was getting up from her chair, as if she too would leave when he did. 'Don't go. Stay and keep Andrew company. I don't know when I'll be back. Perhaps straight away. Sam may not want me. On the other hand, I might be gone some time. Andrew, get Felicity a drink, will you? I'm sure she'd like one.'

He left them, and two or three minutes later they heard the BMW drive away.

Felicity had said that a drink would be very welcome and Andrew had supplied her with whisky. He was thinking that Mollie's hope that Ian might turn from her to Felicity had not been realistic. He had seen no sign of anything between them but an almost casual kind of friendliness.

She sipped her drink in silence for a moment, then looked at Andrew with a sad sort of smile.

'Were you expecting this too?' she said.

'The break-up between Ian and Mollie?' he said. 'No, I'd never have come if I had been. These things don't really need an audience.'

'No, I suppose not. You haven't exactly had a happy visit, have you?'

'One certainly couldn't call it that.'

'Well, I've only been wondering how long it could be before Mollie did something definite about the situation. I've got to know her rather well during the last couple of years, and I've known Brian longer than that. I saw it happen almost at once. But Mollie tried very hard to be loyal to Ian, and Brian never tried to put any pressure on her. And Ian didn't force the issue. I'm glad it's sorted itself out at last, even if it took a murder to do it.'

Andrew gave her a puzzled glance. She nodded her head thoughtfully.

'Oh yes, I'm sure it's that that did it,' she said. 'There's been a lot of explosive emotion in the air, which brought Mollie's feelings into the open. And when it turned out that there was a risk that Brian might be suspected of killing his brother, she felt she had to show her feelings at once.'

'She's sure of his innocence, is she?'

'I wouldn't say for certain that she is.'

'So you think she could go to live with a man who she knows just might be a murderer?'

'Don't a lot of the worst murderers have loving families? But you've said you're fairly sure of his innocence yourself. Is that because you think you know who did it?'

'I believe I do.'

She gave him another of her appealing smiles.

'You don't feel like telling me in the strictest confidence...?'

'I'd very much like to. I'm sure a discussion with you would be very helpful. But I've made up my mind that until I get certain information I'm going to keep my cogitations to myself.'

'You haven't even told Ian what they are?'

'No, not even Ian.'

'But he knows you've thought of some sort of solution for the whole problem?'

'I suppose he does.'

She finished her drink and stood up. A little colour had returned to her face, though it still showed lines of strain.

'Well, I must get home. I hope Ian doesn't stay away too long.'

'Let me see you home,' Andrew said.

'Thank you, but I have my car.' She turned to the door, but paused as she reached it. 'I was sitting next to Luke Singleton, Professor. Have your cogitations anything to do with me?' She waited a moment for him to answer, but when he said nothing, said, 'I see, you really won't talk. And I suppose you're right to stick to that. But I understand that I'm an excellent suspect. Goodbye.'

He saw her out to her car, then returned to the house, a heavy frown gathering on his forehead. Going into the sitting room, he poured out some more whisky for himself.

'I'm a bloody fool,' he muttered. 'Why did I have to say anything about it at all to anyone?'

Chapter Nine

Sinking into a chair, he began thinking about what he and Ian should have for supper. There was some cold chicken in the refrigerator and the makings of a salad. He prepared these, leaving them ready in the kitchen for when Ian came in, then returned to the sitting room, helped himself to another drink and sat down again.

Almost at once he found himself beginning to brood on the question of whether the idea he had had that there might be some interest in writing the life of Eleanor Clancy's great-grandfather was not after all a possibility. It was a question really of what there was in the letters that he had written home and which she had said that she had kept. If she had, they were probably still somewhere in that cottage that had been so badly wrecked. They might be among the wreckage, crumpled and torn, and if that had happened to them, Andrew would have to abandon his idea straight away. Anyway, perhaps it was not really a very good idea.

In case it was, however, he thought that he ought to go to the cottage next day and see if he could find the letters and if he did, find out if they stirred his imagination at all. He supposed that he would be able to get into the cottage. The lock on the front door was broken, and unless the police had put some kind of seal on it, there should be no difficulty about getting in. All the same, before doing much about it at all, he would have to discover to whom the letters belonged. He could not remember that he had heard anyone say anything about Eleanor's next of kin, and she might not have left her belongings to her next of kin, even if she had any, but to some friend, if it happened that she had made a will. And in either case there would have to be discussions on the matter, and probably a contract, and perhaps other complications. So it looked as if the idea was not really a good one after all.

But he must find something to do. He thought of how bird-watching had helped Ian to face the gradual disintegration of his marriage, and of how photography and making jams and chutney had helped Eleanor to face the emptiness of her solitary life, and of how he himself had been helped to endure the shrinking world of old age by writing the life of Robert Hooke. What a fool he had been ever to let it get finished. How contented he had been, working at it. Surely he could have found a lot more to say if he had not had the absurd idea that it would be a good thing to finish it. Well, he would go to the cottage tomorrow, but his hopes of what he might find there were not very high.

It was about half past nine when Ian returned to the house. They had their cold supper in the kitchen. Then Andrew made some coffee and they settled down to drink it with some brandy in the sitting room. The meal had been almost silent. Ian muttered something about it being pretty well impossible to do anything for someone who had just gone through what Sam had, then seemed not to want to say any more about the time that he had passed with him, and Andrew did not press him to talk.

But after a little while Ian suddenly observed, 'She'd tried it before.'

Ian's round, cheerful face seemed to have become hollow-cheeked and his large, dark eyes, which normally looked so shrewd and observant had a dull, almost blinded look, like those of someone with the beginnings of a cataract.

'Tried to commit suicide before?' Andrew asked.

'So Sam said—twice,' Ian answered. 'And he's blaming himself now, because he didn't take it seriously. The first time was soon after they first came to live here. She took an overdose of sleeping pills, enough to scare him, but not nearly enough to kill her. Felicity was her doctor, and between them they kept it pretty quiet. Sam thought it was just the dodge some people go in for to get attention, but Felicity told him it was because they'd decided not to have children. That business of being cousins—it seems he was more scared of it than he let on. Anyway, Anna seemed to recover, and then about two years ago she threw herself in front of a car in the road near them. If the driver of the car hadn't been a bloody genius she'd have been done for, but he managed to drive the car almost up into the hedge to get round her, then stopped and went for help, because she'd fainted. And the official story that time was that she'd slipped on an icy puddle—it happened there'd been a bit of frost in the night—and had hit her head on the road and passed out. But Sam said he guessed she'd done it on purpose even though by then she was swearing it was an accident, and he began to take the situation more seriously. But he did think just possibly she'd really slipped on the ice and he didn't do much about it. And that's what he's blaming himself for now. I mean, that he didn't pay her extra attention, but kept on with his fishing and his Parson Woodforde and his quite busy life, when she was lonely and longing for children and so on. She was very shy and didn't easily make friends, and the things she really cared about, cricket and so on, aren't possible for a woman to keep on with once she's getting into middle age. Well, that's what Sam poured out this evening, and I suppose it may have done him good to talk. For a time he kept saying he didn't understand what he'd been doing to her, but after a bit he just dried up and seemed to want me to go away. He's alone in the house now.'

'The police aren't there?' Andrew asked.

'They were for a time, but they've left,' Ian said. 'There's no question that it was anything but suicide. Sam himself was actually down by the gate, chatting to a neighbour, when they heard a fearful scream, and both went running up to the house, and there she was spread-eagled on the ground with a top-floor window above her open. They went inside together, and of course the house was empty. So, as I said, it's no question that it was suicide.'

'Did Sam tell the police about those other attempts?'

'I don't know. I didn't ask him.'

'Does he think that the events of the last few days had anything to do with it?'

'Singleton's murder, you mean, and Eleanor's?'

'Yes.'

'I'm not sure what he thinks himself. I'm inclined myself to think they helped to tip her over the edge. Specially Eleanor's. She had that schoolgirl crush on her once, and that may have boiled up again, suddenly meeting her here, and then her dying as horribly as she did. But Sam says he believes she's been a bit abnormal ever since the death of her parents. They were killed, you know, in a plane crash, and she was brought up by grandparents.'

'I remember her saying she was very happy with them, that evening when she was here,' Andrew said.

'But it could have been a blow she'd never got over, even if she didn't know she hadn't,' Ian said. 'Isn't that common enough?'

'I believe so. And I'd a sort of feeling, as I believe you did too, when we were with the Waldrons this morning, that when she tried to prove that Singleton's death was suicide and that Eleanor was killed by some chance prowler, she was trying to exorcise some feeling of guilt. I'm not sure why I felt it, but I did.'

' "The burden of guilt"—wasn't that what Felicity called it? But she can't have been feeling guilty all these years for her parents' deaths.'

'It doesn't seem likely. But one can feel guilty about all sorts of irrational things.'

'I wish I didn't feel as guilty as I do about the way my marriage has cracked up. Is that irrational?'

'Probably.' Andrew poured out more brandy for himself and Ian. 'I don't believe any marriage cracks up without a certain amount of guilt on both sides.' He gave Ian's haggard face a thoughtful look. The day must have put a fearsome strain on him, he looked so unlike himself. 'But I shouldn't nurse your guilt, if it's there. That won't do you any good. By the way, did you tell Sam that you and Mollie were separating?'

'I mentioned it. I also said I'm thinking of going to a solicitor in Rockford tomorrow to get the divorce moving, and he said something about Ernest being a good man, so I suppose he was listening, but then he went straight on to ask me about Brian and how he's taken his brother's death. He can't really think about much else but that murder, except for Anna. Of course, that's only what you'd expect. And by then he was wanting me to leave him alone. Well, I think I'll go up to bed now.'

Andrew was ready for bed too, but he slept restlessly, waking frequently, and he was glad when morning came. He went downstairs in his dressing gown to make the coffee and the toast, and found some cheese for himself, and presently he was joined by Ian, freshly shaved and fully dressed and acting with a briskness which suggested that he had definitely made up his mind about something. This turned out to be simply the decision to make an appointment with Ernest Audley to discuss with him the steps that he must take to obtain a divorce.

'The sooner I get things moving, the better,' he said. 'I'm tired of indecision. I'm going to phone Ernest as soon as his office is likely to be open to see if I can arrange to see him this morning. It means going into Rockford. Would you care to come with me? There's a church that's worth looking at, and there are one or two good pubs if you feel like a drink. We could meet after I've seen Ernest and have lunch there.'

'If you don't mind, I think I'll stay here,' Andrew answered. 'I'm expecting a phone call from my nephew, Peter. That's to say, I'm hoping for one, and it could be important, but I don't know when it'll come. I asked him to do something for me and I know he'll be as quick about it as he can, but I don't really know how long he'll need. Anyway, I don't want to risk missing it.'

'But you won't mind if I go off for a while and leave you here?' Ian asked.

'Not in the least.'

'If I'm not back in time for lunch you can help yourself.'

'That's quite all right.'

'I'm not sure actually if it's a good idea for me to go to Ernest,' Ian said. 'He's a queer chap and he may try to make the divorce a much more acrimonious thing than I want, but he's the only solicitor I know in Rockford. Of course, there are the people in London whom the family have been going to for several generations, but I don't even know if they handle divorce, and I like the idea of being able to talk things over when it's necessary with someone near at hand. So I think I'll risk handing the whole thing over to Ernest.'

He made the phone call for an appointment soon after he and Andrew had finished breakfast, but was unable to arrange to see Ernest Audley before twelve o'clock. Andrew had spent most of the morning reading *The Times* with half his attention on the telephone. As it remained silent, his impatience grew. He knew that this was foolish. What he had asked Peter to do for him might well take him more than a day. Yet he felt as if by concentrating on the instrument in the hall, he must surely be able to make it ring.

At the same time, he felt that this very behaviour of his might actually prevent it doing so. He tried to stop himself thinking about it and gave his attention to *The Times* crossword, but he was never very clever at crosswords at the best of times and that morning he was badly defeated by it.

A bell ringing suddenly brought him instantly to his feet, only to realize at once that it was not the telephone but the front doorbell. Ian, who had not yet set off for Rockford, went to answer it and brought in Inspector Roland. He took a chair by the fireplace and looked around the room. It almost suggested that he was looking for signs of Mollie's departure, though Andrew did not know for sure if the Inspector would have heard of this by now. What he said first, however, made it plain that he had.

'So your wife's gone,' he said to Ian. 'I heard about it from Waldron. Seems you told him about it yesterday evening. I've been in with him again this morning and found him pretty shattered, as you might expect. I went along to see him to find out if he could explain a rather curious fact we've stumbled on, but that'll have to wait. He isn't in a state to talk rationally about anything much. I believe he was devoted to that wife of his, though he blames himself for her suicide. He told us she'd tried it twice before. If that's true and he didn't get her into the hands of a psychiatrist, perhaps he's right. Not that I've all that much faith in those boys, but there doesn't seem to be any alternative.'

'That curious fact you've stumbled on,' Andrew said, 'are we allowed to know what it is?'

'I don't see why not,' Roland said. 'It's just that Mrs Waldron happens to have cashed a cheque for a thousand pounds several days ago.'

'A thousand pounds!' Ian exclaimed. 'The amount that was in that handbag of Eleanor Clancy's that they fished out of the river! But look, that doesn't make sense. Why should Mrs Waldron have given Eleanor a thousand pounds?'

'That's what I hoped I could find out from Waldron,' Roland said. 'But he stubbornly refused to believe she'd done that. Said it must have been coincidence, and of course he could be right. The bank hadn't got the numbers of the notes. And if Mrs Waldron did give the money to Miss Clancy it seems most probable that it was an act of generosity, and not, as one can't help thinking, the situation being what it was, the payment of blackmail. By the situation being what it was, I mean the fact that Miss Clancy must have got herself killed very soon after she received the money, because I can't imagine her going about the countryside with a thousand pounds in her handbag. However, there's something against the blackmail idea, but which is difficult to explain. It was last Friday that Mrs Waldron cashed that cheque.'

'Friday?' Ian said questioningly, not immediately grasping what that implied. Then he suddenly understood it. 'Friday! That was the day *before* the Waldrons' dinner party. *Before* Luke Singleton was murdered. So if by any chance Anna Waldron was paying blackmail to Eleanor Clancy, it had nothing to do with his murder. They'd met here at a party we gave on the Thursday and recognized each other, though they hadn't met since Anna was a schoolgirl. If you've been thinking that Anna could somehow have been involved in the murder, though God knows how she could have been, she wouldn't have cashed a cheque for a thousand pounds in the expectation of being blackmailed for that, would she? I believe you're going to find it was what you've just suggested yourself, an act of generosity.'

Roland nodded. 'Could be, could be.'

At that moment the telephone rang.

Andrew leapt to his feet and reached it before Ian was out of his chair. But it was not Peter Dilly who was on the line. A man's voice asked if Inspector Roland was there. Andrew returned to the sitting room.

'For you, Inspector,' he said and subsided into his chair again.

Roland went out to the hall, was heard to say, 'Yes,' and 'All right,' and 'Right away!' Then he came back into the room.

'That may be interesting,' he said. 'A sister of Miss Clancy's has turned up. A Mrs Jevons. She's at the police station in Rockford and I'd better get there as soon as I can to see her. Meanwhile, Professor—' he turned to Andrew with a faintly ironic smile—'if you have any bright idea about why that thousand pounds was cashed before the murder, I'd be grateful if you'd let me know. I've been waiting hopefully for you to have one of those bright ideas of yours which have been so helpful in the past, but you don't seem to have come up with anything yet.'

'I'm sorry,' Andrew said.

'Just keep on trying,' Roland said. 'Try, try again.'

He went to the door and Ian saw him out of the house.

Returning, he said, 'I'd better be off to Rockford too. I'll get back as soon as I can, but don't wait lunch for me. And help yourself to a drink.'

He went out and made his way to the garage, leaving Andrew alone in the house with the silent telephone.

❈ ❈ ❈

By the time that Andrew had had his lunch, still listening for the telephone to ring, he was growing tired of his own impatience. On the principle that a watched kettle never boils, he was becoming convinced that his very listening for the call was making sure that it would not come through. Besides that, he was very restless and wanted to get out of the house for a time. Soon after he had cleared his lunch away, he decided to go out and see if he could get into Eleanor Clancy's cottage.

He wanted to see if the letters from her great-grandfather were anywhere to be found there. If they were, and if a quick glance at them suggested that they might be interesting, he would try to make contact with the sister who had arrived in Rockford to see if she would allow him to get to work on them. If they seemed dull and colourless, however, there was no need for him to take any steps in the matter. He set off briskly, and in a few minutes was at the door of the cottage, which it turned out was quite easy to open as the lock on the door had been smashed, and watched by a number of children who were in the playground opposite, he pushed the door open and stepped inside.

It looked much the same as when he had seen it last, except for a grey dust of fingerprint powder everywhere. The place to look for the letters, he was inclined to think, was the bureau in the sitting room, where Eleanor had kept her box of old prints. He started towards it but was immediately checked by a shrill voice calling out, 'Who's there?'

He stood still. The voice, he thought, had come from the bedroom.

'Who's there?' the voice repeated on a note of anxiety, but no one appeared.

He called back, 'My name is Basnett. I'm staying with some neighbours of Miss Clancy's, the Davidges. If I'm intruding, I'll go away.'

A door opened and a woman came out.

'What do you want here?' she asked.

She was presumably Mrs Jevons, Eleanor Clancy's sister, but there was very little likeness between them. She looked as if she might be the older by several years and was heavily built, with a large, pale face and features that looked as if they had been clumsily modelled in it by an unskilful hand. She had heavy brows and she was frowning, but her light blue eyes were apprehensive. She wore a knitted suit that, stout as she was, hung a little too loosely on her.

'I was hoping to find some letters that Miss Clancy told me about,' Andrew said. 'Some letters written, I believe, by her great-grandfather. She was wondering if they might be worked up into a book and asked me if I could help her with it. They sounded interesting and I came here to see if they'd survived the wrecking of the place. But I'll abandon the idea if you'd sooner I did.'

'Oh, those letters,' Mrs Jevons said. 'Eleanor was always talking about making them into a book and she always asked every new person she met to help her with it. But they're hopelessly dull. They're the sort that say, "I hope you are very well, I'm very well, hope to see you soon…" You know what I mean. Of course, there's a little local colour in them, but not enough to work up into anything, even with the photographs, which really are interesting. If you want the letters, you're welcome to them. Would there be any money in a book of that sort, d'you think? I mean, one that was mostly photographs, with bits from the letters just saying what they are?'

'Not very much, I imagine,' Andrew said.

'Well, come and sit down.' She led the way into the sitting room, righted a chair that had been knocked over and planted herself on it.

Andrew followed her and sat down on the edge of a sofa that had not been overturned.

'You don't think she might have got a contract for a book like that, with an advance agreed on—a quite handsome advance?' she asked.

'I would find that surprising,' Andrew said.

'Well, so would I, yet she was expecting money from somewhere, you know. She wrote and told me about it just a day or two before her death. We'd money problems, you see. I'm a widow, living on an annuity I bought with what my poor husband left me, and it doesn't come to much, and Eleanor, as you know, was a games teacher who gave up when she didn't feel up to the job any more, and she was living on some life insurance she'd saved up and a bit of a legacy an aunt left her and finding things pretty tight. And we'd a mother to look after between us. She's got an old-age pension, of course, but she's always lived with me because, as a matter of fact, she and Eleanor never did get on, but Eleanor always paid her share to me to help look after her. Then suddenly she wrote me this letter last week telling me that our money worries were over, she'd had a bit of luck and I was going to get my share of it, and we could put our mother into an old people's home, if I'd like to do that. And of course, it seemed too good to be true. I love my mother, but it gets more and more of a strain looking after her. And the fact is, I didn't really believe it, because Eleanor was always one for exaggerating things, if not telling downright lies. Perhaps I shouldn't say that now she's dead, but it's a fact. She lived in a sort of fantasy a lot of the time, and often did the most ridiculous things. So I thought probably she'd been gambling in some way and had a bit of a win and thought she was going to go on making lots more. But now there's this queer business of the thousand pounds in her handbag that the police have been telling me about, and this frightful thing about her murder. So what am I to think about all that, will you tell me?'

Her flow of speech stopped abruptly and she stared at Andrew as if the whole situation were somehow his fault.

'Have the police told you what they make of it?' he asked.

'Yes, would you believe it, when I told them all this, which I thought it was my duty to do, that man, Inspector Somebody, asked me if I thought she could have been blackmailing anybody? Blackmailing! Honestly, that's what he said.'

'And does it seem to you quite impossible?'

She took a few seconds to reply, then she gave a kind of snort, which might have been a sort of laugh.

'All right, it wasn't impossible, but what a thing to ask *me*! I mean, I'm her sister. It's not likely I'd tell them a thing like that, is it?'

'So you didn't tell them?'

'Well, actually, I did in a way. I just said nothing's impossible in this world, is it? But I've been thinking about it and I know it's a thing she could have done if something dropped right into her lap, as it were. I mean, if she found she knew something about someone who was doing something that wasn't altogether legal or whatever, she just might have tried to cash in on it. When I was a young girl and took to going out with a boy and letting him go a bit farther with me than was thought proper in my family, and Eleanor found out about it, she threatened to tell my father, who'd just about have killed me for it, if I didn't pay for her to have her hair done every week. She used to care about her appearance in those days, and boys, and a lot of things she grew out of later. But I remember I suddenly got fed up with paying up for those hair-dos and told her to do her worst. And she didn't do anything. And that's what I think may have happened here. She frightened somebody, and they paid up, but if they'd called her bluff she wouldn't have done anything.'

'Not even if whatever she found out was a good deal more serious than you going out with your boyfriend?'

'As to that, I couldn't say. Perhaps I'm wrong and her threat was serious. Anyway, someone thought it was, or the poor girl wouldn't have been murdered, would she? Oh dear...' Tears suddenly welled up in her pale blue eyes. 'I don't know why I'm talking to you like this. I don't know what you're thinking of me. I don't often talk much. Mother's deaf, you see, and doesn't listen, and I've had to give up my work—I was manageress of a very nice little coffee shop and met lots of stimulating people there—because mother couldn't be left all by herself. Even to come down here today I had to get neighbours to promise to look after her. So that money Eleanor said she'd be sending sounded wonderful. I wanted so much to believe in it. But it's lucky for me now that I always had my doubts, isn't it?'

'About those letters...' Andrew said tentatively.

'Those letters, of course, I was forgetting about them. They're probably in the bureau.' She drew a chair up to the bureau, all the drawers of which had been pulled open and their contents scattered on the floor. 'If not, they may be in the cellar. There is a cellar, isn't there? I don't really know my way around yet. This is the first time I've been here.'

'What brought you?' Andrew asked.

'Well, as I told you, I thought it was my duty to tell the police about that letter of Eleanor's. A policeman had been to see me at home—I live in London—but I thought I ought to get in touch with the people here. So I came down this morning, and as I was in Rockford I asked them if there was anything against my coming out here to look round, and they said no, they'd done everything about fingerprints and so on. Apparently there are the fingerprints of lots of people, people who probably just dropped in to visit her now and then, so they aren't much use. Perhaps there are some of yours among them. But I thought I'd have a look to see if there was anything here worth keeping, but apart from the damage that's been done, there really isn't anything. When the police say I can, I'll just get some clearance people in. There's nothing I'd want to keep. Now those letters...'

While she had been talking, she was turning over what was left inside the open drawers, shutting them and after a time shaking her head.

'No, they aren't here. We'd better look in the cellar. She was great at hoarding things. They may be there.' She stood up and looked uncertainly about her. 'Where's the door to it?'

Andrew led her to the cellar door, switched on the staircase light and said, 'Shall I go first?'

'Yes, please do,' she said. 'I've never cared for cellars. I think I suffer a little from claustrophobia.'

There was another light at the bottom of the staircase which lit up the devastation there. He heard her gasp as she saw the shattered negatives.

'But who could have done this?' she cried out. 'A madman, surely.'

'I think we may be dealing with someone who's at least a little mad,' Andrew said. 'Now, let's look for those letters.'

It did not look like an easy thing to do. There were all kinds of boxes on shelves and on the floor, some wooden, some cardboard, some overturned with their contents spilled on the floor, some untouched. The letters might be in any of them. Some had contained photographs that looked as if Eleanor Clancy had taken them herself. Some held odd collections of china and glass, most of it cracked or chipped. One of the boxes held some old shoes and another some sweaters that looked as if moths had feasted on them. It seemed that Eleanor had been one of the people who are incapable of throwing anything away. After stirring about in the rubbish for a while, Andrew felt like giving up the search, when Mrs Jevons suddenly exclaimed, 'Here they are!'

She had found them in a small and battered looking brief-case on a shelf, and held it out to Andrew.

He was disappointed to see how few letters there were, but taking the case from her, he sat down on the only chair in the cellar and took out one letter after another. The paper on which they were written was of the brownish colour of old age and the ink was faded and they were very short.

After a moment he said, 'I'm afraid you're right. There's nothing much interesting here. They're just the sort of letters you said they were—'

'Ssh!' she interrupted in a fierce whisper and gripped his arm. 'Listen!'

Andrew heard it at once, the sound of a footstep just over their heads.

He thrust the letters back into her hands and walked to the bottom of the stairs.

'Oh, take care!' she whispered into his ear, standing just behind him, shaking with apprehension. 'God knows who it is.'

'Who's there?' Andrew called out.

'It's all right,' the voice of Peter Dilly answered, 'it's only me.'

'Peter!' Andrew began to laugh, then started to mount the stairs. 'What the devil are you doing here?'

'Trying to find out what you're up to,' Peter answered.

'Who is it, who is it?' Mrs Jevons demanded, still in a frightened whisper.

'It's a nephew of mine and he's quite harmless,' Andrew answered. 'Come and meet him.'

She mounted the stairs behind him, to come face to face with Peter Dilly in the little hall of the cottage. In his neat, small way he had his usual appearance of considerable charm. His fair hair had tumbled forward over his forehead and he was just thrusting it back.

'Peter Dilly, Mrs Jevons,' Andrew said. 'And I've no idea what he's doing here. Mrs Jevons, Peter, is the sister of Miss Clancy, the poor woman who lived here and was murdered. Now, tell us why you've come.'

'Didn't you want me to find out certain things for you?' Peter said.

'But I thought you'd telephone. I waited in all the morning, expecting you to telephone.'

'And I didn't much like the sound of things, so I decided to come. In the light of there having been two murders here, some of the questions you asked sounded decidedly sinister, and I didn't want you getting into trouble. And I didn't know if you'd be able to take my call in private, or if there was a risk that you might be overheard.'

'So you've found out what I wanted, have you?'

Andrew was uneasily conscious of Mrs Jevons beside him, feeling more nervous of being overheard by her than he would have been if Ian had heard him at the telephone.

'I think so,' Peter answered. 'You made only one mistake. You told me to go to Somerset House. But you don't go there any more for the register of births, deaths and marriages. You go to St Catherine's House, at the corner of Holborn and Kingsway.'

'I'm sorry,' Andrew said. 'That comes of not keeping up with the times. It was always Somerset House in the past. How did you find I was in this cottage?'

'Well, I went to the Davidges' house first,' Peter said, 'but there seemed to be no one there, so I asked one of the kids on that playground across the way if they'd seen anyone come out of the house, and she said she'd seen an old man come out and go into the cottage she pointed out to me, but she hadn't seen Mr Davidge or anyone else. So I thought it might be you, and when I saw the broken lock on the door, I thought I'd arrived on the scene of the crime. And what do you want to do now?'

'Yes, what do you want to do?' Mrs Jevons said. 'I'm sure you want to have a talk without me hearing it all, and what I want to do is get back to Rockford and take the next train back to London. Do you think there's a chance I could phone for a taxi to pick me up here? That's how I got here, but as I'd no idea how long I'd be staying, I didn't ask him to wait for me.'

'Peter, how did you get here?' Andrew asked.

'By car. I drove down,' Peter replied.

'Then you could drive Mrs Jevons back into Rockford, couldn't you? And you could take me too.'

'Of course,' Peter said, 'but what do you want to do in Rockford?'

'I want to speak to Inspector Roland. I promised him that if I had one of the bright ideas he seemed to keep hoping I'd have, he'd be the first person to hear of it. And after what you've just said I think the time has come for that now.'

Chapter Ten

'I don't know where to begin,' Andrew said.

He was in Inspector Roland's office, a bare room furnished with a big desk, several chairs, some filing cabinets and some posters on the walls, mostly of men who were wanted for a variety of misdemeanours. He and Roland were facing each other across the desk. He had had lunch with Mrs Jevons and Peter Dilly in the Black Horse in Rockford, then Peter had driven Mrs Jevons to the railway station, and Andrew had presented himself at the police station, asking to see the Inspector. It was annoying that he felt a little foolish.

'You understand that it's only an idea,' he said. 'I haven't a shadow of proof of any of it. But you did ask me, in the event that I had any possibly interesting ideas, to tell you about them.'

'Yes, indeed,' Roland said. 'Take your time. No need to rush at it. Ideas are what I'm dead short of at the moment.'

'Well, I think I'll start with something I heard said,' Andrew went on. 'It couldn't happen, so it didn't happen.'

The murder?' Roland said.

'Yes.'

'Luke Singleton's murder?'

'Yes. It sounds nonsense, of course.'

'I'm afraid I agree with you.'

'But you see, if you state more exactly what you mean, it isn't nonsense at all. What couldn't happen is the *deliberate* murder of Luke Singleton.'

Roland shook his head. 'You'll have to elaborate.'

'Suppose it didn't matter who got murdered,' Andrew said.

'That's something that does occasionally happen, but it's unusual. It's generally the work of the insane.'

'In this case it was sane and calculated. What is it that's foxed you completely over Singleton's murder? It's how cyanide could have got into the cup that was put down in front of him by one of those innocent women, when that same cup might have been put down in front of anyone in the room. I'm assuming, of course, that you've accepted the fact that no one but the Bartlett sisters got close enough to Singleton during the dinner to have dropped poison into his coffee. I know that you were close enough to have done it yourself, and so was Dr Mace, but if either of you had done it you'd have had to come to the dinner armed with the cyanide for your purpose, and neither of you could have known beforehand that you'd be sitting anywhere near Singleton. So even if you or Dr Mace happens to be guilty of murder, you'd have had to be prepared to use the poison on whoever your next-door neighbour chanced to be.'

'I'll grant you that, and I'm glad to find you don't seem to suspect either of us. But go on.'

'Well, suppose there was someone who actually was prepared to do just that, to make sure that someone at the dinner was killed, but it didn't matter who. Suppose the fact that it was Singleton who got the poison was sheer chance. It might just as well have been me or the Lady Mayoress.'

'So we're back to insanity, are we?'

'Certainly not. Consider. What was the actual result of the murder? What did you yourself and everyone connected with the case immediately start to do?'

'We started trying to find out who'd murdered Singleton, didn't we?'

'Of course. And to do that, what did you do?'

'Asked a bloody lot of questions, for one thing.'

'Exactly. And what were those questions about? The usual old things, weren't they, motive, means and opportunity? The means was obvious, cyanide in a cup of coffee. Opportunity was apparently nonexistent, leaving you thoroughly baffled. And that left motive—that's what you concentrated on, wasn't it? Who had a motive to kill Singleton? Of course, if it had been the Lady Mayoress who'd been killed, you'd have asked the same questions, but got quite different answers, and your thoughts would have gone in a quite different direction. As it was, you found out that Singleton's brother had a motive as he stood to inherit a considerable fortune, which was particularly convenient when he wanted to leave his job and take off with someone else's wife. And Ernest Audley, a Rockford solicitor, who'd never made any secret of his hatred of Singleton, who'd taken off with Audley's wife. And just possibly Mrs Davidge, who had the same motive as Brian Singleton. And I think a few, not very convincing rumours circulated that Dr Mace might have had some relationship with Singleton at some time, but I don't think we need pay much attention to them. Now, going back for a moment to opportunity, some thought was given to the possibility that Brian Singleton might have managed to flick a capsule of poison into his brother's cup when he was reaching out to pull a flower out of that arrangement on the table to give Mrs Davidge, who was sitting next to him. That seemed to be just possible, because Brian Singleton was a bit of a conjuror and might have done something clever with sleight of hand. But Audley was sitting at the far end of the table and certainly had no chance of doping Singleton's coffee. I don't know if you gave any thought to Eleanor Clancy, because she'd once known Singleton when they were young, and it happened that she'd a lot of old photographic equipment, including a certain amount of cyanide, but you certainly thought about her later, because she herself was murdered. And what did you immediately think about that?'

Roland had been growing increasingly interested, though the frown on his forehead showed that he did not know where all this was leading.

'We were inclined to believe that she'd seen who had murdered Singleton, or at least knew how it had been done,' Roland said, 'and was trying her hand at a bit of blackmail.'

'Which was exactly what you were meant to think,' Andrew said. 'It seems obvious, doesn't it? And naturally it wouldn't have been done by anyone who was demonstrably innocent of Singleton's murder. And who was the most certainly innocent of that?'

Roland's frown had deepened.

'If you mean what I'm beginning to think you mean...'

'I probably do. The person who most certainly could not *deliberately* have killed Singleton was Sam Waldron. He was in the kitchen throughout the dinner. He didn't touch the coffee cups. He didn't give either of the Bartletts any instructions about giving any particular cup to Singleton. But it would have been the easiest thing in the world for him to have put some cyanide—supposing he had some, I don't pretend to know how he got it—into a cup out in the kitchen and leave it to be put down in front of someone in the dining room, it didn't matter whom, just so that you should act as you did at the time and try to solve that person's murder. Then later, when you found Eleanor Clancy dead, you were to assume that she'd been killed because she knew the answer to that problem. In other words, the real motive for her murder would go unsuspected, and it was that that mattered to Waldron. He had no trace of a motive for killing Singleton, and out in the kitchen couldn't possibly have done it, but he had a very good reason for getting rid of Eleanor Clancy, as you'll be able to check for yourself if you'll go to St Catherine's House in London and investigate their register of births, deaths and marriages. I've just had a nephew of mine doing that for me and he found out what I thought was probably true. As I told you, I haven't a shadow of proof of it, but I'm quite convinced Waldron's your double murderer.'

Roland was tapping his teeth with a ballpoint pen that he had picked up from the desk. He shook his head.

'If you're going to tell me that Waldron and his wife weren't married, and the Clancy woman found it out, that's hardly a motive for murder nowadays, is it?'

'No, but wouldn't you say incest is?' Andrew said. 'Sam and Anna Waldron were brother and sister.'

Roland looked startled for a moment, gave a brief, hard glance at Andrew's face, then got up and went to the window. He stood there silent, looking out.

At last he said, 'What put you on to that?'

There was faint scepticism in his tone, but no outright rejection of what Andrew had said.

'It's hard to say just when I began to think about it seriously,' Andrew answered. 'Looking back, it's easy to trace the things that put it into my head, but at the time I didn't take much notice of them. For instance, there was something that struck me about Eleanor Clancy the first time I met her. It was a way she had of looking at people as if she was trying to fix their image in her memory. And later she boasted to me about how good she was at recognizing people. She seemed to imply that it was almost a trick. But then, as soon as she'd said that, she seemed to get a little scared at what she said. It didn't mean anything special to me at the time, but later I thought of the way she'd looked at Waldron when she met him at the Davidges' party. It was with what you might call a surprised sort of thoughtfulness. And I began to think it looked just as if she'd recognized him, but that he wasn't what she'd expected. And I think the fact was that she did recognize him, though it was years since they'd met. You know Anna Waldron had lost both her parents in a plane crash and was brought up by her grandparents. They sent her to that school, St Hilda's, and it's quite common in such schools for relatives to come down and visit the children and take them out for lunch and so on. Well, that was what Waldron, a cousin, might have done and Eleanor might have met him and then recognized him at the Davidges'. But if so, why didn't she simply greet him and remind him of their meeting, as she reminded Anna? And why didn't he give any sign either that he remembered having met her at the school? It's true she may not have made any impression on him, and that he genuinely forgot her, yet Anna had a crush on her, so we've been told, and would probably have made a point of introducing them to one another, of course telling Eleanor that he was her brother. But it was Eleanor's silence about what I began to feel sure had been a meeting with him that interested me more than his not remembering her. Was that diffidence on her part? I didn't think so. She wasn't in the least a diffident woman. There had to be a reason for it of some sort.'

Roland turned and came back to the desk.

'So that's all you're depending on,' he said. 'Clancy's silence about possibly having met Waldron once before?'

'It was all I was depending on until I got my nephew to get some information for me, as I told you, at St Catherine's House,' Andrew said. 'You'll find there that Martin and Agatha Waldron died when their daughter was ten. They left two children behind them, a son, Samuel and a daughter, Suzanna. There was a big gap between the ages of Sam and Anna. But there's no evidence that Anna ever had a cousin called Sam, or for that matter, any cousins at all, and also there's no evidence that she ever married anybody. When Sam and Anna decided to settle down together and come to live in a place where nobody knew them, they didn't actually go so far as to go through a marriage ceremony.'

'But why did they pose as a married couple?' Roland asked. 'Why didn't they simply settle in here as brother and sister, and keep their sexual relationship to themselves? No one would have suspected anything.'

'Wouldn't their servants have caught on pretty quickly that there was something strange going on?'

'Hm, yes. I suppose so. If you feel you've got to have servants, I suppose you've got to be careful about things like that. So you think Clancy understood what the situation was and tried her hand at blackmail.'

'That's how it looked to me and this morning I had a talk with her sister, Mrs Jevons, which made me sure of it. She's got very little money and has an aged mother to look after, and recently she'd had a letter from Eleanor telling her that she'd had a bit of luck and that her sister needn't worry about money any more. Hasn't that the smell of blackmail, in the circumstances?'

Roland nodded. 'Mrs Jevons told us about that letter from her sister this morning, but blackmail hadn't entered her head. But I agree with you, it seems pretty obvious that that was the reason for her murder. Blackmail that had nothing to do with Singleton's murder, as we were meant to think it had, to put us off thinking of anything like the incest business. And that explains why Anna Waldron cashed a cheque for a thousand pounds before that murder. She'd already been threatened by Clancy and got ready to pay a first instalment. But how did she persuade Clancy to meet her on the common in the evening, when there'd be no one about, and why was the cottage wrecked?'

'I think Eleanor agreed to meet her when she suggested it because she had no suspicion of danger. I think Waldron himself was keeping in the background, so that Eleanor felt she had only Anna to deal with, and if she worried about danger at all, she'd have thought she was much the bigger and stronger of the two. But I think the probability is that Anna, prompted by Sam, managed to make things sound as if they were on a friendly basis, I mean, that Anna was quite ready to help Eleanor look after her poor old mother and they might meet for a little walk on the common and sort things out without any ugly talk of blackmail. So they met, and Anna steered Eleanor towards the bridge where Waldron was waiting among the trees, and it was only at the last moment that she realized that in fact she was in deadly danger. And it was then that she thought of saying that she'd left a letter in the cottage, telling the truth about the Waldrons' relationship and that if they killed her the truth was certain to come out.'

'Why didn't they simply kill her in the cottage? Why do something so risky as kill her out in the open?'

'Because they were afraid of being seen going into the cottage. They're quite well-known hereabouts. If they'd met anyone they knew, it would have spoiled everything. An approach along that quiet lane beyond the lake must have looked far more promising. And then, after dark, they did go to the cottage and hunted for the letter and didn't find it, probably because it never existed, and Waldron, going into a blind rage, which it must be rather easy to do when you've got into the way of committing murder, smashed everything he could find. It was Clancy herself he was killing all over again, because she'd come along and ruined his nice satisfactory life with his sister.'

'It can't have been all that satisfactory to her, or she wouldn't have committed suicide.'

'No, that's true. It's possible the incestuous situation was really more than she could stand. That would explain why she'd tried to kill herself twice before. But she did her best to clear her brother of murder before she tried for the third time. When I saw her last she went into a hysterical state in which she insisted quite violently that Singleton's death was suicide and that Eleanor had been killed by some prowling pervert. But perhaps she did that simply because she couldn't face the fact that she herself had been accessory to two murders and was really as guilty as Waldron. Her solution of the crimes may have been simply what she desperately wished was the truth. Poor woman. A rotten life from the start.' Andrew paused and gave Roland a quizzical smile. 'Well, how does it strike you, Inspector? I told you I'd no proof or anything. It's all just one of my ideas.'

'Except for the little matter that Sam and Anna were brother and sister,' Roland said. 'We can check on that.'

'Yes, and I think you'll find there's no mistake there.'

'What we need are some witnesses. If you're right about Singleton's murder, I doubt if we'll ever be able to prove it, but we may have better luck with Clancy's. Anyway, many thanks for your help. It's been a very interesting conversation. If you should ever feel inclined to take up a hobby, Professor, you might try the solving of crimes of violence.'

❈ ❈ ❈

To Andrew's surprise, the witnesses that the Inspector required were in the end forthcoming, though it took them more than a week to make up their minds that it was their duty to tell the police what they had seen. They were a boy of nineteen and his recent girlfriend of fifteen. He came from Rockford and she from Lower Milfrey and they had met at a dance only a few weeks before. At the time of Eleanor Clancy's murder they had been together in the trees beside the stream that flowed out of the lake, behaving in a way that would have deeply horrified the girl's parents, and as her father was given to a certain degree of brutality she was terrified of allowing him to know what she had been doing when she and the boy heard Eleanor's one scream. Even when they heard it, the girl had stayed hidden where she was, refusing to come out from the trees to see what was happening, but the boy had gone running towards the bridge, to see a man and a woman making off down the lane. He did not know either of them, but later, when he and the girl had decided to face the wrath of her parents and tell the police what they knew, he had picked out Sam Waldron's photograph from a number that he was shown, and again had picked him out in an identity parade.

That Sam Waldron and Anna had committed incest had told heavily against him, and although he was ably defended when his trial for the murder of Eleanor Clancy eventually came on, he was sentenced to imprisonment for life.

However, as Inspector Roland had predicted, the murder of Luke Singleton was never officially solved. Roland believed that Andrew had arrived at the truth of it, but he was sure that no jury would be convinced of it. In the meantime, as soon as he could after the inquest, which had been adjourned, Andrew had returned to London, and one evening he and his nephew Peter Dilly had dined together once more in a restaurant in Charlotte Street. Peter had been leaving for his villa in Monte Carlo next day and had tried to persuade Andrew to visit him there.

Andrew had felt almost tempted to accept the invitation, but had been checked by a feeling he had had that his life had a way of being more peaceful, calmer, more serene, in St John's Wood than anywhere else.

'Well, at least come out for Christmas,' Peter had said. 'There's nothing to keep you here.'

'Oh yes, there is,' Andrew had replied. 'I've just started on a new and very interesting study. It takes up all my time.'

'You mean you've actually got a hobby at last?'

'I suppose you could call it that. Anyway, it's the sort of thing that really suits me.'

'What is it?'

'Just the life of Malpighi. It's something I've been wanting to do for a long time, even though I don't know if I shall ever live to finish it.'

We hope you liked *A Hobby of Murder*. If you seek more mysteries that feature deft social observation and an educated air, the Sarah Deane series, by J.S. Borthwick, may be just your style. Though dear professor Basnett is British and Sarah is American, she's an academic, too—a classic amateur sleuth with a scholar's mind. To give you a taste, we've included an excerpt here of her first adventure, *The Case of the Hook-Billed Kites*. Enjoy!

The Case of the
Hook-Billed Kites

Friday, March 15

The mid-March day that closed with a corpse imperfectly
hidden by the chaparral growing near the trail began in an
ordinary way for a certain number of people making their way
toward Doña Clara, the new National Wildlife Refuge that
lay along the Rio Grande some twelve miles south of Boyden,
Texas. The travelers came from Massachusetts and Maryland,
from Idaho and Connecticut, from New York State, and from
Texas itself. They were, all of them, moved by a variety of interests having to do with the flora and fauna of the Texas border,
but what would bring them together was murder.

I

Those who hate to fly find it necessary to keep a wary eye on
the plane's equipment. Now it was time for another engine
check. Sarah Deane, from her aisle seat, leaned past the bulk of
her seat companion and peered through the window. Yes, the
engine was still there, fastened to the underside of the wing and
seeming altogether too ponderous an object to be held in place
by a few bolts and rivets. Sarah frowned at the wing. Was metal

fatigue visible at this distance? Or did everything just give way all at once? She leaned back once more in her seat and considered the life expectancy of a rivet—a rivet under stress.

A disembodied voice sounded from somewhere in the middle of the plane. "This is Captain Barnes. Ah hope y'all are enjoyin' your trip on Texair Flight 53. Right now, folks, we're flyin' at twenty-one thousand feet over Anderson County. It's a little dusty down there, but we ought to get us some rain tonight."

Reminded again that she was a considerable distance above the ground, Sarah swallowed hard and tried to breathe deeply as she had once been told to do when coming out from an anesthetic, but now some unhappy process in her stomach demanded attention. Fourteen inches from her nose sat the remains of a Reuben sandwich on its plastic plate, strings of sauerkraut draped over its curling crusts. This object had mismated with an unaccustomed piña colada taken at the Dallas airport to quiet jitters. The whole, working in synergism with a central emotional lump, had assumed a life of its own underneath Sarah's ribs and seemed uncertain whether to participate in its own digestion or to take the return route.

Trying not to hear the rattle and tap of other passengers' knives and forks, Sarah closed her eyes. Vertigo. She opened them and, sighing, reached for a small knapsack at her feet and lifted out the top member of a pile of books, all field guides from Philip. A book mailer had arrived two weeks ago, together with a note: "Dear Sarah. Looking forward to Texas. Be sure to go through the description of those species of birds common to the Gulf coast and the Rio Grande Valley. Take notes on the characteristics of each. Bring insect repellent. All my love, Philip."

Well, she certainly didn't feel up to taking notes on a bunch of strange birds, but Philip had been very kind, taken care of everything. She opened her book, *Roger Tory Peterson's Dozen Birding Hot Spots.* Even she, indifferent birder that she was, had heard of Mr. Peterson. A hot spot, it seemed, had nothing to do with the tropics or a fungus infection; it was just a good place in which to see a lot of birds. Sarah swallowed again, turned a page, and stopped at a paragraph headed "Worth It All."

Apparently anyone could bird-watch anywhere, anytime...on the job as governor, telephone lineman, or dentist. Sarah paused, and the picture of a bird-watching dentist halting in the middle of a cavity to spot a blue jay presented itself unpleasantly. But it certainly was a compulsive activity. She remembered Philip, the most serious of tennis players, once dropping his racket at set point and shouting, "A goshawk!" They lost the set.

Sarah yawned, replaced the book in her knapsack, and drew out another. Mr. Peterson again. *A Field Guide to the Birds of Texas.* She turned at random to a plate entitled "Heads of Terns" and confronted row on row of bodiless unsmiling birds. Sarah glared at the picture. They were all exactly alike. She closed the book.

A flight attendant gathered in her tray, a gong sounded, a voice urged passengers to return to their seats and promised turbulence.

Sarah's window-seat companion, a vast lady of middle years packed into a pink pantsuit, tugged at her seat belt and then produced a length of crochet work from a cloth bag. Her face was that of an unbaked muffin, her hair a variation on the beehive, and her eyes decorated by slanted silver-rimmed glasses with a feather motif.

"Visiting southern Texas?" Pink suit swung her wool smartly around the hook. Turbulence manifested itself in a sudden drop and bump.

Sarah blew through her teeth. Perhaps conversation was better than huddling in misery. "I'm meeting a friend down in Boyden," she said. "We're going to visit some of the wildlife sanctuaries."

"Now isn't that nice." Sarah's companion beamed. "I'll bet it's a special sort of friend, you traveling all the way from Dallas."

"My friend is a former colleague of mine," said Sarah with dignity. "We taught at the same school in Maryland last year. But I'm not from Dallas. I just changed planes there. I'm teaching in Boston this year."

"And your friend is still in Maryland without you? But, dear, you have such a young face, much too young to be a teacher. You look like a student yourself."

Oh God, thought Sarah. Why did I get into this?

"And do you have a special interest in wildlife, dear?" Sarah's companion executed a series of loops and spins with her crochet hook.

Sarah sighed. This woman could never be snubbed into silence. Better behave and be polite. "We're going bird-watching," she replied. "My friend will be leading a school group on field trips, and in his free time we'll visit some of the refuges."

Pink suit nodded and smiled. "Well, now! I look at birds myself. Cardinals and those cute chickadees, my favorites, come right up to the feeder. It's by the kitchen window. And the titmice with that tiny crest and lots of others. There are so many names I just don't know, and the price of sunflower seeds..."

Sarah, an English teacher by trade, shuddered. Aloud she said, "I'm a beginner, too. We're going to Doña Clara and to Aransas to see the whooping cranes."

"You couldn't do better, dear. I know that." The woman began to fold up her crochet work, and Sarah saw that yellow daisies alternated with what seemed to be chocolate kisses.

"What's your name, dear? Sarah? That's a real nice old-fashioned name. I'm Iris. I'm meeting my brother down in Boyden. He just loves to bird-watch, and he's almost a professional. I mean he gets paid to do it. I'm coming down to see him because Orwell passed away a year ago February, and I just have to get out of the house."

Sarah was too enfeebled by indigestion to pursue Orwell's widow through her bereavement. Wearily she returned to her field guide. The wretched birds were blurring into masses of speckles, stripes, spots, and wing bars. At the end of the book, Sarah found an account of "Extinct and Unsuccessful Birds." Perhaps, she thought, I can become a specialist in those. She closed her eyes and pictured herself standing in the center of an admiring group of ornithologists, Philip, silent for once, listening while she conversed knowledgeably on vanished birds. "*Francolinus pondicerianus*," she would say, "was really a brown partridge, thickly barred above and below, with a rufous tail and..." The gong sounded again, and a voice began its ritual reminders about seats and belts and no smoking. "We will be landing," it concluded, "in four minutes, one-ten Central Time."

"There it is, Sarah. Corpus Christi." Sarah's seat companion patted her shoulder. "Remember, I'm Iris. Maybe we'll bump into each other somewhere looking at birds."

Sarah wiped her perspiring hands on the knees of her new safari-cloth pants, pressed her elbows against her ribs, and jammed her head against the seat back. Corpus Christi rose around her...bump, thump, whirr, bump. Down on dear old lovely ground again. "Thank you," said Sarah aloud.

The plane rumbled with decreasing speed toward the terminal and stopped. Sarah grabbed her knapsack, her camera, her handbag, and shoved herself into the aisle behind Iris, relict of Orwell. From somewhere on that ample person a narrow yellow folder drifted down into the tangle of legs.

"Hey," Sarah called, "did you drop this?" But Iris, in the short interval of Sarah's bending down, had pressed ahead and become lost in the forward-moving crowd of passengers.

"Y'all have a nice day," said the flight attendant at the door.

Sarah peered from the top of the boarding ladder for Iris, but the pink suit had vanished, so, bag, pack, camera case slapping at her side, she made her way down the metal stairs and into the hazy air.

II

Alex McKenzie finished his glass of beer, rose to his feet, and reached for the check. The plane was coming in. Again he wondered why, in the middle of what was a part-time holiday, he had offered to make a detour to the Corpus Christi airport to pick up and drive Sarah Deane to the Texas border. There were shuttle planes, weren't there? But he had promised Philip, and, of course, given more favorable omens, he might have welcomed her. But Sarah seemed not much aware of his existence, and now she would be hastening with his help into the arms (clutches? sleeping bag?) of his old friend Philip Lentz.

Alex shouldered his way to the top of the entrance ramp. There was Sarah now, hastening forward, her face flushed, her dark hair in damp wisps against the sides of her face. Even with her long legs and the almost defiant tilt of her chin, she looked to Alex more like a cross child after too long a trip than a purposeful adult. Alex fought an irrational surge of annoyance and smiled at her.

"Sarah, hello. Good flight? Right on time. It's great to see you. Let me take that." Alex reached for the knapsack, but Sarah snatched it away from his outstretched hand.

"I'll keep that. Thanks, it was a hellish flight, I hate flying. Is there something to drink here? I've got a sandwich stuck halfway down."

"Not right here, there isn't." Alex, his role as porter rejected, turned and walked away.

Sarah knew she wasn't being friendly; after all, here he was ready to drive her all the way to Boyden. She trotted after him.

"Have you seen any birds yet?" This question proved irresistible. Alex's face lightened.

"Matter of fact," he said, pushing his way toward the luggage-claim counter, "there are three long-billed curlews by the airport fence."

Sarah tried to sound delighted. "Curlews? How great."

Alex looked down at Sarah from the advantage of seven inches. "Have you ever heard of a curlew? Well, you'll have to hold on because the luggage isn't in yet. Go and get a drink from the water fountain, and I'll buy you something cool when we get out of here."

Sarah departed and returned with water dripping from her forehead and the tip of her nose. *She looks fourteen,* thought Alex.

"That should fix the sandwich," said Sarah. "The curlew would be, what do you call it, a life bird? Philip is trying to make me keep a life list, but he wouldn't let me count a dead owl we found last week."

"Philip is very strict. After all, there are rules."

"And the rules are stupid. I mean it was a perfectly good owl. I picked him up, and he was so beautiful. I saw him a lot better than I ever do those warblers bouncing around in the leaves."

They stood together and watched the luggage trundle into sight. Alex allowed Sarah to wrestle a lumpy green duffel off onto the floor. "I won't ask to help you and insult an emerging woman," he said.

Sarah frowned. "Give me a break. I'm so tired. You can carry any damn thing you want. I had to leave Logan at seven and then had a long wait in Dallas. Don't ever drink a piña colada before flying."

"I'd as soon drink crème de hemlock," said Alex, picking up the duffel. "So let's get the show moving."

They made their way outside to the parking lot, and Sarah watched as Alex rummaged about making space in his elderly red Volvo, finally settling her duffel beside a small battered black bag.

Sarah eyed this object dubiously. "Do you always travel with that thing? Isn't it almost asking for trouble?"

Alex slammed the back door. "I always take it…feel unfinished without it. Where are your binoculars? You can't see a curlew properly without them."

"Back in Boston, all out of whack. Philip is bringing me his father's old ones. He's had them fixed up for me."

"Philip is always thoughtful. But in the meantime we have miles of birds to go before we sleep, and I've got an extra pair too—from an uncle. For emergencies like this. There, put the strap under your collar. It's a single-wheel adjustment. The curlews are over there. We'll move up quietly. This curlew has a sickle bill twice as long as the whimbrel's, no striped crown, and when it flies look for the cinnamon underwing."

"Cinnamon, yet. You don't say." Sarah lifted her binoculars, and together they moved slowly and discreetly toward the fence.

III

At one-twenty-five, a green minibus pulled into the parking area of the Doña Clara National Wildlife Refuge and rolled to a stop. The air in the refuge, in common with most of southeast Texas, was on the opaque side, owing to unfavorable western winds.

But the thickness of atmosphere did not prevent a listener from hearing the calling and screeching of birds, for here along the road's edge, in the brush and in the tree canopy, was the treasure that drew bird-watchers from all over the world to Doña Clara.

The green bus, door open, was disgorging the twelve members of the Hamburg, New York, Bird Club. Despite the blowing dust, the legend on the side panel of the bus was still clear: "READY TO TOUR—Ready Tours, Inc., Boyden, Texas." For a good round sum, the members of the tour had been promised "exciting birding, first-class accommodations, well-chosen meals, and experienced leadership." The prospectus had also assured them that Arthur H. Ready himself, "well-known ornithologist, author of the monograph *Migratory Patterns along the Rio Grande*, and his assistant, Major George Foster, of the Boyden Bird Club, will be your guides through selected refuges and parks."

The fortunate members of the Hamburg Club, now free of the western New York snow belt for two weeks, and hatched from their bus, stood about blinking in the hazy sun, grateful to be warm. They clutched binoculars, cameras, hats, telescopes, and field guides. Some raised their binoculars in a tentative way in the direction of the bird calls. Several began to sidle quietly in the direction of the restroom sign.

Waldo Plummer, president emeritus of the club and trip captain, began waving a map over his head and making little glottal noises. White-haired, angular, with ears suggesting flight, he was a bottomless source of information on the world's flora and fauna and had strong opinions about everything else. He now rapped loudly on the side of the bus. The driver, Eduardo, slumberous after the drive from Dallas, sat up.

"Welcome to Doña Clara. I have a few ideas to share with you about the remnants of the subtropical forest in which we find..."

Only a faint shuffling of feet on the gravel could be heard, for Mr. Plummer, although long retired from teaching, still had the power to command.

"Good Lord, I've got to get to the john," whispered Mrs. Bailey to her sister-in-law Mrs. Goldsmith.

Ostentatiously apart from the group, Jeff Goldsmith, thirteen-year-old bird-wunderkind and nephew to the two women, stood at the perimeter of the parking lot and fixed his binoculars on the center of an ebony tree. His younger sister Nina, shaped like a basketball in shorts, wandered up to him, jaws moving, and blew slowly and with intense concentration a large bubble. It collapsed over her round face like a discarded skin.

"Nina... God," Jeff snarled from the side of his mouth. How could a person look like a professional with this creep around?

"Screw you," said Nina.

Mr. Plummer raised his voice. "If the two children in our party would like to run down the road for a distance, they may." Jeff moved away toward the ebony tree.

"Shit head," yelled Nina.

Mr. Plummer arranged his face in an expression well known to old students. He peered at his flock and resumed in a threatening tone, "Doña Clara is home to the black-spotted newt, the giant toad, the ocelot, and the jaguarundi. The eastern coral snake is rarely seen." Here his audience began to look at its feet and uncertainly at the nearby undergrowth. Mr. Plummer paused, struggling in advance with the problem of publicly enunciating the names of such flora as tepeguaje, guayacan, and huisache.

Lois Bailey and Constance Goldsmith slipped quietly away.

❉ ❉ ❉

Waldo Plummer, having wound up his résumé of the wonders of Doña Clara, held up his hand. "Major Foster, our guide for the first week, will bring our lunch. Now we must all wear our name tags." Mr. Plummer indicated a label stuck to his jacket that announced "Hi! I'm Waldo Plummer—Ready to Tour." "Now, we all know each other, but to Major Foster we are unidentified species." Here Mr. Plummer beamed at his group, and Mrs. Plummer laughed obediently.

Suddenly from the fringe came a cry, "It's a golden-fronted!"
"Where?" Binoculars were raised, fingers pointed.
"On that branch. But it looks like a red-bellied."
"No. Zebra back, white rump. See that orange patch?"

A tan Dodge van turned in to the parking lot and stopped next to Mr. Plummer, who waved a knotted hand in welcome. "Major Foster, well met!"

Major George Foster, known in the Valley as "Big," wore two hats. After pulling his van to one side of the Dike Road, which lies north of Doña Clara, he had done his quick-change act. The friendly salesman of hotel glass and china had shed his outer skin of business attire and changed into the khaki costume of the field leader. The patch of the National Audubon Society decorated the major's right sleeve, the triangular emblem of the Boyden Bird Club his left, and the effect, borrowing as it did from the Boy Scout uniform, was altogether reassuring. Big Foster, now arrived before his troops, squared his shoulders, inflated his chest, pulled at his belt, opened the door of his van, and heaved himself out.

"Yessiree. Y'all got yourselves a golden-fronted woodpecker. Hope that's a life bird for some of you." Several hands were raised. "Now here's an oriole comin' in. Anyone know what kind of orioles we have in the Valley? Young fellow, do you know an oriole when you see one?" Big Foster, who liked to include the children in his discussions, now pointed at Jeff, who skulked at the edge of the group.

Jeff, thus addressed, came forward, looked directly at the major, and announced in a hoarse voice that threatened to crack, "That's the Altamira oriole. It used to be called Lichtenstein's oriole. *Icterus gularis*. It's listed as common here and at Santa Ana. Then maybe we'll see the hooded oriole and the black-headed oriole, though they're both listed as uncommon to rare. That's *Icterus cucullatus* and *Icterus graduacauda*," he added.

There was a moment of silence while Major Foster considered what fortune had allotted him in the guise of a thirteen-year-old boy. Then club members, long inured to Jeff Goldsmith, began to talk and move about. It was well past lunchtime, a fact not lost upon the major. He called them to order.

"Okay, folks, the picnic is all packed in the van. When you finish washin' up and visitin' the restrooms, I want everyone back in the bus. Eduardo will follow me, and we'll go over to Long Bone Lake where there's a picnic ground." His tone became serious, fatherly. "After lunch I'll talk about a few little old rules we have. Don't want to lose anyone—these trails can be mighty confusin' at times—so we ask the group to stay together." The major looked at Jeff and Nina Goldsmith and smiled. "No solos. Okay? Up and at 'em. Chow time."

IV

By two o'clock in the afternoon, the parking space behind the Casa Queen Diner in Raymondville was almost empty. Only a vintage Buick shared the space with a new blue Club Wagon. This latter vehicle, like that used by the Ready Tour, announced that it, too, was in the bird business; the inscription on each flank read: "Cactus Wren Tours—Madison, Connecticut."

Across the booth table inside the diner, Mrs. Addie Brent put down her fork and confronted her associate and co-director of the Cactus Wren enterprise. "Now, Midge, stop it. You have been in the dumps since we left home. You didn't get out of the car at Antietam, you stayed in the motel at Natchez, and I don't think you even looked at the whooping cranes yesterday at Aransas."

"Yes, I did, Addie. I don't neglect my birds." Margaret Fellows poked in a moody way at the limp body of a burrito. "And I've seen battlefields before. They're depressing. As for Natchez, it was raining."

Mrs. Brent pushed her plate aside and peered at her companion over the tops of her glasses. They were a curious couple. Mrs. Brent was a small square woman with a small square face framed in swatches of brindle hair, the effect being rather that of a miniature schnauzer. And, like that breed, she could be both fierce and combative, a fact she had impressed on successive classes of the girls of Miss Morton's Academy in Butler, Maryland, over which she had reigned for thirty-three years. Miss Fellows, however, was tall, large-boned, and large-featured. Her hair, still almost entirely brown, was looped around her head and into a bun at the rear. She had the countenance of an elderly and troubled ruminant; her top lip protruded slightly, and nature, in an act of balance, had caused her chin to recede.

Margaret Fellows, intelligent without being clever, had been labeled almost from birth as one of those girls who had best be given strong academic training with a minor in field hockey and fitted for pedagogy. When, however, she found herself unequal to the stress of doctoral orals, fate arrived in the person of her old college classmate Addie Brent, who flushed Miss Fellows from the university backwaters and gave her the vacant post of history chairman at the academy. There, as teacher, leader of field trips (she was an informed amateur naturalist), and field hockey coach, she had rested content until the past year. Academy girls of the past decade, alert for signs of aberration, had given Miss Fellows a nickname: "the Great Gelding."

Addie Brent, spared such by the facts of marriage and early widowhood, had long recognized the sensitivity of her old friend and her need for a strenuous occupation in a safe place. She also knew that her colleague required careful handling in moments of distress. There had been many since last June.

Miss Fellows, head down, regarded her burrito.

"Midge, look at me," commanded Addie. "That's it. It's not your fault that we lost the Hamburg Club. My dear old Margaret, you are letting your resentment run away with your sense. We are business people now. A fine business ... as good a way to teach conservation as any there is. But we have no time for temperament."

Miss Fellows's eyes were moist. Her large hands pulled and shredded her paper napkin. "I said it wouldn't work, Addie. I'm a fish out of water. I can't handle men, especially when they're being difficult. As the girls would say, I'm just a drag."

"A drag? Nonsense! I never want to hear you use that word again." Mrs. Brent beckoned to a waitress. "We'll have some of that nice-looking cheesecake with the strawberries."

Miss Fellows looked up and addressed the waitress. "*Por favor*," she said distinctly.

Mrs. Brent, unrebuked, continued. "You have cold feet, Midge. We will be a success. Tours are big business in Texas, and we will have our tiny share. Now use that good head of yours. When you heard that Mr. Plummer dithering, you should have called me. Never mind. We start anew. This is excellent cheesecake."

"But I'm not hungry, Addie."

"Of course you are. That Mexican food was not edible. Eat the cake and keep up your strength. I'm quite glad, really, not to have the Hamburg group. Mr. Plummer talked too much, you said."

"He did seem to be an expert on Texas birds."

"So we are well rid of him. After all, it's our first time on the Texas circuit, so we must learn the territory in a hurry and be ready when a group comes along. In the meantime, we can register at the motel and see if we can pick up one or two tourists."

"At least we have the Morton girls next week." Miss Fellows's voice had more vigor, and she cut a piece from her cheesecake.

"Yes, indeed. Quite providential…like being in harness again. I've had a note saying that Miss Lucas will be at the motel with four or five girls, and we are to work out a schedule with her."

"Will Mr. Lentz be there?" The question was barely audible.

"You know he will be. He's the only decent birder they have now." Mrs. Brent removed a small notebook from her handbag. "Here's the plan. Philip Lentz will take the girls for morning field trips, Miss Lucas will do botany in the afternoons, and we will be fitted in as substitutes. The last week is ours entirely when we drive the girls to Big Bend National Park. It's just as well to get Philip Lentz over with. Don't let him know that you feel a thing. Forward march. Remember, 'How dull it is to pause, to make an end…' "

"I knew you were going to say that, Addie. I just knew you were going to throw Tennyson at my head."

" 'To rust unburnished, not to shine in use!' " continued Mrs. Brent firmly. "So we must … if things as old as we are can shine. For heaven's sake, Midge, don't droop. Big people should never droop. You knew we would see Philip Lentz again; we've both been invited back to graduation. Finish your cake. It's time we got out into the world. Perhaps he did us a favor, after all."

But Miss Fellows shook her head and then struck her fork savagely into her cheesecake, impaling a strawberry en route.

"No, Addie," she said.

V

Philip Lentz pulled his car off to the side of the road and cut the motor. He was pleased. Everything on schedule. Because, really, it was just a matter of planning. Field trips needn't turn into a shambles—lost trails, forgotten maps, missed birds. This year he had taken the Saturday morning bird walks at the academy and wrought order. He had turned those rambles, formerly conducted by Miss Fellows, into disciplined investigations of the world of ornithology. Of course, on this trip he would ease up on the girls—perhaps tennis at the motel. He hoped Eleanor Lucas wasn't going to be difficult; she certainly had a talent for it. But they were adults, weren't they, responsible adults.

Philip ran his pencil down his Laguna Atascosa Refuge checklist. Satisfying, with a fine view of a least grebe in the pond at the end of the Paisano Trail. He hummed softly to himself as he entered the details of time and place in his field notebook.

Starting his car, a blue rental Escort, Philip saw with annoyance that a film of dust had coated the hood. He would have to see about a car wash tomorrow. Which brought his attention around to Sarah. He swung the car back on the road and considered her. Yes, Sarah, too, had to be attended to. Some gentle management. This Philip was ready to provide. Physically, she had everything going for her—on the thin side, but good bones, tall, and with roundness where necessary. Intelligent, perceptive. But an odd sense of humor. Sometimes she laughed when he saw absolutely nothing funny. All in all, though, she was everything he wanted in a woman. He'd made mistakes with females before, but now, with Sarah, this was it.

Even with all that mess. Bags, notebooks, trivia, lost and found objects unraveled and swirled about her. But this was going to be a good trip, without all the bother of school pressure and those hurried trips to Boston. He would help her find out what a joy it was to have life running smoothly; for a start, he would put her bird list in order, help her make coherent notes. It shouldn't be difficult. Sarah was a responsive person. And, although he didn't want to rush her, if all went well, he hoped they would be sharing a bed at the end of the two weeks. What could be more natural? She probably expected it, and he certainly wanted it.

Philip suddenly slowed and pulled again to the side of the road. Was that a swallow-tailed kite? Yes, the black-and-white pattern, the wide split tail. There it was, balancing in the air just beyond that knob. Philip leaned out of the car window, raised his binoculars, and adjusted the focus. The swallow-tailed kite skimmed close over the ground and then rose into the air. It arched and dipped and soared low again over the furrows of a distant field. Philip, unmoving, watched the bird until at last it vanished over the rim of the field. For a moment he sat smiling and then looked at his watch. Almost three, but still time for another stop, and then an hour or so left for a sortie to Doña Clara. After that, Sarah.

VI

Sarah had expected Texas to surprise her, to bare its chest and say "I am the Lone Star State." She had hummed "The Streets of Laredo" while packing back in Boston, but as Alex turned the car south onto U.S. 77 and the landscape began unrolling, she felt let down. It seemed quite ordinary, farm country on a wide scale. Here and there a windmill stood by a water trough, cattle dotted a grazing stretch, a cluster of farm buildings broke the expanse, and now and then a line of pumping jacks appeared, moving up and down like hammerheaded robots.

Even with the car window open, the air was stifling, and Sarah felt heavy-eyed and sleepy. She tried to count the tank cars on a siding and then to read the message on a historical marker, but she could only make out the first line before they drove past. Something about Zachary Taylor and a march to the Rio Grande. He was the one, she remembered, who wore old straw hats and died after drinking cold milk and eating raspberries—or was it cherries? What was he doing marching to the border? It was all a long time ago. Sarah yawned. Even Philip seemed a long time ago. And far away. Not a real person, just a commitment of time and place. That's what flying did to you; it cut connections.

Sarah tried to conjure up Philip as she had last seen him, standing in the drive next to her apartment in Boston. It had snowed hard all that Sunday morning, and Philip was brushing the snow from his car before the drive back to Maryland. She had stood at the door and watched because she had a cold and Philip had ordered her not to come out. He had kissed her goodbye cautiously, just a light touch of a mustache across her forehead. Sarah closed her eyes and blotted out Texas. She could see Philip in his new tan coat pulling up the alpaca-lined hood over his fair hair. She saw him brushing the snow, working methodically with the wind from the rear to the front of the car, and then waving to her with a flourish of the long-handled brush. She remembered thinking that, even with the snow blowing puffs around him, he seemed competent, decisive. His car started at once. It always did. Philip saw to things like carburetors and batteries and he spoke seriously to Sarah on the subject of "proper maintenance" because her old VW never started without a struggle.

"We're making progress," said Alex. "Three towns gone through while you were daydreaming. Clarkswood, Driscoll, and Bishop."

Sarah looked over at Alex and nodded. She had forgotten all about him in researching Philip. At the airport, Alex had seemed almost a stranger, although she had known him about ten months. But in Boston she had always seen him in the insulating presence of friends of Philip. She studied his face. Older than she remembered. From the side view it seemed to be all corners and planes, no curves, and the dark hair was cut shorter than was fashionable with Sarah's male friends. The eyes were set deep under heavy brows. Genus Heathcliff, she decided. But she saw that the long uncompromising mouth was relieved by a humorous lift at the corners, and one thing about Heathcliff, as far as humor went he was a dead loss. She suspected that Alex could be sardonic. Genus Mr. Rochester, perhaps. Not, said Sarah severely to herself, types that interest me. Thank heavens she had gotten over that Byronic nonsense long ago. In a mood of clinical detachment, Sarah shifted her attention to Alex's hands—square, nails short, scrubbed, a mark of his profession.

"Look," said Alex, pointing ahead to a huge sign reading "WELCOME TO KINGSVILLE" over which was suspended the bleached skull of a cow. "You're in Texas, Sarah. Now, shall we hit the side roads for variety? Look for some birds. What's your schedule?"

"I'm not meeting Philip at any particular time. He said that he might not even make it for dinner—he's checking out a couple of refuges for the students' trips. But I'd like to make it by five-thirty...to clean up, take a swim."

"Fine. After we get through the King Ranch, we'll turn off and wander around and still have you in the swimming pool before dark."

Alex was aware of Sarah sitting next to him, her left knee, her shoulder, only eight inches away. But, he thought, she might as well be in a glass case. I could be any taxi driver that happened along, while she hangs in waiting for Philip. With an effort, Alex turned his attention back to the road and silently pointed out to Sarah the wildflowers showing by the side of the road: clusters of cream, lemon, blue, wine, coral—phlox, storks-bill, bluebonnets, star violets, scarlet paintbrush. Sarah smiled and turned her thoughts again to Philip.

VII

Back home in Idaho, Janice Axminster found little room for her artistic inclinations, and her job as secretary at the Amber Park Methodist Church was a penance for a free spirit. However, loose on vacation as an assistant to her husband, Professor Leo Axminster, she could let go. Despite the discomforts of brush, thicket, and insect life, Janice chose for a field costume a printed dirndl as an outward and visible sign of a sensitive and girlish nature. This dress she enhanced by open-toed sandals, ankle socks in a pastel shade, and a series of beads and chains that tinkled and clicked as she moved. Janice's hair, confined by a net in her church persona, was now released aft in a gray ponytail that bobbed behind her when, plump and uncorseted, she moved and bounced. Her husband's profession—he was a lepidopterist—was her delight. Each butterfly espied, each one netted, each thorax pinched brought excitement.

Today Janice and Leo were headed southeast on their tenth trip to the Rio Grande Valley to augment what was known as the Axminster Collection at Middle Moscow College. They had not found the number of specimens hoped for on their sweep through western Texas but the promise of the Mexican border kept their interest at pitch.

"Motel first, sweetheart?" asked the professor, turning to his wife and so guiding the Land-Rover into a pothole with enough of a jolt to cause his wife's cheeks to joggle.

Janice, recovering stability, shook her head. Her features, which for a time in her late teens might have been thought pert, were now blurred into a series of soft rises and hollows from which an upturned nose emerged looking unrelated. As a faculty wife she was, however, among the more presentable, particularly on the arm of her mate. Professor Axminster, with the return to favor of the beard, had rescued a nondescript face with a gray Vandyke. This change in appearance, plus a natural indecisiveness that alternated with spasms of irritability, was put down now to character by those students who had not known the professor earlier.

"Almost three-fifteen," persisted the professor, "and we're coming up to Boyden now. Shall we stop?"

"No, Leo. Straight to the refuge," said Janice. "After those ridiculous letters from the people here, we shouldn't waste time. We can call the motel from the Visitors Center."

"But which refuge? Santa Ana, do you think?"

"No. Doña Clara. A smaller staff and not so tourist-conscious. We can park away from headquarters."

"Janice, you're absolutely right. Have you got a list of the species we're still missing?"

"Yes, and the ones for which we need replacements. This should be our year. Five weeks. The grant came through just in time."

"Amen, sweetheart." The professor accelerated and shot the gray Land-Rover into the passing lane. "I think we'd better run over our *modus operandi*," he said. "More problems this year."

"Piddle," said Janice with scorn as she tossed her ponytail. "Nothing we can't handle with a little imagination."

VIII

Sarah and Alex had stopped once for an iced tea (Sarah) and a Dr. Pepper (Alex), and now a second time to examine a light-colored hawk that obligingly stayed for several minutes on the branch of a dead tree next to the road. Back in the car, Sarah shook her head and made a face.

"Hawks are worse than sparrows. All those spots and stripes, only bigger ones. I suppose I'll have to write it up in my logbook. Philip wants to put my bird-watching habits in order ... and the rest of me too, I guess."

"Is this a vacation or an overhaul job?"

"That doesn't sound friendly. I thought you two were good friends. Philip said you were. You were roommates at college, weren't you?"

"For the last two years. You got to know him at Morton's Academy for gracious girls, didn't you?"

"Not always gracious, but yes, we both taught there. Philip did wonders for the place. He reorganized all the departments and cleared out some of the faculty deadwood."

Alex looked over at Sarah. High cheekbones, strong chin, wide mouth, eyebrows set well over dark-rimmed eyes. It was

the sort of face that Hollywood used to cast in those aloof spin-
ster roles: high-collared lace dresses, unworldly, then suddenly
passionate. Was she as unforgiving as she sounded when she
spoke of "faculty deadwood"?

"That sounds a little brutal," said Alex quietly.

"But Miss Morton's was stuck in about the 1890s—especially the history department."

"In terms of literacy that might be an advantage."

"Alex, you can't sit back and let an all-female school sink
into the genteel mud of good manners and getting ready for
marriage and the azalea festival—no, let me finish. Now at least
the girls have a modern curriculum and a faculty that doesn't
hobble on canes."

"Sarah, you sound like—"

"I know. Like a real bitch, and I do think Philip came
down pretty hard, but that's what he was hired for. It wasn't
a solo; he headed a committee for the trustees. Pensions were
paid, proper notice given, silver trays handed out. Everything
in order."

" 'How thoroughly departmental.' "

"Are you in a Robert Frost phase? The well-read man. But
yes, you're right. I was only in my second year of teaching, so
I didn't get too involved, but most of the younger faculty felt
that the senior citizens should move on. And I did enjoy the old
ladies. Honestly. Old pros, interesting, intelligent, but they'd
been there since I was a student. And hung up—you wouldn't
believe. Most of them resigned without a fuss; only the head of
the history department had to be pushed. And Philip tells me
that she and the headmistress have started a bird-tour business
and will be down in Boyden helping out on some of the school
field trips. So you see, a happy ending."

"I doubt that. But why did you leave? Not old age anyway."

"A chance at an M.A. I got a job teaching at a day school
that left time for grad classes at B.U. Maybe I'll go back to
Morton's someday. Philip tells me that all the dust has settled,
wounds are healing, and some of the beheaded faculty have been

invited back for graduation. We'll all sing school songs and talk about what it was like in 1923 or 1937. Sometimes the whole scene gives me the creeps."

"Tough Miss Deane."

"Not so tough. I start giggling when we sing 'How Firm a Foundation,' because it makes me think of those girdle ads, but by the time we've worked up to the school hymn, a tear is brimming."

"Nostalgia is a powerhouse. It'll get you every time. How about one more bird stop and then motel land?"

And the Volvo sped over a rise and pointed south.

IX

Old Settlers Village squats near the center of the Doña Clara. The broken-down buildings, crumbled walls, and rusted iron railings are of negligible interest to the historical archaeologist; the village dates only from the 1870s and was abandoned in the 1950s. A condominium scheme was defeated by a conservation bloc, which subsequently established the refuge itself, and now the village is one of the favorite stopping places, perhaps because there is always something to sit on.

"Thank God," said Constance Goldsmith, collapsing on what was either a step or an overturned gravestone. "I've had it."

"I see an eastern yellow coral snake," said Nina Goldsmith, hopping in a circle around her aunt.

"That's the fifth coral snake you've seen," said Mrs. Goldsmith without moving. "See if you can find a python."

"This heat is murder," said Lois Bailey, sitting down next to her sister-in-law. "Major Foster's still looking for those groove-billed things."

"Anis. Groove-billed anis. Here's the picture." Mrs. Goldsmith opened her guide. "Ugly, aren't they? I hope," she added wearily, "he doesn't find them. My feet are going to explode." It was past four, the temperature had gone to 88 degrees, the dust had settled, and the air was heavy. The Hamburg Club had hiked long and

hard, sighting birds and swatting bugs. Bird lists had length-
ened, necks were stiff with craning, and hiking boots pinched.
Enthusiasm had quieted, and most were grateful for a respite.

Two college students sat on a brick wall and puzzled over
their lists; next to them sat Mrs. Milton van Hoek, who for her
first birding trip wore an Inverness cape and was bitterly regretting it. She was now slumped like a collapsed tweed mushroom
on the edge of a ruined well. Nearby was Mrs. Enid Plummer,
consort of Waldo, who called Mrs. van Hoek "dearie," and
was placidly readjusting a strap on her husband's pith helmet.
Others sat, leaned, looked for ticks.

A kiskadee flycatcher swooped from a branch and disappeared, rattling his noisy "kiss-kee-dee," but only two heads
turned. Everyone was an old Texas birder now, and this was the
sixth kiskadee. The tour members chattered: "How can you tell
if you've got chiggers?" "Are you using the new Peterson?" "You
can just unscrew a tick. Counterclockwise." "It's the same bird,
but one has a black crest—you can't count two. They're both
tits." (Here Nina Goldsmith giggled and poked her elbow into
the rib of an aunt.)

"Now, people," interrupted Waldo Plummer, who in his
reclaimed pith helmet looked like someone pausing in his search
for the source of the Nile, "we must trust the A.O.U. for species
nomenclature."

"Goodness, what's an A.O.U.?" asked Mrs. van Hoek in a
stifled voice from around her cape.

"That's the American Ornithologists Union. They settle
species debates," said Jeff Goldsmith with the air of a tenured
professor informing a freshman. "The black-crested titmouse
and the tufted titmouse hybridize, so they're the same species."

"Jeffrey is correct," said Mr. Plummer, "but now we must
all be silent. Major Foster is trying to find an ani for us."

"He moves quietly for such a big man," observed Lois Bailey.

Jeff rounded on his aunt. "Any good ornithologist moves
quietly. Only stupid people make a lot of noise and talk all the
time."

Lois Bailey and Constance Goldsmith sighed in concert. Not for the first time did they regret their invitation to take their niece and nephew on the Texas tour. Jeff, of course, was an avid birder, but an impatient one. Thirteen was an uneasy age, and the difference in years and what Miss Austen might have called "habits of address" made social moments distinctly sticky. As for nine-year-old Nina, she was overheated and bored stiff.

"It's time for the motel and the swimming pool," said Mrs. Bailey, and she wiped her forehead, leaving a wide streak of dirt.

Major Foster reappeared on the brink of the group and held up a hand for attention. "Can't see hide nor hair of those anis, but we'll try again tomorrow. Now, folks, it's after four, and I'm goin' to check out some other trails for new arrivals. Eduardo will drive you to Lupine Lake where there's a photo blind. Then he'll take those folks dyin' of heat to Progreso for a milk shake or a cone. For those that stay, I suggest goin' around Lupine Lake or Dodder Circle over by East Lake—they're both close to the Visitors Center. Don't go off'n your own. We've been havin' a mite of trouble here on the border. Be at the parkin' lot by six and I'll meet you there. Then we'll drive up on the Dike Road and try and get ourselves a pauraque just when it's turnin' dark. That's a bird'll tickle you. It sits sideways on the road with eyes that look like little red taillights."

"Isn't it sort of a whip-poor-will?" asked Lois Bailey.

"Yes, ma'am," said Big Foster. He looked squarely at Jeff. "Order Caprimulgiformes; family Caprimulgidae. The pauraque is *Nyctidromus albicollis*. All right, folks, into the bus. Left foot, right foot, hay foot, straw foot."

"He's certainly a dynamo," said Constance Goldsmith. "Well, I'm ready for a change. Jeff and Nina, how about something cold?"

Jeff looked up from his study of the refuge map. "I'm not going to waste time with ice cream. The birding just gets good now."

"All right, Jeff. Nina and Aunt Lois and I are going with Eduardo. You stick with the tour group, understand?"

Jeff did not answer.

"Did you hear me, Jeff Goldsmith?"

"Yes, Aunt Connie." Jeff aimed a short kick at his sister's shins, looked at his watch, and then resumed his inspection of the trails of Doña Clara.

X

Cheryl Cabot had one simple policy regarding dress: if it fit, it was too big. As a consequence, Cheryl always appeared as a sort of sausage forced into too small a casing. Now the last thing that Carlos Allen, the manager of Vacation Villa, wanted on the desk was a sexpot, but clerks who could type, keep accounts, and speak English and Spanish were valuable, so, for the time, he held his tongue.

It was almost five o'clock, and the telephone at the reservation desk had not rung for at least twelve minutes. The lobby was empty, and Mr. Allen had seen fit to improve a dull hour by quizzing Cheryl. She was bent low over the reservation charts and was concentrating on keeping a wad of gum secure in the cheek away from Mr. Allen. To anyone within a hundred yards, it was obvious that the motel's strictures on modest necklines had been ignored. Mr. Allen, however, was all business.

"Good. We're almost booked except for the rooms behind the Rotary Room and the Annex. Now where are our bird groups going? Let me see. We have the Cactus Wren leaders for tonight and on through next Friday. Then we have the Morton Academy students with two instructors and an adult guest, a Miss Deane. Then there's the new Ready Tour group, also for one week. The Hamburg Bird Club this time. Someone has put them off on the second floor. That won't do."

Mr. Allen shuffled sets of floor plans. He was stout, under five foot six, and his hair was sparse and combed across a bald spot. But under the exterior of a mouse lurked a motel lion. He had been with the Vacation Villa chain only a few years but had risen like a rocket. Mr. Allen's gimmick was the care and feeding of the nature-lover. He made a point to gather the tired, the hot, the bug-bitten into a better trap, and by dint of this single vision the Boyden Villa had gone from a mediocre tourist bin to a refuge for those weary of the refuge. Guests dined in the Avocet Room, were quartered on the likes of Warbler Walk, raised their spirits in the Roadrunner Bar, and were catered to by the Grackle Gift Shop. In short, Mr. Allen had wrought a nature-lover's Xanadu.

He now spoke sharply to Miss Cabot. "Get rid of that gum." Cheryl sulked.

"In the wastebasket, Cheryl. It makes a bad impression. Now look at these charts. We always give our tour groups the best. Tour groups are our bread and butter, Cheryl."

"So how can I fix it up?" Cheryl yawned. Birds were for the birds. All this jazz about tours was a pain in the ass.

"I will do this over now, Cheryl, but I want you to make yourself familiar with our reservation priorities. And it wouldn't hurt you one bit to go out to one of the refuges on your day off."

Mr. Allen, ignoring the look of horror on his clerk's face, bent to work with his eraser. He lifted the Cactus Wren ladies from Kingfisher Row and slipped them into safe nesting on Warbler Walk. He took the members of the Texas Gay Alliance Directors' Conference, operating under the name of Alternates, Inc., out of their slot next to the girls of Miss Morton's, and, humming softly, wrote them into a series of chambers behind the Rotary Room. The Ready Tour people he tenderly rubbed out from the second floor and replaced them in units on the Oriole Hall, which gave out on the garden and pool. Miss Eleanor Lucas and Mr. Philip Lentz, he separated and placed on the starboard and port flanks of their students, who remained on Caspian Turn. Miss Sarah Deane, whose reservation had been made by Mr. Lentz, he moved to Warbler Walk, which should make a stiff hike for Mr. Lentz were he amorously inclined. Mr. Allen was old-fashioned when it came to children being proximate to cohabiting adults. An apparent stranger to all these, an A. McKenzie, M.D., was left on Warbler. Mr.

Allen smiled and pushed the charts under the desk counter. The telephone rang, and he snatched it from Cheryl's hand.

"Vacation Villa. Yes. Indeed, yes. A nice room in the Annex. All just finished. So good to hear from you again." Mr. Allen turned to Cheryl with satisfaction. "That's Professor Axminster and his wife. Here every year. They're butterflies."

"What's butterflies?"

"Professor Axminster is. A lepidopterist. A new word for you, Cheryl. As a matter of fact, I'm thinking of using butterfly names for the corridors in the Annex. Swallowtail, monarch...something like that. There's a butterfly called sleepy orange."

Cheryl was bored with the Axminsters. One hand quietly sought the open pack of gum cached under the counter.

The glass door of the lobby glided open, and two persons came over the threshold, stepping warily as people do when not sure about self-opening entryways. They were each hung about with leather cases and canvas baggage. Cheryl Cabot thought they looked like a couple of tramps who had wandered in by mistake—those dusty boots, crumpled hats, and bandannas. But Mr. Allen always kept a weather eye for expensive optical equipment and the safari look; such promised cash flow, grist to the motel mill.

"Good afternoon." Mr. Allen nodded and rubbed his hands.

The tall man dropped a knapsack at his feet and lowered a green duffel. "Hello," he said. "I'm Dr. McKenzie, and this is Miss Deane. We both have reservations."

Mr. Allen smiled a tight little smile. "Welcome to Boyden. Now let me see." Mr. Allen slid his chart a small way into the open. "Here we are. You have a nice corner room on Warbler Walk, Doctor. And you, Miss Deane..."

"Philip Lentz made the reservation for me," said Sarah.

A faint shadow settled on Mr. Allen's face. He frowned at his room chart, but, eraser artist that he was, he could not, having once lifted Miss Deane from the purview of Mr. Lentz, now keep her out of the sphere of Dr. McKenzie. He shrugged. At least the Morton girls were at a discreet distance. Perhaps

Miss Deane was sharing her favors in one of those three-somes he had heard so much about. And Miss Lucas? Was it a four-way affair? Well, as long as everyone was quiet about any bedtime frolic, he was not one to object.

"Ah, yes, Miss Deane. I have your room. Warbler Walk, number seventeen, with a nice view of our patio."

Alex turned to Sarah. "I'll leave you now. I've an appointment in Boyden. This was fun. Hope the birds didn't bore you to death."

Sarah looked up at Alex, then let her glance slide toward a sign reading "POOL AND GARDEN." "Yes—oh, thanks, Alex. For meeting me and everything…the iced tea and all. And the birds were great. I hope we'll see you around birding somewhere or maybe dinner tonight."

"No, not tonight. I'm going over to the station to see Tom Pérez about that drug project I'll be working on, and then going back to his house for dinner. But keep in touch. If Philip can get loose, perhaps we can make a day of it later on."

"Maybe we can." Sarah smiled a bit vaguely, reached out, and shook his hand. Alex was already a little out of focus. She thought of a shower, a swim, and a cool drink. Then, perhaps, Philip and dinner. She turned back to the desk. "Has Mr. Lentz checked in?"

Mr. Allen consulted his file. "No, we haven't heard from Mr. Lentz yet, but we have his deposit and will hold his room."

"He'll be here," said Sarah, "but maybe not until much later. Please tell him to call my room when he comes."

"Certainly, Miss Deane." Mr. Allen indicated the binoculars hanging around Sarah's neck. "I hope you have rewarding birding during your stay, Miss Deane."

"Oh Lord," said Sarah. "I forgot to give Alex back his binoculars." She ran to the door, but the Volvo was just turning out of the drive. Never mind, she thought, he has his own; I'll give these back later. And she moved to follow a small person in a blue uniform, who, encumbered with her duffel, was vanishing down the hall.

XI

Eleanor Lucas, present colleague of Philip Lentz at Miss Morton's Academy and instructor in botany, tennis, and fencing, had been hiking since three o'clock in the Doña Clara Refuge. In this activity she had been joined by her traveling companion and most promising pupil, Dory Williams, but at four o'clock they split up after making plans to meet in the parking lot and return to the motel in time to meet the small clutch of Morton students who would be arriving from the airport.

Cactus Wren Tours, in the persons of Mrs. Brent and Miss Fellows, arrived just before five o'clock and launched themselves onto the maze of paths that wound through Doña Clara. Shortly afterward, Professor and Mrs. Axminster, now assured of a motel room, plunged into the thicket south of Heron Pond laden with nets and bottles. By five-thirty, Philip Lentz had put up his telescope, opened his notebook, and settled himself on a folding stool in the part of Bobcat Marsh that he believed favored the appearance of wildlife.

By five-fifty, those members of the Hamburg Bird Club who had voted to skip the ice-cream trip had begun to emerge in wilted condition from the nearby trails and to make for the parking lot and the six o'clock rendezvous. On the returned bus, Nina Goldsmith, victim of heat, boredom, and a strawberry soda, was asleep on a rear seat. Her two aunts, sticky and numb, sat next to her, beguiled by visions of showers and tall frosted drinks.

Jeff Goldsmith, after the departure of the bus, had immediately asserted his independence from the tour, and at six o'clock was running hard across the Lupine Lake boardwalk leading to the Auto Tour Road. He arrived more than ten minutes late, to face the ire of Major Foster, who had just pulled up his van ready to lead the group across to the Dike Road.

By six-thirty, cumulus clouds that had begun to form earlier in the east Texas sky appeared, the edges luminous in the fast-departing light. The heat had lessened, thunder was grumbling somewhere in the direction of Brownsville, and a northeast wind was rising. As if nudged by the change in the weather, most of the remaining visitors to the refuge converged in the parking lot, climbed into their cars, and left.

At six-fifty, dusk had almost changed to dark, and the wind moved forcefully through the brush and rattled the tops of the trees beside refuge headquarters. Inside his office, refuge manager Sam Hernández walked to a side window and heaved it open. The wind hit the screen furred by the day's dust and sent a storm of dirty air into the room. Sam sneezed, closed the window, sat down heavily at his desk, and collected the papers scattered by the wind, then opened a field guide and bent over it. Assistant refuge manager Bud Wojak was balanced atilt a wooden chair, his legs resting on a low file cabinet. Holding a flyswatter ready, he was watching a spider move across a large wall map of the refuge.

"That clinches it." Sam slapped his field guide on the desk top.

"Clinches what, Sam?"

"Clinches the kites, old buddy Bud. Hook-billed kites! Two of the devils. Male and female—first time in the refuge. Hot damn! *Chondrohierax uncinatus.* That'll keep Santa Ana in its place. They've had kind of a monopoly on hook-bills along with Bentsen State Park."

"Where d'ya see 'em?" Bud took aim with his flyswatter.

"South end of Bobcat Marsh, just before five. I'd stopped the Jeep, and, goddamn, there they were. Two on the big dead oak near the edge of the road. Light wasn't great, but okay for coloration. I had time to check the field marks, but wouldn't you know, a family came along asking about the restrooms—nobody reads signs—and by the time I looked again they'd gone to a tree up the marsh. So what d'ya say?"

Bud Wojak brought the flyswatter down hard on the map, and the spider disappeared hastily behind the wooden frame.

"Bud, if you'd spend more time on your field I.D. work you'd get a real buzz from this. God, hook-billed kites at Doña Clara."

"You said that, Sam."

"They've only been seen at Santa Ana and Bentsen in the last few years. First reported in Hidalgo County in 1967."

"So now you can write 'em up, Sam. Me, I like trees and plants. They don't fly off on you."

Sam snapped off the lamp at the edge of his desk. "Let's close her up, Bud. Only six cars left in the parking lot, and I guess they belong to the Kansas biology team. I gave 'em permission to stay in the campground and park in the lot. Trails were almost empty when I went through just after five. Think the weather's scarin' 'em."

Bud lowered his legs, keeping his chair on point until the last possible moment. He was young and unruffled by the trials of a refuge manager's life. "Where's Art Ready's bus?" he asked.

"Probably still out on the Dike Road. Big will try and find some night birds if the weather lets him. A helluva hot day for that bunch. From somewhere near Buffalo...you know, that snow belt. I saw 'em in the Settlers Village and they were shot."

Bud stood up and stretched. "I got me a girl waitin' in Boyden. You goin' sweep the trails, Sam?"

"You got too many girls in Boyden. Yeah, I'll sweep early tonight. Hell, anyone in here after seven is probably making damn sure he isn't found. Well, one thing for sure, anyone hidin' out is goin' get a good soaking. Looks like a helluva storm comin' in."

XII

Sarah woke to a siren screaming somewhere beyond the motel encampment. Confused with sleep, she pulled her pillow back over her head. The siren faded, and a heavy machine rumbled past. Suddenly she was completely awake. She groped for her bedside light and held up her watch. Almost midnight. She had slept through dinner, through the whole evening. Exhausted by the long day, she had, after her swim, put on an old kimono, flung herself on one of the beds, stuffed the telephone under one pillow, pulled another over her head, and, like a stone dropped in deep water, fallen asleep. Damn, now she had missed Philip. She'd only meant to take a short nap. If he'd come by dinnertime, he'd be furious. With the pillow over her head she wouldn't have heard him knock. But no, he wouldn't be furious—he'd be kind and talk about taking responsibility for a relationship, and smile and say let's start from here. Well, it was too late to call now; he'd be long in bed.

Sarah sat up and pulled the flowered counterpane around her shoulders—it had turned quite cool. Vacation with Philip. What was he like on the loose? A freewheeling Philip was almost a contradiction. Were they going to sleep together? Did he think so? Did she? But here Sarah reached a block. She couldn't even picture Philip in what the previous century had called a "state of undress." The clearest image that Sarah could muster was of Philip in pajamas. Then a pair of slippers covered his feet and a dressing gown, neatly tied, closed around his figure. Sarah tried again and placed Philip next to the motel swimming pool, but she had never seen him in a bathing suit, and a picture rose irresistibly of Philip in a swimming costume of the 1920s—the Jay Gatsby look—dark trunks, white webbing belt, striped top; then a towel appeared across his shoulders and high white sneakers on his feet. By the time Philip was in a terry-cloth robe and holding a beach umbrella, she saw that rather than disrobing Philip in the usual sexual fantasy, she was smothering him in garments. A case for Dr. Freud, she thought, and chuckled. There's something wrong with you, Sarah, my girl; you can never imagine Philip mussed up. She unwound the bedding, rose, and shuffled to the bathroom. Coming back, in an afterthought, she went to the door to see if any friendly note from Philip had been pushed into her room. Yes, there it was a—small card folded in half. Opening it, Sarah read with a slight sense of irritation: "Hi. Think you said Philip would be tied up with the girls at Doña Clara in the A.M. Glad to drive you to refuge for hike and lunch. Will then turn you over to P. Lentz. Breakfast at 7:00. Will knock. Alex."

I might as well, thought Sarah. I don't want to sit around the motel all morning. She walked over to the half-open window and saw that the rug under the sill was wet and the window streaked with rain. Across the motel garden the light from the terrace lamps was reflected in standing puddles of water on the flagstones. An extra puff of wind blew suddenly into the courtyard and sent a garden chair spinning. Thunder cannoned somewhere to the east, and a burst of lightning lit the tops of trees and the roof of the motel. Sarah winced, pulled the window down, and climbed back into bed and replaced the pillow over her head.